THE BOOK CODE

DAN NOBLE

"The type of mind that can understand good fiction ...is willing to have its sense of mystery deepened by contact with reality, and its sense of reality deepened by contact with mystery."
  -Flannery O'Connor

———

Polonious: What do you read my lord?
  Horatio: Words, words, words.
  Polonious: Though this be madness, there is method in it.
  -Shakespeare, Hamlet

———

"You've gotta be stronger than your story." –The Killers

PROLOGUE

THERE'S SOMETHING IN THE MIND THAT KEEPS US TRYING TO MAKE
sense of everything, to find the code in the random. The secret
center. The reason we're here. And that's what's had me hooked
on this mystery. But that can lead to trouble.

Whether or not you're a Reader with a capital R, it is better
to think of a book like a wonderfully engineered car driving
through a new land with no itinerary. And no roads. The good
news is Reader can wind up with an excellent guide. It is
possible to recognize an excellent guide immediately. If this
guide can show Reader a character who travels back in time
along a telephone connection and Reader buys it, hook, line,
and sinker, then he can be confident he has an excellent guide.
He knows the rules, this guide, and he can choose which to
follow and which to bend because he knows what's important
about these rules and why.

He knows he can make anything happen, because in the
story, it is the experience that matters. But to Reader, everything
is so dazzling, this is easy to forget. The journey is eye-opening.
The brain is careening off in different directions. As Reader is
propelled along these roads, he feels himself changing. Wanting

to try that Indonesian dish mentioned in The Novel. Interested in taking a tour of Perugia, like the heroine has. Skinny-dipping in a neighbor's pool at midnight. Or having a life-awakening affair.

There is something not quite right about the way Reader is glued to all he encounters in The Novel, and yet, aches to race through the pages to see where it is he's going. But Reader realizes, if he does that, gobbles it all up ravenously, it will be over too soon.

And suddenly it is. Abruptly, like a fall with lots of bruising. And that's when the question haunts most: which is the reality? The dazzling, eye-opening journey that sent Reader's heart racing, or this lonely bedroom, where Reader faces a pile of unwashed laundry and an alarm clock that will go off with such monotonous regularity in a few hours that Reader doesn't even need it anymore to signal the start of another soul-destroying day?

Surely, there must be something more to it all than that. That's all any of us want: for it to *mean something*. How to harness the magic of the story and keep it when the alarm bell rings?

Terrible as it all was, this is what she taught me.

1

MILLIE

"What can I do for you, ma'am?" I ask Rose, my three year old daughter.

"I told you not to call me ma'am." Isn't it amazing that even at three and a half, we don't like being called that? I don't understand the pleasure I get in taunting her with it. It might have to do with the ripple that etches above her nose and the way the skin around her eyebrows goes red. Apparently, I do the same.

"All right, ma'am. I'm sorry, no more. I promise."

She jams her hands on her hips and hooks her thumb through one of the belt loops on her seersucker pants, which I notice, are about half an inch too short already. It is only eight a.m. and already she has lost a sock.

"But, Mum, you just did it again!"

"Did I?" I tease.

"Yes, you said, 'All right, ma'am. I'm sorry, no more. I promise.'" I stand just in time to see her green eyes—Kennedy's green eyes—bulge with sheer hatred. The kind kids show us several times a day though they spent months gnashing our nipples to bits and puking in our hair. Our little angels. Sometimes, though

3

as soon as I think it, I force myself to *un*think it, she scares me just a little.

I pull her to the sofa, onto my lap. Her tiny bottom, newly swathed in big girl panties, doesn't span the width of my thigh. "You know what it's time for?" I ask dramatically.

She's giggling already—hysterical, throaty peals punctuated by wild shrieks. "No!" she tries, but her smile gives her away.

"A million kickles!" I say and begin the frenzied choreography of kissing and tickling we've thus coined after rejecting tissing (me) and dickkiss (Rose after switching the remote to HBO without my noticing).

She's yelling and laughing and transmitting sounds to shame a screeching train. As I await her endearing crescendo snort (see? Nothing to be scared of),

Writhing in laughter, she slides to the floor. "Ouch, my bum!" Rose says. Kennedy dropped Australian terms all the time when Rose was learning to talk: bum, bloke, snorker. "I want her to be bilingual," he said, deadpan.

I follow her into the kitchen where things are all clearly explainable, where I've lain Rose's raisin toast on the table, cut into checker squares arranged over Winnie the Pooh and Friends. Next to that is her drawing tablet where she'll "write" copies of Winnie and Tigger while her raisin toast hardens and the butter congeals.

Once she's seated and busy, I step into the adjoining laundry room. The washing basket is overflowing, so I wade through, yanking out my prematurely enormous maternity pieces and Kennedy's button-ups. Grabbing a pair of his jeans, a densely folded paper slithers out and I rescue it from a dark and dusty fate behind the dryer. My diligent husband files every receipt for tax write-offs, but endearingly, sometimes washes them by mistake.

Feeling useful, like Kennedy's money-saver, head financial

minister of domestic affairs, I unfold the sheet and lift it to the tray overhead where I collect these effects for him. Belatedly, I register the word "oncology."

I picture an egg under a spotlight. I say it slowly to myself.

"WHAT?" Rose yells, her back to me.

"Nothing, sorry."

"Sheesh. Mom, can you put more butter next time!"

It's just melted, I want to say, but the O word's gruesome counterpart intrudes. Cancer. A shock of energy bolts my chest. I do the most ridiculous thing: I wipe my hands, as if removing something sticky and unpleasant. What in God's name is this thing of pink ribbons and holiday telethons doing in my laundry? In this family, we do different kinds of unspeakable, invisible illnesses, which may or may not cause costume jewelry to detach itself from necks and lie on chair arms. We've put our time in with that, and in return, we don't have to do cancer. Even thinking the word, the hard C sticks in my craw, echoes in my head.

I reach into the tray, my chest thudding, and retrieve the creased sheet from the top of the pile.

Dr. Leonard Kramer, Oncologist

Sloan Kettering Cancer Center

It's a computer-generated receipt with a breakdown of services rendered: Bloods and Urine, CT Scan, PET, Lymph Node Tissue Analysis. I've never realized how scary capital letters can make words look, especially when they're stapled to a yellow carbon credit card receipt with my husband's signature and an appointment card with a follow up in eight days' time.

This is Kennedy's full name, the one I usually laugh over when I see it in print: John F. Kennedy (his parents are a couple of *those*), his insurance carrier, and co-payment breakdown. But they're only words on paper, I tell myself. Only I am too experienced to think they could never hurt me, Mrs. John F. Kennedy.

I scan for a calm, rational thought thread, something I can grab onto, but nothing comes, so I refold the receipt, taking care to follow the creases, replace it exactly where it belongs in the tray, and look for something, anything else.

"Mum!" Rose yells, on cue. I run toward her in the living room, and away from the words on that page.

My American daughter, who thanks to her father, fancies herself fluent in *Aussie*, is frantically groping at her neck: a sign she has again misplaced her magic charm necklace from *The Magic Charm Book* about the girl who—taking a page from Dumbo—can't ice skate without it. Skipping my mother's troublesome advice about grounding books in real life, I instead have concentrated on the ways in which stories encourage imagination. Simpler, I thought. Harmless. I'd like to think my father—should I ever see him—couldn't say anything about this little girl and her books.

Right now, I'm glad for the distraction. I am shaken by the oncologist receipt, but I don't want to panic. People go to oncologists for all sorts of things, don't they?

"Don't worry, Mommy will help you."

Rose stands back, as if this is something I need to be given space for.

You'd think I'd have wanted nothing to do with books after Mother's vanishing, and at first, I didn't. But it didn't take long to find out that without them, life didn't make sense. I tried to avoid stories altogether for the first few days after I brought Rose home. Right now, my head under the sofa, looking for this blasted necklace once again, I'm thinking I should have tried harder.

I'd lock onto her searching eyes and sing songs. Songs—in that high-pitched voice we swear up and down we'll never use with our kids—about anything that got her little fists pumping and feet kicking. *There once was a girl named Rose. She had a berry for a nose! The dog came by and gave a sigh and ate it. Down it goes!* It only took me a week to realize these songs told stories, that avoiding such a thing was impossible.

Besides, I caught Kennedy reading to her on the sly. He has a penchant for a board book named *Incy Wincy Spider: The True Hollywood Story*. At least, that's what he calls it.

"What are we without the stories we've grown up on?" he asked me. This didn't seem to jive with the Kennedy who'd so denounced Mother's fancies, and it threw me. So I gave in to the stories. And what did I get? Hours spent hunched over her crib, and eventually her big girl bed, painstakingly extricating from her sleeping body tarnished costume jewelry that turned her neck green, to secretly replace it with a spare that was not yet at that stage. Already books were trouble.

From the corner of my eye, I spot the twinkle of the locket's faux-ruby rhinestone.

Why is it there's never a moment of motherhood that doesn't get filtered through our daughterhood? As I take in the neck-lace's delicate placement—the charm over the chair arm, the lengths draped over the side—as if it alighted there on a raft of snowflakes, I see my eager young self crouched over that same arm, when this was Mother's house, searching eagerly out the window for the elusive tree swing my father had promised the night before.

Mother used books to distract me from disappointments on that occasion, and others when I was young, on that very chair, running her finger under the text until I realized those black marks held the meanings, that they told Mother what to say. Going through the early stages of reading comprehension with Rose has given new meaning to Mother's odd communiqués and all that ensued, it's certainly enriched the way I comprehend and express myself too.

I shake off the past and concentrate on the discovery that has surely been staring me in the face for months now: Rose would never remove the necklace herself. *No. Don't think it.*

"Stop, Mum," she breathes, then waits, tensed in like a crab, for me to do get some more tissing in, a wide-eyed smile poking up despite her attempt to restrain it.

"Okay, ma'am," I say, my hands freezing—one on her belly, one under her knee.

"Mu-uuum!"

"I know you can say mom," I say, twisting to see her face.

"Hmmph," she grunts.

How have I gotten myself a daughter who says *hmmph*? Never in my wildest dreams would I have said such a thing to my own mother—even when Mother and I spoke in actual words. I don't know where Rose gets her audacity; probably from Kennedy, a little from *Amelia Bedila*. But a part of me takes pride in it, tells me she's comfortable, safe enough to hmmph me. And that was no easy feat.

"Hmmph," I mimic. Maybe she needs a bit of shaking up.

"Mom!" she grumbles. I've stepped into her role and she doesn't like it. We want our mothers to be precisely what we think they should be. Don't I know it?

I hoist her over my head. She's getting heavier these days, which I don't like, but her smell of powder, caramel squares, and baby shampoo is consistent. I lower her to rest against my baby bump, where, despite the five months I have to go, the baby feels restless and about to burst free. Still, that could be the onion bagel I ate earlier.

Rose pats around my belly button in a circle, the way she's seen her father do. "Beebe," she says, a mix of French and silliness.

"I see your necklace," I say, expecting to spend the next hour tweezing together a slippery stretched link.

"Yippee!" she exclaims, which is a line from *Trouble in the Ark*, a book she wouldn't unclench her fingers from for several months. We had to wrap it in a Ziploc for bath time, which isn't as airtight as one might think. Her head jolts. "Where?"

I creep with her over to the armchair, using our exaggerated suspense walk.

Beyond the chair and through the old-fashioned cross-sash window, the winter sun is so bright, the view's obscured and the surface reflective, casting trees, Rose's blue tree swing, weeds and grasses, mirror-like upon us. The junky locket's chain is once again surprisingly intact, catching the sun like a jewelry ad, sending a shiver up the backs of my arms. How did it get here, I wonder again, though I'm trying desperately not to. *It is a piece of junk and it merely broke. Don't read anything into it.*

"Yahoo!" I yell to distract her, and myself, expecting her to hop on my knee while I finish the book's line for Noah. She throws herself on the chair and scoops up the necklace.

"Yippee! Should I 'do the thing'?" I ask, referring to the horsey bounce I do when we read the story.

"No, Mom. Do up the necklace." She's upset, fumbling with the clasp though she has no chance of latching it.

"What's wrong, honey?"

I place my hands over her rubbery fingers, which pinch at the ends of the chain, which thankfully is not broken. "Can you do up the necklace?" she repeats, as if she hasn't heard me. Has she caught onto my odd thoughts? I hope not.

She spills the chain into my outstretched palm and then holds her hair up while I fasten the latch and shove down the strange thoughts, focusing instead on the fine hairs at her nape, wanting suddenly to kiss both her polished and unpolished nail stubs.

"What's wrong?" I ask once more. Soon enough, Rose will be someone all her own, and she'll be making her own connections that I won't be able to save her from. Perhaps she already is.

She exhales like a practiced starlet, then turns to examine my face, our noses centimeters apart, identically scrunched. I feel her congested child breath on my upper lip. Is she considering whether to share her concerns? Her palm wiggles in the crook of my arm. "Is there anything you'd like to say to me?" I whisper. *You are nothing but the wonderful girl I see before me. Gestalt.* I say these words and inhale deeply and it seems to work. I feel like everything is okay.

I try to speak, but my mouth goes dry. After a false start, I have to try again. I shake my head. The past is never far behind.

"Mom!" If she's not teasing, she's seriously perturbed. "You are naughty."

"What would make you say such a thing?" I say, already failing to cram back the fears, the unanswered questions. She's just a child, I tell myself. She's probably angry with me for forcing her to eat peas. Still, on some level, I'm always lying to her, and children have excellent instincts about such things. There it is, all around us: this indignant feeling of knowing the seemingly impossible is what's happened, and the coordinating instinct to simply deny it.

"You moved my necklace."

"Me?"

"Yes."

"Why do you think that?"

"I saw you. You thought I was upstairs, but I wasn't. I'd already come down and I saw you take it off the kitchen table and bring it in this room."

"Don't you tell fibs, Rose. That is a very naughty thing to do."

My heart is racing. I don't like the feeling of someone making me unsure of myself. It's too easy to let the doubts begin.

"I guess I'm sorry," she says, slowly, strangely, feeling the nap of my wool sweater in her pincer grip. *How do you know what's real, Millie?*

"Now, go eat your snack," I say, patting her behind, my heart racing with the undeniable conclusion: it's back. I've pushed it off but here it's come after me.

Mother's secret.

Back in the laundry later, the buzzer goes. pausing with my hands atop the dryer, I try to picture myself at the time Rose mentioned: when she'd gone upstairs. But I was just in the kitchen. The incident disturbs me. Why would she say that? Has Kennedy been saying things about me that would make her doubt me? This is a terrible, awful thing. I am the good mother. I have dedicated my life to being everything my mother wasn't.

I have to stop thinking about it. Nonsense. Hormones. I'm sure of it. There are more important things to fill my head with. Like, how I am going to bring up the subject of cancer with my husband. Still, I can't stop thinking that maybe Rose is like Mother. Maybe there is something different about her, too.

2

MILLIE

As a child, it all seemed innocuous enough. Mother drilled the same words into me as she buttoned me up at the front door: "Do you have your book? Always carry a book with you, so you can ground your reading experience in real life," she'd say. How cultured. How well-rounded.

"But why-uh?" I wanted to know. I'd stopped plugging my ears with my fingers long ago, but there were always things I couldn't explain, and thinking of them only made me feel like a failure, a simpleton who couldn't get it.

"Never mind why-uh. Like most things in this life, you have to work it out for yourself." I was six. I had my book, but often no snack or extra underwear. I assumed she thought I'd eventually find a way to read myself out of sopping pants. I never doubted she loved me, but she was self-contained, and specific about what was important (books).

"Mom! Mom!" I'd yell once she'd turn and head for the school gates.

"What is it?"

But it was never anything. I wanted everyone to see this formidable woman was my mother.

My readiness would get tested, the way we did in school for atomic bomb explosions. In line at the echoey bank, under the gothic ceiling, I'd ask, "Can I have some goldfish?" She'd fish in her purse for a moment before saying, "Sorry, darling. I forgot them. Do you have your book?"

"Do you have *your* book?" I'd ask back when I felt stroppy. But she ignored such things. She knew I didn't mean them and I didn't need to apologize.

Between the queue's velvet ropes, my mind careening between the exact likeness of my hair—dark, thick, and ropy— to Mother's, though hers was braided and mine in two ponytails, and those square cushions of bubblegum in the machine at the door. I watched as another girl's mother pinched a penny from her pocket and handed it to her hopping daughter, who carefully placed it in the slot and cupped her hand beneath the chute as she turned the dial that set the gum cascading.

I made a face, but Mother wouldn't look at me.

What could I do but start reading my book? I'd enjoy it. The time would move faster; still other times, I'd get bored. But I couldn't see what the big deal was. Why should I stick my face in a book when I could play with her, pretend this bank was our castle, and we the queen and princess?

I started to equate books with isolation. When Mother read, she wasn't with me. And before I could understand how I felt, or what it might mean, I would lose my temper, stamp my feet and yell terrible things like, "If you don't pay attention to me, I'm going to cut your head off!"

"If that's how you feel," Mother would say. And her disappointment would be enough. I'd regret it immediately, tears filling my eyes and my arms wrapped around her leg. How could I mean those words so much in one moment and feel such incredible remorse the next?

Beneath the gaze of those capacious eyes, Mother's dark

features at their most severe, my face tingled, my stomach lurched.

She said, "I'm not messing around, Millie. This is serious stuff that will make or break your life." I'd read all the more, to please her, but I only felt lonelier, and like more of a failure.

If I had only known how bad the "break" was going to be, maybe I would've listened more carefully.

3

MILLIE

IT'S NO USE TRYING TO WRITE OFF THE COINCIDING DISCOVERIES OF the necklace where I know Rose had not left it and the receipt as unimportant. I can't bring myself to believe one can't help the other. It's my first thought: I can fix this. I can leave his cancer (god, that "c" really is terrible—*kuh, kuh, kuh* it echoes) wherever Mother left her depression and her speech. There is a way. I don't know what it is, but in her young obliviousness, Rose has stumbled upon it. She is a Reader. But to what extent, I have no idea. The years of therapy beg me not to go here, but they lose.

The pull is so strong.

In the kitchen, I slip on my foil-lined gloves and try to find catharsis in Palmolive suds fighting grease in the sink. It's all I've got. In the living room, I can hear Ernie's earnest voice. Everything makes sense on *Sesame Street*.

I repeat: I'm here, grounded, sane, providing a stable environment for my husband and daughter, who may now need it more than ever. *Fiction is fiction and fact is fact.* God, I hate those words Dr. Samuels taught me so many years ago. Why do I always say them?

My husband may have cancer, *Cancer, Kancer*. A shiver rocks me. And whatever it is Mother had done all those years ago when she finally disappeared, healed my broken ankle overnight. Either she's passed on the power to Rose, or I'm just as crazy as she was and it's manifesting right now, in a moment of extreme stress. Can my daughter do what I believe she can? The time prior to seeing that fucking receipt feels like an oasis I should be able to reach again. Despite everything, I have to at least try.

I scan my memory for something grounding to focus on. My mind rewinds to last night, Kennedy and I in the bedroom. It's my favorite part of the day, when Rose is off to sleep, all the domestic duties have been done, and it's just the two of us, peaceful, more joyously satisfied with our lives than two people deserve to be.

Propped up with my litany of pregnancy pillows, I looked up from the book I was reading, *The Culture of Motherhood*, to share with Kennedy the nugget I'd just read.

"In Sumatra, pregnancy is considered an 'in between' state —not yet a mother, no longer simply a virgin or bride. She is liminaire—of the threshold—and must undergo rituals to both protect herself and others from the contagion of danger she presents." I shared this line because it sounded beautiful to me. The image, not exactly concrete, but attractive, kept presenting itself to me throughout the night. Don't forget me, it said.

"That's why I've got a mistress," Kennedy said. "To protect myself."

"You'd better not." I kissed him. He pulled me to him.

"Yes, I remember history giving us some great remedies— much better than today: What have we got? Leeches, blood-letting, lobotomies, and my personal favorite, female genital massage."

I wriggled my brows and let my knees fall open. When he reached for me, I snapped them shut and continued talking. I loved the genuine smile I brought to his face—dimple and everything. I didn't see him reproduce it much outside of Rose's and my company.

"I've been taking a multicultural angle on protecting this pregnancy. I'm follow the Jamaican tradition—no coconuts lest the baby be cross-eyed, no stretching my arms overhead and risk grotesquely stretching the baby's neck." But in my head, the lovely sounding word *liminaire* still seduced me. I often felt that way—of two worlds.

"No Fox News lest Bub be Republican," Kennedy said. The dimple was so big I could stick my thumb in there.

"Says JFK. Anyway, I thought we'd see what tossing in one of those conservatives to the family dynamic was like. It's so boring being an all-red household in a red state," I said, then finished off the book's no-no list: avoid ugly things or the baby will be born in kind.

"Okay," Kennedy said, "I guess we won't be seeing any of your friends from Rose's school."

I rolled up the book and whacked him with it.

He scoffed. "What? Should I say that one with the cleavage up to her neck and the velour track suit tight in all the wrong places—you know the one I mean—is attractive? Are we—"

"Are we what?"

"Liars," he said. The dimple vanished.

"What's wrong?" I asked.

"Nothing. Just thinking about unzipping that woman's hoodie." He smiled but didn't manage the dimple. Odd. "Also, I didn't pick my own name. My mother should have thought a bit harder. Names are important. They have significance, weight.

Just look at the name of that doctor your mother had. Who goes around in life with the surname Pinocchio? Especially if you're going to become a doctor. How can anyone trust a person named for a wooden puppet known for lying?"

"Well, I never trusted him. Maybe the name clouded my view." I didn't want to go down that path. Not with how good everything was presently. "Back to the book," I said, steam-rolling on to tamp the nerves beginning to pulse around my eyes. "I steered cleared of ugly stuff for a week," I told him. "But I found that left me mostly at home or walking around with my eyes fixed to the ground, bumping into things. So that one didn't work out well."

"Not fair to blame the remedy. You always walk around bumping into things."

"Do not." Maybe we *are* liars, I thought as I stood and stubbed my toe on the nightstand.

4

MILLIE

A LITTLE LATER, WHEN ROSE GOES DOWN FOR HER TWO O'CLOCK nap, I tiptoe to the door, swing it swiftly closed to avoid the creak, and retreat to my office next door to quietly think. I'll have at least forty minutes before she wakes and I need to make the most of it.

Turning on the soft, faint light of the anglepoise, which is positioned with the neck tucked away from me, I sit in nearly as much darkness as my daughter. In the lamp's circle of light, I see the persistent dance of those fibers of our lives that resist cleaning, their victory dance, and can't help thinking of Mother and when this office, exactly as it is now, was hers.

This fear of losing the one I love and need most is breathtakingly familiar in here; Mother was my first lost love. I can literally feel the sensation of my brain seeking out solutions. We. Can. Do. This. And I don't even know the problem yet.

Next door, Rose's breathing must be slowing, her rear end skyward. I hear her mouth muscles involuntarily sucking every now and then.

I pick up the phone to dial Kennedy. Any normal wife would insist on knowing the truth immediately. But I hold the receiver until the dial tone gives way to a busy signal. Kennedy is not the kind of man who wants his wife to share in his burdens. In fact, healthy or not, we wouldn't have the relationship we do if I didn't let him take care of us his way.

I recall the day we met as if it were yesterday. I rest my head on Mother's desk and conjure it. We met at my most aimless time, only months after Mother's disappearance. I was trying on a simple life and arranging myself the best I could to make it fit.

During my first office job, though it was a fifteen-minute walk past dozens of perfectly good diners, luncheonettes, and delis, I always went to Three Guys' Diner on Madison and 93rd to fetch Mr. Tyler's ridiculous lunch. My employer ate the same thing every day, and I'd learned not to get it wrong.

When noon rolled around, Chico, the Three Guys' counter man, and the two grill cooks waited for me. "Hola, beautiful lady," Chico would say. And then he'd wait. He liked me to repeat the order, even though he knew the drill.

On one of those days, there was a handsome man in brown pants standing off to one side of the counter, reading a neatly folded section of *The Times*, as if waiting to pick up his own lunch. I waited a second before ordering, in case Chico would let me off the hook with this guy standing there. He didn't.

I grimaced. "Tuna fish on lightly toasted rye with one slice of tomato, two paper thin purple onion rings and a pickle spear—sliced into strips and spread across the sandwich, three centimeters apart."

Chico rolled his hand out for the finale.

"And a chocolate chip cookie—slightly raw." The three of them in white kitchen jackets applauded.

They gave me a hard time, which I pretended was a big bother, and in exchange they always got the order just right, which meant a peaceful afternoon. I placed a high price on peace back then.

After Chico and the grill cooks settled down, the man looked up from his paper, flashing me a conspiratorial smile as if he'd been listening and decided he was on my side. He had thick dark hair and the kind of skin that looked like it always needed a shave; I wasn't sure if it was this, or something deeper that gave him that aura of gravitas. He was a bit older than I was, maybe ten years, but still I took notice of him.

"You're weird," the man said.

"I know," I said, "but that isn't my lunch."

"Oh," he said. His eyes blinked a mix of confusion and amusement. He had a pleasant glow and all the right angles, like he could advertise soap.

We both turned our attention to the sizzling grill, the thick, greasy smell of which scented the whole place.

"Then why are you weird?" he asked.

"You don't want to know," I answered.

"I do."

I was so used to pretending to be this simple secretary that this exchange caught me off guard. Why had I been my actual self with this stranger, told him the truth? Perhaps because he seemed sincere, and his directness was refreshing.

I said something bold like I never had allowed myself to since Mother's disappearance, which was about five months earlier by that point. "Well, I'll meet you for a long dinner one night and tell you all about it." I couldn't imagine what brought me to say something like this, the kind of thing the teenaged me used to say at moldy basement keg parties, envisioning Mother saying as much to her Parisian men nearly twenty years earlier.

Maybe it was the dream I'd had of my mother—smoking in the garden, a rhododendron sprig woven into her braid—the previous night that had propelled me. I always had the most vivid dreams, and bits of them would flash up throughout the day as if still playing out somewhere.

All day, I'd heard her words from back in the era my father had been around, stirring in me the most potent mix of desperation and solidarity: "It's you and me against the world." How it must have shocked my father to witness such a transformation in her.

He squinted, spreading his lips into a bright smile. "Depends what you consider long. I've only got about two days, three tops."

Overpowered by his gaze, I looked down, my eyes landing on his pants' zipper. A jolt shot through me, still I didn't look away. I couldn't tell if he noticed or not, but when our eyes search each other's out once again—long after he'd gone back to his paper and I pretended not to watch—something in his stare penetrated deeper, as if in exchange for my bold behavior. As if we'd bypassed the usual boundaries.

As he accepted his I heart New York bag from Chico, the man held my gaze long and steady before turning toward the exit. I watched his shirtsleeve tighten at his shoulder and bicep as he pulled the door. I noticed it tremble slightly and wondered if this meant he was as affected by the meeting as I was.

Sashaying back to the office, I swung Mr. Tyler's I heart New York bag, redolent of tuna fish, in loop-da-loops as I began to dread the mound of paperwork which amassed the bulk of my job. It was the smallest of comforts to me that Mother would never know what I did for a living. Meaningless words were anathema to her.

At least my mother wouldn't—if we discussed such things—scold me for having left without making a date with that man who said he had two days, three tops for me. She wasn't like that. When it came to men, in the real world at least, Mother was a lot more like me. Old fashioned.

She believed in letting things happen naturally. Relationships were complicated, tactile things, not some generic concept. I had this fact memorized by the time I was five.

Remember this, I thought. *This is a significant moment.* I couldn't articulate why. But I felt it. And I saw his shuddering. It fit into a pattern in my life: things I could not explain. And as always, I was pulled toward the mystery, needing to see where it all led.

I went back and forth on the whys and the hows, but I was one hundred percent certain: I felt ready for action. I felt I could begin my story, that this collision with the handsome newspaper reader was a starting point, my inciting incident. Despite my desire to be everything Mother was not, I couldn't help but think in terms of story, books, words. These were as much a part of me as my own feet, and I couldn't shed them, though I tried.

I had a sense my life was only just beginning. This meeting with the newspaper man broke the rules. But I didn't know which rules to follow anymore. It had been a long while since I had.

Rose is still napping, and though I've reminisced, I haven't found any sense of purchase or way forward. I am reeling still. And I certainly can't approach Kennedy about his terrible secret in this state of mind. Panic never helps a situation. So, I open the laptop and click around on Google, the way everyone looks for answers today.

The scans Kennedy paid for were used to diagnose so many cancers and problems that it was impossible to glean anything specific they may have been after. Thirty-five minutes down this rabbit hole, I realize this is only making things worse. And that's when I type something very different into the search bar: liminaire, the word that had enchanted me yesterday. The first entry is from Wikipedia. And I click on it:

"In anthropology, **liminality** (from the Latin word *līmen*, meaning "a threshold"[1]) is the quality of ambiguity or disorientation that occurs in the middle stage of rites, when participants no longer hold their pre-ritual status but have not yet begun the transition to the status they will hold when the rite is complete."

There's something hypnotic and attractive about the words, a beautiful equation of meaning. I snap the laptop shut and lie on the sofa on the day a receipt might change my whole world and try to let the beauty and promise of them calm me. Next thing I know, Rose's creaky calls wake me, and for a brief, welcome second, I forget about the big cancer question.

When I remember, I know immediately I need to work out what's wrong with Kennedy on my own, and as quickly as possible. I can't go much longer feeling as desperate as this. And if he's hiding it, I don't want to disturb whatever delicate balance is allowing him to function.

Rose and I do lunch, painstakingly slow sips of water punctuated by dramatic sighs, and a particularly poignant round of kickles before I have the chance to sit at the kitchen table with the receipt again. This testing could be about anything. It could be a funny-looking freckle that needs to be lasered off and never thought of again. It could be administrative clearance for health or life insurance. There's even the possibility of hypochondriasis. There is only one way to find out.

"Doctor Kanter's office. This is Cindy."

"Cindy, I'm calling on behalf of a patient of yours—John Kennedy."

"And this would be—"

"His secretary. Excuse me. Yes, I have her on the phone right now, Mr. Kennedy."

I take a risk. "He says hello, Cindy."

I can sense her blush. I've seen it so many times.

"Yes, well. What can I do for Mr. Kennedy?"

"He asked if you could fax his records to his home number. His insurance carrier is giving him a hard time about some of the bills."

She clucks her tongue. "Disgusting isn't it?"

"A dirty, dirty business."

"Well, normally he'd have to sign for it, but seeing as he'll be here in a few days, I'll just go ahead and grab his John Hancock then. You tell him that'll just be our own dirty little secret."

"Yes, of course." Floosy. I give her the number, set our home machine to receive the fax and hang up, holding the handset in my fingers for a long while.

The fax says it all. Non-Hodgkin's Lymphoma. Hasn't presented mortal danger until now. Atypical case. Lots of students following up in the lab. Could be helpful for other people. The upcoming appointment is to repeat tests, and looking ahead, to prep for surgery—fill in forms and take blood tests.

An hour later, I'm washing serving bowls I will never use just for something to start and fucking finish. Easy. And I'm startled by a connection my brain fastens together. When Kennedy disappeared all those years ago, he was very sick. How could I have overlooked this? I recall my conversation with Angie as if it were four weeks ago instead of four years.

I'd brought up sickness as a possibility. But it went the way of other excuses we conjured: maybe he joined the circus or decided to become a top-secret boutique cheese maker and had to cut all ties for marketing cache.

People have always disappeared on me. I've found ways to deal with it. But I wasn't happy. With Kennedy I *am* happy. Surely, if he came back, I could excuse one little disappearance without too much bother. If I didn't, I couldn't have had everything else—the peace, the love, the happiness with which Kennedy had crashed into my life, which had previously been just a list of backstory, foreshadowing, darkness, and intentions with no structure. By the time I'd run into him at the diner, I'd become excellent at compartmentalizing. Sometimes it scared me, what I could not think about.

Rose is singing *stupid-califragilistic-crispy-salad-oceans*. One day someone will have the heart to correct her interpretation of *Mary Poppins*. But for now, we idle away hours arranging our imaginary sea: sometimes with arugula, sometimes iceberg tossed with frisée. Is it so bad to keep our salad oceans crispy a bit longer? Kennedy, what is happening to our salad oceans?

I keep my hands submerged in the sink full of steaming water. Just words on a page, I tell myself, though this runs counter to everything I've ever believed, despite trying to talk myself out of it. I force myself to feel the water's burn, if only to prove I'm still here, that my life hasn't yet dissolved around me. To prove that I can take the pain. Just not yet.

Nearly as soon as he's in the door, Kennedy starts in on his dinner at full speed—probably wanting to tick off the days to get whatever he's doing at the oncologist next week over as quickly as possible; take that cancer!—and I feel rushed to get started with the talking, or put it off for another night, or, I don't know what.

When he's finished, he gets up to put on the news, but Rose intercepts him squeaking with delight, and perhaps he remembers there's still a life vying for attention; a wife, a daughter, and all the mundane rituals that keep life tacked down. He sits with what yesterday would have been an innocuous sigh.

"Why don't you help me with the dishes, Rose?" She can't

resist squeezing the dish soap and swirling the sink water into bubbles.

He nods a thank-you and envelops Rose in a hug, carrying her to the stepstool that allows her to reach the sink. No sooner has he put her down than he swoops her up again, twirling her, her tiny legs blurring with speed; she's watching me to make sure I notice how loving they are. I can't help but think of her accusation earlier. I feel the shift in his energy, in her energy, in mine. I am reminded of the butterfly affect. He's worried we will lose him. Am I crazy or does he smell different, slightly acidic, the way he does when he's got a sore throat? Wouldn't I have noticed that before?

I watch them, my feet stuck to the wood planks, reminded of the early days of Mother's mutism, when I was glad for the showing over the telling, the beautiful unsimple simplicity of it, for the lovely, if lonely, infinitely-nuanced power of it. There was always pleasure in deciphering her intentions, as if she were a fictional character herself. She had me hooked from page one. That night, I can't bring myself to say anything to Kennedy.

5

MILLIE

THE NEXT DAY, KENNEDY'S MOTHER AND I PREPARE TO SERVE lunch in Kennedy's childhood kitchen, in the family home that he and I refer to as the Kennedy Kennedy house, because I've grown so used to calling him by his surname that it always jars to say Mr. and Mrs. Kennedy, which they still insist I do. With the signed portraits of the real JFK in the family room, you'd think they might be related. It'd be creepy if Kennedy didn't joke it off so compellingly. *Welcome to Camelot,* he whispered in my ear right as his mother opened the door on my first visit.

"Will you plate up the crudités?" Mrs. Kennedy says to me. "I just learned that term 'plate up' on the cooking channel. It's what you say for the way you serve everything. Isn't that great? I love to watch language change."

I like it to stay the same, but who am I to say how things work in Camelot, so only say, "Sure. I'll plate up for you." I also leave out the comment about perhaps updating your recipes while you're watching the cooking channel; there aren't too many households where you can still find Jell-O molds clotted with cottage cheese and canned fruit cocktail.

Through the doorway, I see Kennedy helping his father to

adjust the lock on a window. There is nothing *kuh-kuh*-kancerous about this scene. I catch him watching me through a window as I arrange vegetables in a retro baking dish, losing myself in the creativity of it, wondering what kind of birthday gifts Kennedy will receive and how each will play against the context of the ominous receipt. This day could have been so different.

"You're so good with that," his mother, Mrs. Kennedy, says. But behind every comment is the menacing shadow of kancer.

"Oh, it's not very different than decorating."

"Is that something you're interested in?" Though worn, I've always thought our house lovely, enchanting; though this is just the kind of passive-aggressive way she has of making her opinion known, it still stings. She has a way of keeping me at arm's length. I could counter with a comment about not knowing her son's got *kancer*. But I don't. I may not be so innocent in this area myself.

"It is," I say. Kancer, kancer, kancer. Why hasn't he told any of us? It is ruining everything, even the fun of comebacks I'd give if only she weren't my mother-in-law. "It's a family thing," I say before I know I'm about to.

"That's lovely, isn't it?" She can really hurl that word. And I hurl her first name at her in my mind: *Diane, Diane, Diane*. Diane opens the squeaky oven door and pulls out the roast that's been resting there. She waits there a moment too long, as if taking a break from everything around her—it looks almost as if she's lost consciousness. Should I poke her?

"Isn't it lovely to have everyone together?" she says, finally, returning to me, to *lovely*, as if she hadn't just zoned out.

Now I'm the one playing pretend. I tell myself it was nice for a minute to have a break from bristling over her canned lines punctuated with jabs in place of proper talk—all on a day when all I can think about is the possibility of her son dying.

Before I know I'm going to, I say, "It's good to have light conversation at the ready, isn't it? In your young housewife days such hollow commentary was probably all that was expected of you." I guess this is the kind of thing that comes out in place of that which we shall not speak. Maybe this is how Mrs. Kennedy came to be this way? I'm immediately sorry—not to have thought it, but to have said it—though I don't say so.

"Why don't you take the salad out to the table?" she says, using her power of diversion for my benefit now, and hands me a china bowl that must have cost a fortune.

I nod and smile, not quite sorry, but not exactly proud, my chest tugging with tenderness for Mother, a special woman— perhaps too special—who would look at this macerated salad in this priceless bowl and say, "Curly parsley? Who bothers with curly parsley? Only you, Millie, would manage to find in-laws who garnish with curly parsley."

And again, my mouth goes rogue. "You know about the Kancer, don't you, Mrs. Kennedy?"

"I do," she says. "Don't forget the salt and pepper shakers."

———

At the table, Kennedy leans in to kiss above my blouse's high neckline. My hair is up, and my entire neck breaks out in goose-flesh. Sadistic possibly, but there is something erotic in not knowing how long you'll have with the person you love.

He jiggles his fussy Queen Anne chair closer to mine and keeps his hand at the base of my back all through the salad course. Our palpable intimacy is striking to his brothers and their staid, capri pants-wearing wives who we barely get a straight look from.

Kennedy turns to smile at me every few minutes as if the prize in some contest he's won. Despite everything, I feel the same. He makes his way to Rose, two seats down, and hands her a plate of finely chopped roast beef, though we both know she won't eat it. The day before the receipt, she declared herself a vegetarian. She pronounced it *refrigeration*, but when she pushed away her ham sandwich, we knew what she meant.

"Good thing we've got oceans of crispy salad," Kennedy had said. We all sang Stupid-califragilistic-crispy-salad-oceans, and Kennedy said, "God, I love that refrigeration song."

His arm brushes mine now as he returns to his seat, and vertigo rips me. I have to sit on my trembling hands, wait before I attempt to pick up my fork. It's too much, the way I love him. He knows, and I swear, in front of his family, he flaunts it, as if to say, "This is the way it's done, folks!"

Before, though, he never would have been so in-your-face. Perhaps he feels there's only a short time left to show them the way; he will not die in vain. Stop, I tell myself. You don't have the full story. I put my fork down and kiss him on the ear. He beams. *Teamwork!* Rose would say if she understood the gesture. Sometimes it's like she's following a script.

"What a roast!" Diane says with the slightest tinge of annoyance in her tone while Kennedy's smile gleams. Nobody likes change in real life, even if they don't think it's so bad in language. I certainly understand this, and for her benefit, I shimmy slightly away from Kennedy. He yanks my chair back. Fuck, I love him.

We pass the platters, tuck in, compliment the various side dishes, laugh when Rose and her cousin Stewart launch into a conversation about whether roast beef (which she is ignoring for her peas) is considered a white meat because a lot of white people they know like it, but so do a lot of *brown* ones, so they start to call it "everybody's meat," which we all agree is much better—except for Stewart's pre-teen sister, Kim, who thinks we're all criminal for supporting factory farming, and for not explaining to a couple of three year olds about the term African American 'right this instant.'

Kancer.

For a subject change, Kennedy, with whom I've shared Mother's view on parsley, runs effusive about how pretty it looks. I kick him under the table.

How can humor rear its head now? It's criminal. Or delusional. He lays his fork against the rim of his fussy floral plate and takes a knife to his wine glass. "I've got an announcement," he says as if my toe in his shin has just reminded him of something.

Kennedy's energy flows well in crowds and diffuses the sudden tension. "Roast beef is officially the new mascot of this family."

The table erupts in laughter, probably too effervescent. Even Kim smiles.

"No, really," he says, taking my hand, looking at me. Is he going to speak about the Kancer? To be so direct about it with his family, it must be as bad as I suspect.

"The Kennedy family is expanding. Millie is having a baby."

My exhale is audible. Rose claps though she looks unsure. Fair enough. Everyone else applauds loudly and whoops. I am just beginning to show and we agreed today would be the day we shared the news, but I forgot about our plan, amidst the receipt and everything.

I look back to Rose, who spears a carrot with her fork—the special silver one Kennedy used as a child. I remember the way he apologized when his mother made a big deal of showing me how she'd kept it all these years. "Don't be ridiculous," I'd told him. I wanted him to have a wonderful life. It made me happy to think of such care taken on his behalf. Still does. I would never want my mother for him.

After, Kennedy secures the wilted, sleeping Rose in her car

seat and then loads his gifts in the back: a barrage of electronics, an Over the Hill tee shirt, some hand drawn cards from the nieces and nephews, and gift certificates to two of the three upmarket national department store chains. When he sits next to me and starts up the car, I look at him and nearly spill it.

"So, tell me how you feel, Millie." Is he *asking* me about the Kancer?

"How do I feel?" I say. "How do I feel?" I look out at Third Avenue. "Isn't it obvious? I love you and all I want in this world is to continue our lives together with Rose and the baby. And I'd do anything it takes to do that."

"I hoped you'd say that."

Are we talking about what I think we're talking about?

6

MILLIE

IN THE YEARS LEADING TO MOTHER'S SECOND SUICIDE ATTEMPT, I mastered the art of carrying my book around, had one of her old satchels for the purpose. God, I loved the worn canvas of that thing, sucked its strap almost as much as the ear of the stuffed beagle I'd carried around throughout childhood. By the time I was in junior high school, I was wearing ribbed turtlenecks and vintage floral skirts, my nose in a book by my own accord. Emulating her containment, I amassed my own admirers, who didn't realize I was all show.

The act crumbled soon enough. When I pretended to master the magnificence of books (err, had one with you, acted like you understood why), she started in on something else.

"How do you know what's real, Millie?"

I always offered the wrong answer. She wouldn't speak to me all afternoon, so I could take time to work it out. Which I wouldn't. I often took my dinner alone. She didn't tell me where she was going. She'd just be there, and then she wouldn't. It would have been too juvenile, too much of a failure in her eyes for me to hate her. Besides, I couldn't.

And so it began.

Something I did learn from books is that you must trust that eventually everything will come together to make sense, and though I couldn't understood exactly why Mother was so focused on "experiencing" books, and separating fact from fiction, in the meanwhile, the learning curve made me into a clever party trick.

"Tell them," Mother would say.

At least I felt special then. No one in that room knew Mother took this show seriously. None of them suspected she was up to something the way I did—even if I didn't know exactly what. I would tell them, in my frilly dress with its floral sash, that Jane Eyre is forever entangled with the rear-facing back of our Volvo station wagon, and Robinson Crusoe with the small electrics department of Bloomingdale's Lexington Avenue. I'd heard Mother recount my performances, and these were proud words she used. I didn't understand them all but I sounded lovely when she spoke of me that way.

This was all before the divorce, and of course, I never noticed how this act drove my father out of the conversation. I just listed off these book/life associations and soaked up the attention. "*Are You There God? It's Me Margaret* and spaghetti carbonara," I would say, eventually getting the dramatic pause right. "*Bedknobs and Broomsticks,* and *Intercourse,* at the Pennsylvania Dutch Country." When my parents split, I figured, eventually, this kind of talk is what drove him permanently from the conversation.

Our flashy neighbors and the trio my father referred to as Mother's holdover hippie college friends laughed into a cloud of menthol cigarette smoke and started to sing out their own pairings. When the comments became more obviously inappropriate for a girl my age, Mother assumed I wouldn't understand,

and chortled along with "Anais Nin and furry handcuffs," shooting me barely a glance over her gin and tonic.

But even if the *Intercourse* double entendre was over my head, I sensed what this last comment meant. By ten, I'd read the slim volume with the bow-topped, mary-janed girl on the cover, and terrifyingly, felt my body respond. Books had taught me everything. Even—if I'd noticed, which was hard to do in the shadow of Mother—why someone like my father would be hunched awkwardly in the corner, fumbling with the pull-tab of his Budweiser. Alienation is a novelist's pet theme.

I didn't understand, but it certainly made Mother happy. And back then, that made everyone happy. Even my alienated father—for a while anyway. He either didn't understand enough to question or knew enough not to. I couldn't work it out. I didn't want to. But later, I understood how he felt being on the outside.

Nothing was as it seemed. My father used to say to me, "Some of us don't have the luxury of being depressed," though he'd never dare say that to Mother, and it made me hate him a little when he tried the phrase on my ears, even as Mother's talk of reality and grounding books into the real world infuriated me. I wasn't *getting* it, clearly. Whatever *It* was. And she was losing respect for me, I could tell. Little things like cooking foods I didn't like or forgetting to tell me when she'd be gone for several days. I tried to be tough—just look at what Crusoe had survived!

And then Mother tried to kill herself. The first suicide attempt, when Mother swallowed her Prozac supply and nodded off reading her favorite Lorrie Moore short fiction was different than her second attempt. I remember my fifteen-year-old-self thinking bravo, how well you've grounded that book forever in our lives, Mother.

Leading to that first time, she'd spent days of her life trying to work out how a writer could be so articulate, could get everything so beautifully, painfully, right. There'd been an excess of disappointment in my inability to *get* how one would ground their reading into reality, and of course, my pathetic attempts to explain how I knew what was real. And then there she was, the print transferred onto her face where she'd let the book rest, her vomit adhering the words to her in a whole new way. This seemed to answer both of her insistent questions at once. Would she have tried to kill herself just for my benefit? It was quite a spectacle. A terrifying one.

If my marvelous friend Angie, who was always troublingly attached to Mother, and I had found her—our mouths agape— even seconds later, she'd have died then and there. The vomit had blocked most of her airway.

"You saved her life, girls," the EMT with the immaculately groomed goatee had said to us as we rode along to the hospital; he called her puking *emesis* and patted our backs hard in a reas-suring way. Still, my best friend and I weren't convinced. Though she wouldn't say, Angie looked angry at Mother, while I thought her disappointment in me, and in compensation, our schemes at enlivening post-divorce Mother had not only been a failure, but perhaps had landed her here. How many times had she asked, "Just leave me alone girls, please?"

Was the whole wordsmithing and narrative structure thing just a mania? Something to focus her intellect and hyperactivity on? The psychological manifestation of the depression of a failed writer? It couldn't be: one look at her office, the compelling flow charts of one theory giving way to another, the incredible concordances, and that was clear to me.

After the divorce and before the first suicide, when I spent hours hovering over her, drinking ginger ale through bending straws and trying to beg her off the sofa, she'd say, "Millie, show, don't tell." I already knew the basics of fiction craft, though I couldn't name off the full fifty states. Mother had a book in her. I grew up knowledgeable of that fact. "If only we could medically remove it," my father said to me in confidence after he let me pull the ring on his Budweiser for that satisfying carbon discharge.

But going over those days, which she spent lying in bed or watching reruns of *The Love Boat*, it felt she couldn't have been clearer if she'd tried. I was her last hope at happiness, and I was a failure. In turn, I saw what I wanted her to be and I'd rant, pointlessly ticking off items on my own agenda,.

"Why don't you just get up and do something?" I'd yell. "And how about drinking some juice instead of ginger ale for a change?" What an example I was setting sliding my own Canada Dry can behind my back.

I'd show Mother by dancing the tango while sipping cranberry juice out of one of the Star Wars glasses from Burger King —usually the Princess Liea—and Mother would actually laugh. More satisfying than the Budweiser carbon discharge. God, I loved to hear her shocking guffaw. These are the moments I try to hold onto.

"I'll say one thing for you, you've got a wonderful sense of humor," she said once, as if it were a magnificent gift. In my darker moments, I still treasure that compliment. Sometimes she'd cry a little after and say, "Get your old mom a tissue, would you?" Like I really touched her with my humor.

I'd carry the tissue like a knight's sword, but I'd wonder why my humor, if it was so wonderful, wasn't enough. Was there anything I could ever show that would be enough? No. It would never be enough for her. I began to score the number of times I could be of assistance to Mother alongside the number of times Angie could. I didn't like the results. Angie understood the books much more than I did. "Exactly!" Mother often said of Angie's take on a metaphor, or a turn of phrase. I began to see why people discussed the similarities between love and hate.

Mother lived after the first suicide attempt, but no longer was she the woman who'd fallen asleep reading of a faded starlet in a Midwestern motel who somehow touched the tender spot of Mother's own troubles.

Somewhere in the transaction—the reading, the pills, the vomit, the crossing over, the crossing back—Mother had abandoned her depression, like a duffle bag left behind on a train platform. Now she was a ball of energy. I should have been happy for her, but really, I wanted to take that book and shred it. I knew it was somehow to blame. But how?

How could a book, pages printed with words, albeit articulate words, but words all the same, be to blame? *You're thinking too black and white, Millie.* But I couldn't get my mind around how.

I should have been thrilled to leave all that behind. But without it, I had to get to know her all over again. And not in the way Angie and I had hoped during all those years plying her with outlandish proposals for aerobic activity.

It was as if without her books Mother was nothing. Perhaps the worst surprise of all though, was that she didn't seem to need me in the way she had. I could stay in my room all day, smoking cigarettes I pretended to want and like, and she wouldn't notice my absence. I took it to mean she'd given up on my understanding her book world. She would no longer bother trying.

Suddenly my father's catchphrase took on a new sense: "Beware a well-read woman" he used to say when Mother said the thing about carrying a book. I'd never understood, and to compensate, I'd laughed. Surely a woman and a book was nothing but harmless. Just look at all those men with their guns, Mother used to say. And that made sense to me. But once she began to exclude me so completely, I couldn't help but feel there was something sinister afoot. But what?

After the second botched "suicide," the one that took her speech, Mother was transferred far from our Long Island home to New Jersey General Hospital's psychiatric wing, where she'd spent time after the divorce and again after the first suicide. Thirty days into this latest sentence, stumped by her loss of speech, and my threats for the questionable ethics of their treatments, the doctors released a silent Mother into my custody. Despite the doctor's insistence, I simply couldn't buy that she was doing this on purpose. Surely she wouldn't cut me off so severely?

I'll never forget the way she looked sitting in my passenger seat, her hands folded on her lap, waiting for me to strap her in, as if this type of thing—an ordinary car ride—was no longer a part of her world, as if she could completely cut me and everything that came along with me out of the world *she* inhabited.

Still, I couldn't help myself and kissed her on the cheek after I'd leaned through the open door to click the belt. She looked at me and smiled. It was the last time she'd do so. I sometimes wake up screaming to this image of her, clear as day. It was the most dismissive smile. The kind you'd flash at a simpleton you felt sorry for.

At first it was nerve-wracking, the silence. There were days so quiet, I'd forget I could speak myself. Every sound became a feature: the crunch of a chip, the tinkle of a fork. I wanted to hate her. What the fuck was she doing to our lives?

But I'd catch a glimpse of her through her office door, once again so studious with her blackboards swirled with connective charts—tying all her reading into such meaningful looking flows—and her books, and I felt overwhelmingly that she was being the only person she could be. But that didn't stop me beginning to hate her for it.

I hated her for not sharing whatever it all meant with me. But her passion glowed, and it was impossible to think of her in the same way as other people. She was here, but she wasn't. Sometimes I wondered if she was real. And then her question would come to me: *how do you know what's real, Millie?* If you bleed when I cut you, I'd think. But such thoughts scared me and I tried hard not to have them.

Angie handled it differently. To her, Mother's silence was reverential. She studied Mother's boards, often copying them long-hand. "It's a test, to see what we can understand on our own," Angie would say.

"You're drinking the Kool Aid," I'd say because this looked desperate to me, and in contrast, I swore off my curiosity. Pretended to shut it down completely.

"Isn't your mother expecting you?" I'd often say to her. It felt more like Angie was there for Mother than for me most days, and my anger amplified. Once, I locked the front door and didn't let her in. I sat on the other side in tears throughout her banging. She was, after all, the last person I had.

And when she finally retreated down the driveway, I was sorry. I loved Angie, and it wasn't her fault she understood Mother better than I did. I didn't always hate her, and I certainly didn't admit it, despite Dr. Samuels, my therapist, advising me it was okay to do so. I'd repeat that to myself a lot later on. *It is okay to hate.* "You don't know her," I'd say.

"But you *do*," he said. And eventually, this made me consider the ways in which I, as witness, might translate Mother's experience. My senses engorged, for the first time, I felt I wielded some power.

Unlike the inertia following the first suicide, Mother now had me drive her to rare bookshops, whose addresses she'd rip out of the Yellow Pages and circle in runny black pen. She'd schlep a tote bag to the library in some of her old Parisian getups—all this action, so different from her years on the sofa—and I'd purposefully try to ignore her scanning the card catalogs. Sometimes I rolled my eyes and fingered the crazy person rings at my head.

What book was she looking for? Whatever it was, she didn't seem to find it. I'd see her leafing to, it seemed, a specific point in the books she perused. It took only seconds for her to reject volumes as if there were a detail she was after that was clearly there or not.

Always, she'd come out deflated and empty handed. After such a trip, I once drove to The Olde Ice Cream Parlor—the one with the old Singer sewing machine tables where you could pump the iron foot pedal while you waited for your root beer float.

When I pulled the car to a stop in front, I thought I'd done something right. This, I took from her assessing gaze. But when I turned the car off, she wouldn't budge.

"What? What did I get? Please don't tell me we've been searching these shops for my benefit."

Nothing.

I reached into the tote bag in front of her to see what book she'd just purchased: *Wuthering Heights.* I had read this over a hot-fudge sundae here years ago, then donated it to a used-book store down the street. Did she care or was she fucking with me? The familiar feel of the cover immediately turned my head to the ice cream parlor window. Tears welled, my hand trembled, and I turned more completely away from her, tucked my hand aside my thigh. I wouldn't let her see my emotions.

We had driven to this colonial Massachusetts town a couple times every summer. Mother loved the romance of it. Dad liked the lake. I loved the ice cream shop's sewing machine pedals. My father and I would race them.

It still stung, the abandonment—from both of them.

Still in the car, I looked at the window seat where we'd sat inside. The pane was grimy, but there was a family sitting there and it looked so much like me at ten years old. I could only see the parents' legs, but I swear it could have been us. *Ground your reading in reality.*

I hurried inside. But those seats were empty. How could that be? The woman sat Mother and me there. And yet, I could feel the presence of that other family. I half expected to reach out and hold my father's calloused hand. The experience was beautiful, significant, like the book itself.

All through our hot fudge sundaes, mint chip and coffee scoops with no cherries, I wondered, could that version of us exist somehow? Was *this* finally what Mother had been on about? I shook it off. I sounded just as crazy as her. The rest of the time we sat with our books open. This was *my* copy of *Wuthering Heights.* My name was in it, penned in my earliest cursive. From the first sentence, I was drawn into the romance of the possibility that maybe there was something more, maybe something *magical* to what Mother did with books. It certainly seemed to tick all the boxes of her questions. Even while I explored the enchantment of this notion, I spewed prosaic hatred at her.

"Why did you buy my own book, Mother? I read it here, yes. But so what? What could that possibly matter now that you've ruined everything for us?" I regretted the angry words I hurled at her. It was infuriating to live with someone so reactionless. And on that day, it got the best of me. I felt my anger flare. For her refusal to be out with it, or my failure to get it, I couldn't tell. Mostly, I felt they were becoming one in the same.

More often, I began tugging at the threads of that possibility of magic, of a larger plan and meaning to it all. As the story goes, God created his world in seven days, beginning with light and then supplementing that with birds, sea creatures, and man.

Now Mother was creating hers—using the best stories as a portal. Why not? It made more and more sense. Why else would she have lived the life she did? Treated me the way she did? Mother was a genius none of us could deal with, who'd discovered a wormhole in the universe through which books were the entry. I said this drunk at keg parties. Everyone laughed. *You should be a writer,* they said.

It's a big ask to believe in a point where fiction and fact overlap unless you witness it for yourself. It's a ridiculous amount to take in—especially when we're programmed to develop precisely along the opposite logic route: give up make-believe for the real world. I gleaned that from one of her science of creativity books.

Believers most often begin as disbelievers. I might say it takes one to know one. That's why the *experience* is so important. If I merely told the facts of this story, nobody would believe it. *Show, don't tell.* Yes, Mother. For Christ's sake, I get it. Finally, I get it.

But after all those years of shredding tissues in the cheap halogen light of the very expensive behavioral therapy office, trying to tamp my hope of her return, I convinced myself to stop believing. I clung to that therapist's striated, cigarette-choked words with everything I had. Otherwise, how could I move forward with the lonely, prosaic life I had left?

Instead, therapy gave me this: imagine your worst fear comes true and live with it. That is the survival skill I mastered thousands of dollars later—the way to concentrate on the bits of life that allow you to go on living. It's far more difficult than it sounds. And often, dangerous—living each moment as if it not only may be, but *is*, your last, and still going on with the mundane tasks of brushing your teeth and catching the train. Ignore how it feels. Once it's mastered this tactic is quite a relief.

Later, as a mother myself, I swore there was only one thing I'd never risk: losing myself in the obsession's Mother had instilled in me. Because once down that road, there was no turning back; just look where it led her. I wouldn't do that to my daughter. Never. But we don't really know what we'll do until we're shoved against that brick wall.

7

MILLIE

MY LASTING PHYSICAL MEMORY OF DR. PINOCCHIO IS AN INTENSE and skinny man with a ridiculous name, a big nose, and a hushed voice that underlined the importance of everything he said.

"Under the current system, there are people who have no hope," he said to me that first time in his new office, where a lithograph of Shakespeare hung on the wall. "They aren't going to pull out from beneath the ugly thoughts that drown them. They'll never step outside the constructs they've created to hide from their own grief."

The words hit close to home. Couldn't those words be said for me? I tried to shake it off; he didn't know me. Besides, Pinocchio struck me as someone more interested in the science of how this occurred and the study of how it might be fixed, than the suffering of the people themselves. And yet, he had that vulnerable look that made him approachable. *He'll get it,* people would think. But I was brought up to be skeptical of vulnerability, to respect strength.

He did have modern ideas, and this was better than the alternative I often thought. He always had his nose in *The Oxford*

Companion to Emotion and the Affective Sciences, and from that first meeting, he shared with me tidbits of his research in the field.

"Simulation is a key operation of the mind. Imagining how a scenario—say a public speaking appearance—might play out, creates in the brain a series of triggers in the same regions that would be triggered during the real thing.

"A similar thing occurs when we read stories. It's less intense than the real thing most of the time, but I'm sure there's a way to amp this up, so we aren't just trying scenarios out 'off-line' without the risk, but actually *experiencing* them without the risk.

"Hold on, Doctor P," I said, trying out the nickname I heard the staff and patients use. "This sounds like what dreams do. When I dream, everything seems so real and my body responds as such. I wake up screaming or sweating sometimes. Same reactions I would have in real life. Is that what you're saying?"

"Exactly. Think of all the dangerous scenarios people could get out of their systems without actually harming themselves in the real world. Or conversely, think of the fears that could be overcome, the careers tried out before thousands of dollars in student debt. Anything we want to do in real life but can't."

"Sounds like science fiction. Would virtual reality therapy fit in here?"

"Not exactly. It's a lot more low tech than you might think."

"Interesting. Are you telling me this because you think Mother might have some contribution to the research?" Even as I asked the question, I didn't believe it as a possible reason for this talk. She would hate all this scientific speak. She's all about instinct, beauty, the mystery of how everything works, giving yourself over to the experience. Imagine her giving me a step-by-step walk through like Pinocchio was doing! My own instinct was to look inward for blame. Was he about to justify my self-flagellation? Had Mother already made known to him my shortcomings?

Pinocchio jolted in his chair and dropped the ballpoint pen he'd begun massaging. I eyed the door behind him. The knob wasn't even properly engaged in the frame. I could be out of here in a flash. "Yes. She's key. Her brain is primed to a vastly larger degree than 99 percent of the population to be perceptive to simulative journeys. The initial scans are remarkable. Never seen anything like it."

I should have pretended to be more surprised. That's when I gave myself away. He knew I knew there was something strange she could do. He wasn't denying it. But wasn't saying it either. Why was he being so cagey? Why didn't he just come out and say it: Mother could magically travel into the world of her books? I couldn't see Mother trusting someone like him.

Instead he spoke of terms I hadn't heard of before. "We place all our emphasis in this society on rationality. We treat the mind like a computer, collecting data. We think in terms of rational and irrational. But there's something else, something that taps into our instinct, and this is called suprarational thinking. And we don't pay attention to developing this kind of thinking that allows for intuition—something people can't quite explain— though it's been proven again and again that tapping into it has extraordinary benefits.

"We need the conventional proof to show the world that suprarationality is real. And this is where a collaboration between your mother and myself comes in."

I felt a thrumming in my head. It quickly spread throughout my limbs. It pulsed through me so deeply that I felt like the world was putting all its feeling into my one body, and then suddenly, I felt nothing.

I didn't realize, but I had put myself at his mercy because he understood people, he had the records, and he knew I'd never mentioned a connection between her disappearances and her reading. And so, he must have known I was hiding it. Which meant I was unsure, scared most likely, of what I suspected. I waited on the edge of my seat for him to say it—something magical was happening here. Wouldn't this have been the moment?

One thought led to another: Was I imagining the subtext of this meeting? Was there any subtext? Was there even a Dr. Pinocchio or was this one of those amped-up dreams he was speaking of? After all, his name was ridiculous, especially given the circumstances. Still, maybe this was a signal that he been planted here?

That last thought presented as a red flag. Anyone could see I was manifesting symptoms of paranoia. How much of *all* of this had I imagined? Would it be so impossible to imagine a young girl from a broken home, whose mother tried to repeatedly kill herself, coping by creating some fantastical reason for it all? Something that in the end would make it meaningful? No. I thought of the dedication—to the exclusion of all else—that Mother had given to this cause. And the fact that Pinnochio was singling her out now backed this up: the book world was real.

Pinocchio kept talking, but I was only half absorbing his words. I sat on my hand, which had begun to shake.

"Are you okay?" he asked.

I nodded. But I wasn't so sure. His voice, the sound of the duct heating, the squeal of medicine carts wheeling by, were deafening. I closed my eyes and when I opened them, he was in front of me, on my side of the desk, the colors of his shirt too bright.

"This is where the books come in," he continued, as if he didn't notice how off I was. "It's so clear, I don't know why science hadn't discovered it earlier. We are programmed to learn, to comprehend and interact with the world through story," he continued. "That's nothing new. It's been established through various disciplines, eons ago."

With a wicked sense of déjà vu, and of course, that ever-present possibility of paranoid delusion on the edges, I suspected where this was going. Mother was as important as I'd always known her to be. What had looked like suicide attempts were errors, or occupational hazards, or cover-ups, as I'd always hungered for them to be.

Still, I was skeptical that Mother's personal journey could mean so much to so many people when she'd only ever taken it in the privacy of her own thoughts. If I knew anything about Mother it was that she believed in the individual's journey, no matter how cruel or unhelpful. Magic or not, I was clear on this: it was the reason I'd begun to hate her. This Dr. P did not jive with her credo. Despite the difference in application, I heard him and felt sure I knew where he was going; the term *suprarational* seemed to fit my theory perfectly: the words erupted from within me. "What she does, it's something not art, not life, but a new dimension entered via the combination of the two— perhaps even the *real* dimension." My palm clamped over my mouth. The doorknob called out to me. I'd said too much.

He didn't say anything, just dipped his chin slightly, then pressed a button on his desk. My desperation was a wash over the whole room. Dr. P saw my hunger for Mother's extraordinariness, my shameful normalcy, and he was abusing me for some reason, saying the kinds of things I'd always longed to hear. I yelled as I made my escape, and felt several pairs of hands secure me before everything went black.

8

MILLIE

THE DAY AFTER LUNCH AT KENNEDY'S PARENTS' PLACE, I BREAK THE news about the cancer to Angie, who takes the day off and comes by for lunch.

"Where's my book?" Rose asks even before Angie puts her bag down.

"Rose!" I scold. "Angie doesn't always have to bring you a new book."

My daughter does not look the least ashamed. That's probably because Angie is rolling her eyes in my direction, frowning, and pointing as if I'm from another planet: Disappointment, a holdover from Mother. "Of course, I do. Does your mother see how cute you are? How could I not buy you a book?"

Rose's face turns up in a frenzied smile that bobs her ponytail back as she reaches out for the flat package Angie pulls from her handbag, her stubby fingers tear and crinkle the paper. She pulls out a beautiful hard backed picture book packaged with a stuffed animal: *Diary of a Wombat.* "I know you guys love all this Australian stuff," she says, dismissively.

Rose tries to sound out the letters. "What's a womb-bat?" and looks to Angie for guidance.

"It's what your mom's got in her belly," she says. "It's for breaking all your toys and stealing your parents' attention."

"Mom has that in her belly?" Rose points to what looks like a sleeping baby bear on the cover.

Angie and I exchange smiles. "At least I will be able to tell you two apart," I say. This seems to satisfy Rose's concerns.

"Shall we take it outside and see just what this wombat can do?" Angie asks, pulling the cardboard tabs, freeing bits of Styrofoam and plastic.

"Mom says the ground is wet and the spiders will bite your hiney."

Angie eyes me suspiciously. She sets up Rose to pre-choose the best illustrations. When Rose is consumed on the sofa, Angie and I retreat to the kitchen where she doesn't beat around the bush.

"Now, what the fuck is going on?" She doesn't realize her mouth has come to be sculpted in a permanent frown. "And, hey: spiders will bite your hiney?"

"Sometimes you have to say these kinds of things to kids."

"Spiders. Will bite your hiney."

"Well, when you say it like that." Lying to Angie is like lying to myself. Pointless. But marriage makes you pick sides.

"Millie, you have a family history of mental illness. You can't walk around telling people there are spiders outside your house that will bite your hiney."

I grimace. The psychiatric trained part of me responds to this logic, likes the idea of stringing it out to the logical conclusion in a way I haven't had to in a long while: I didn't do anything wrong to Mother. I have an anxiety disorder that makes me think I did. Still, I can live with the possibility that I did, not concentrate on the feelings.

"Do you remember me reading *Robinson Crusoe*?"

She taps her cheek. "No. No, I don't. *This* is what you wanted to talk to me about?"

"Yes, you do. I talked about it nonstop. If I remember correctly, I even went through a stage of wearing a bandana, thinking I looked adventurous. And no, that's not all I've got." Adventure. That's why I'd been thinking about it in conjunction with Kennedy's Kancer. Power, independence, resourcefulness, bravery. I could use a taste of that.

I don't mention the memory that sticks out most about the *Crusoe* days. When Angie and I had been reading together outside, on our stomachs, our legs kicking in sync, and it began to rain. We'd run in through the kitchen and right down to the basement to grab an old tarp because we wanted to make a fort, be like Crusoe himself. But down there, she found dad's old hunting rifle. She pointed the gun at my forehead. I remember panicking, like she might kill me. But after a long stare off, she lowered it to the ground and began a huge Roxanne style belly laugh. "You totally thought I was going to shoot you, Millie! You should have seen your face."

Of course I laughed too. Angie was often all I had when Mother was inaccessible. I wouldn't have her thinking anything of me that would disappoint her. I learned to go with the flow.

"Maybe," she says now. "Why?" She rolls her eyes.

"Am I annoying you?"

She straightens her back as if snapping herself back to something. "I'm sorry. I thought you wanted to talk about Kennedy."

Something about the way his name rolls off her tongue makes me want to do anything but. As if her words would somehow hurt him, make the situation worse.

"No. I don't. He's sick. Not much else to say." I'd already shared what I knew so far.

"Oh, Millie. You know I'm so sorry for you. He'll be okay.

You'll see. But you must speak to him about it. You can't just ignore reality. You of all people should know that."

Again it jars. His image in her hands is not right. "Let's go see what Rose is doing back there," I say. "She'll be wanting to see how to torture a wombat. So she'll be prepared."

Angie shakes her head and shrugs, like she would have expected this avoidance from me. But she gives in and follows me out back. It's lovely exploring the world of this book with Rose. A great escape.

At dinner, I tell Kennedy about Angie's visit. His jaw tightens, nearly imperceptibly. But I catch it before he calms his muscles. I'm well beyond trying to get those two to like each other. I already feel terrible having shared the news of Kancer with her. Initially, it felt right to unburden myself to her, lightened the load a bit. But now it rankles.

"What did she want? Let me guess, man troubles. Am I right?"

"Of course."

"What a shock." Immediately, he begins to choke.

"Are you okay?" I ask, placing my silverware along the rim of the plate. "Is it a chili? Have you bitten your cheek?"

"Fine," he says. Not *I'm fine.*

I let out a heavy breath and look him in the eye.

He looks handsome, hurt, like he's trying to say something he doesn't think he wants to. How have we become so separate? He smooths his hands over the napkin on his lap, sits straighter and picks up his silver. "Some things," he says, "you don't need to know."

See Angie, you don't understand everything. He doesn't want me to tell him. I've been training for this my whole life: living in the dark, managing the possibility of imminent disaster. It's quite beautiful if you look at it that way—all fitting together so heartbreakingly perfect.

I'm conscious of the way his muscles shift along his arms as he eats, the way his foot taps slightly before he consciously stops it. I feel him watch me.

9

MILLIE

MILLIE

I TOLD KENNEDY WHAT HAPPENED WITH MOTHER AFTER THE THIRD time we laid naked together, catching our breath after frantic, heightened sex. The sort that casts all other such experiences as clumsy, crass acting jobs.

I'd drunk too much sherry—the only liquor left in what I still thought of as Mother's dusty cabinet—and he'd twirled my hair forcefully in his fist and said, "I want to know what you aren't telling me." The level of my attraction to him bordered on mania, and I would have done anything he asked with my eyes and hands thusly in his clutches.

Still, I was surprised to find that once I stumbled upon a way to begin the story, it was a great relief to share the burden of Mother with him. He didn't interrupt me once until I got to the summer of '95, after the Lorrie Moore incident.

I was telling him how I'd become suspicious of all those pungent second-hand books Mother buried herself in. There was something to them I couldn't tap, that wouldn't reveal itself to me. And he only stopped me then to say he wasn't sure where he stood on second-hand bookshops. The smell had always bothered him, and he wondered whether authors should have been worked into a cut of the profits somehow.

"Authors are incredibly underpaid," he said before going silent again. After that, he maintained his silence, rather than spewing the constant barrage of disbelief and questioning I had anticipated, which made the sharing far less terrifying than I'd pictured.

I told him her method for that second suicide, the one that had taken her speech, was a modern rip-off of Hamlet's Ophelia with rocks in pockets, garland of yellow roses from our garden crowning her head, and chains and chains of those blasted rhododendrons (precisely half alive, half dead) around her neck. She'd made the attempt at the creek near the end of the next block and it was quashed by a lantern-jawed fly fisherman.

How could it be anything but tragedy? My mother shedding the parts of herself like a snake slithers from her skin.

"Or a giant, self-absorbed cliché," he said.

No one had ever spoken of Mother that way. I didn't know how to react until a smile planted itself on my lips. After all these years, I was surprised to find I had distilled Mother's untold story into something quite decisive. In fact, though Kennedy's stance was a relief, there was a part of me that instinctively defended the mystery of it all.

I continued. "Still, I know what you mean. Terrible, I told myself as I waited for a ride from my friend Angie's mother to the hospital. Who does something like that to her child? I'd sat for fifteen minutes with the phone in my hand, considering calling my father, and telling myself those weren't my tears soaking my shirt because I was not crying over such a ridiculous woman. Unable to act, I told myself to go to the ladies' room, and when I came back, I would call him."

The word *ridiculous* rang in my ear. It wasn't accurate, but when I told it that way, I allowed it to feel accurate.

"Wait a minute. You said 'ladies' room' to yourself at a time like that?"

"Of course," I said.

"Right," he said. I was relieved when he didn't ask me to explain my father's absence from my life.

"Anyway, on the way back to the kitchen from the ladies' room, I felt a surge of bravery and rushed to grab the handset. Only I tripped on a chair leg—Mother's chair leg, where she always read—and twisted my ankle, which would have to be set. I propped myself onto Mother's chair and called Angie." What I didn't say was that with her, I didn't have to hide the tears, even if she wasn't the softest person around. Instead I shrugged. "Angie knew me."

"This ankle?" Kennedy asked, holding the wrong ankle in an overwhelming way that I had never realized a man's hand could pull off. In that moment, I wondered whether women's lib wasn't just for women who hadn't found the real thing, because all I wanted then was to surrender to him. I nodded and suddenly found myself pinned under him in complete oblivion again.

In two hours, he asked, "Weren't you in the middle of a story before those?" His chin indicated the two silk scarves tied to the iron headboard. "Sorry, Mother Theresa," he said to the painted image in the middle of all the scrollwork. We'd fallen asleep afterward, though it was the middle of the afternoon—somehow time seemed to backbend for us in those early days.

"Do you really want to hear the rest? It gets weird."

"Ah, so this is what you were talking about that first day at Three Guys. As opposed to the other 'normal' stuff you told me earlier. All right, let's have it. I knew this was all too good to be true. Bring on the bunny boiling." Kennedy yanked the blankets around him sanctimoniously, pulling the last bit off me, and fixed his gaze so I'd know he wasn't going anywhere.

I turned over on my side, propping my head up on an elbow to make sure he could see everything. I was love confident. Over confident. "Why do men always use that cliché?"

He shrugged. "There's a reason it's a cliché."

I threw a pillow at him. Disarmingly, he grabbed my hand and kissed it.

"After the second suicide, Mother hadn't spoken. She handed me a volume so old, it looked to belong in a museum archive. As she passed it over, there was something to her look —" I tried to mimic the memory but knew mine had nothing on the effect. "Eyes that seemed to expand to hold everything she knew. A supreme truth." I surprised myself, shivering at the memory of that ghost family in the ice cream shop window. I began to take for granted the way Kennedy indulged my going on about Mother.

"Let me give it a crack," Kennedy said. He tried out a variety of stares that ranged from suggestive to X-rated. If I'd known him better, I'd have thrown a pillow at him.

"Truth," Kennedy said, cocking his head. "Overrated. Reality's a lot softer than that." *Soft?* I wanted to ask, how did he know about that? But he kissed me so hard I forgot what we'd been talking about. What was the point in talking about it anyway? This was real, here, now.

The way he waved off all my escapades with Mother as hogwash was more than refreshing—it was an unburdening that blew life back into me. The words sounded silly to my own ears as I recited them.

My mother disappeared, and I would've believed anything to give that meaning. It was easier to convince myself of that version, and my mind took to it nearly effortlessly, much easier than with all that painful therapy. Who knew all I needed was Kennedy? "Back to the book," I said.

"Oh, let me guess what book it was! Ummm, something really dramatic, and yet, obscurely literary, and yet, fantastical, but with a hip dose of irony. Hmmmmm. I've got it. *The Hungry Caterpillar*. The pickle always annoyed me. I can't buy that with all that food around, a worm would be interested in a pickle."

"Maybe it was Jewish," I said; that's how Mother always explained her pickle addiction.

"I'd have to look back, but I'm pretty sure there was a hotdog in there, which didn't appear to be kosher. Not to mention meat with dairy."

"Pregnant? And how does a hot dog *appear* kosher?"

"Pregnant—interesting theory. That would explain a lot. And if you work on the Upper East Side long enough, you can identify a kosher hotdog by sight. In fact, it's part of the interview process."

"I'm not even going to continue that conversation. You're right. It was. Mother was reading *The Hungry Caterpillar*."

He seemed to forget about the broken ankle, and I, for whatever reason, omitted that part of the story. I rarely allowed myself to dwell on it. It seemed a bridge too far to think, much less say the truth: that my broken ankle didn't heal properly. That I'd walked for a year with a limp that couldn't be fixed until Mother disappeared for good, and I was inexplicably healed. How to explain what the brain can simply write-off? Besides, this lens of Kennedy's was so much more *fun*.

Even as I thought it, I could see myself limping through life like an alternate version of reality. But I kept that bit to myself. Because it sounded wrong, like science fiction or clinical denial. And most of all, because I didn't want that part of my life anymore. I wanted this.

Still, for months on end, we unwound the rest of the story in this way and then I reached the crescendo of my rendition, when Dr. Pinocchio approached me. I told this part in as detailed a manner as I could. I had long since overcome the shame of what I'd been taught by Dr. Samuels to understand as a paranoid manifestation of my grief. It wasn't so rare. Who wouldn't go a little crazy in the circumstances? All the same, I was careful, as I chose my words to share the encounter with Kennedy.

In the telling, I felt I had nearly liberated myself from the whole thing, and I wanted so badly to hear Kennedy's skeptical summation: "Okay, well you thought your mother could cross into another dimension. Who hasn't felt that way from time to time? Now, please pass the potatoes?"

I wanted us to laugh over it and make jokes like "Where are those keys? Did you leave them in the Book World again?" Even the terms I'd come up with—*Book World*, for crying out loud— were so dramatic.

Despite the posturing while I was reciting the story, a dormant image bank in my brain was tapped, and I was back to that cyclonic, banging silence of the weeks after Mother's second suicide attempt. "At first, it had seemed a godsend when I was met by the new guard of psychiatrists—of the Gestalt school—at the Cuckoo Bird Hut," I began. Enter Dr. Pinocchio. I remember that even the dusty Lipton tea in flimsy Styrofoam tasted better in the company of his revelatory approaches to mental health. I don't know what I thought his team could do, but I knew they could do something.

"Ge-what?"

"Gestalt. It's well. . .it's complicated. But the part that's important is that Gestalt therapy is about being authentic and responsible for oneself because everything we touch affects everything in time and space. Some people take this theory to extremes: relating it to field theory where no part of the field is uninfluenced by what goes on elsewhere in the field. You might have heard of the butterfly theory?

And so, this identity we're looking for is constantly changing. We never see the same thing twice, because each experience changes us, and therefore changes the way we see and experience things. We can never be the same. The essence of human nature cannot be pinned down 'once and for all.'" *Softer than that.* "Basically, it's a way of looking at the world that's so complicated that you can drown yourself in trying to work it out. And maybe that's what she did."

"Sounds fun," he said, with a tone that belied his belief it's anything but.

"It's believed that it's possible to free yourself from past associations and experience life 'naively' in a fresh, objective way, that balances the subjective way we are normally limited to with all our emotional baggage.

"Anyway, the goal of achieving such a thing is a new level of awareness. Most people believe it's impossible to achieve. But say someone could get there, they'd see patterns that the rest of us couldn't—with both that objectivity and subjectivity. And they'd be able to manipulate them." *Even across dimensions*, I leave out. Because that's the kind of thing Dr. Samuels had taught me to do. Her version of gestalt was quite different; simpler.

Even expelling it this way, I felt myself being tugged into the mystical promise of it all, the idea of multiple dimensions, where, say, a little girl might still be sitting happily at an ice cream shop with her loving family. Or had a limp. But I allowed that image to stay in the background. "Probably getting too technical," I said.

Kennedy pretended to sleep, a loud snore wobbling his head on his shoulder. I couldn't believe he didn't have more questions.

I elbowed him and his eyes burst open. "What did I miss?" he said, then took my face in his grip and kissed me, looking so deeply into my eyes that any desirability of all that other stuff was eclipsed. There was more kissing, then more other stuff, then a lazy afternoon nap, a steamy shower—the cycle of our early days together.

Our conversation about Mother unspooled intermittently throughout. "There had always been an emphasis on the creative function of the brain at this psychiatric department. But the problem was most of the old testing was done as a misguided observer, from the outside in, the way most creative research had been.

"With new, progressive funding sources, these doctors were encouraged to make revolutionary inroads in connections of emotional health and the arts, in the plasticity of the brain, the exploration of complex creative thinking, of the ideas about those uncharted reaches of the mind, etcetera, etcetera.

"The old guard had wasted years on unusual use tests with Mother, believing the key was in the outcomes, rather than in the processes of recognition and response. Always this black and white: what's the conclusion? She must have hated them, really hated them. It's no wonder she opened up to Dr. P. He was a breath of fresh air with his suprarationality."

"Dr. Pee?" He made a sound-effect to clarify.

"No! P for Pinocchio." I don't know why I said that, but he laughed it off.

"Oh, that's much better!"

God, how natural it all felt.

Creativity, these young psychologists believed, was key to our emotional health, not only in creating art, but in survival. They wanted to test how. When Mother's case was presented,

Pinocchio was enchanted. She had already embraced all these ideas, seemed to live them. They spoke of Kant and Baudelaire and Joseph Beuys with his blackboards that looked so much like Mother's. My definitive narrative astounded me. He seemed to buy it without question.

"So it's all very simple," Kennedy said. "You've had to struggle with a crazy family just like everyone else, is what you're saying."

I actually laughed. All the time. About Mother. It felt fucking great. I let out a big breath and felt like ten years had been expelled. I never spoke about all that field theory and gestalt stuff again, and Kennedy never asked me to. For that I was thankful. I started to forgive myself for the anger I'd harbored for Mother, discarding the ugly images, rather than grow numb at the loss and confused cluster of responsibility I often felt at the thought of her.

Kennedy painted her as a problem I'd been forced to deal with, had done an excellent job of coming out the other end of, and this suited me.

I remember very clearly, in the haze of one of those love-filled afternoons, Kennedy grabbed me and flipped me onto my back. "I will do anything for you."

I blushed. This was the real thing. It was too good to be true.

I looked at him trying to pull off wry, but seriousness, *esteem*. He had chosen me. Of all the people in the world.

I didn't finish the story. He didn't ask, and given his reaction, there didn't seem to be a point. Kennedy accepted me warts and all, and I'd certainly shared enough. My shrink, Dr. Samuels, and I had already gone over what was necessary to share with someone, should I find a man I wanted to spend my life with.

"Your paranoia and anxiety attacks are products of your illness," he'd said. "There is no reason to share the specific manifestations of them. They could just as easily have been giant tortoises taking over the world. We call this need to tell, the urge to *confess*. And in fact, any time you feel that need, I want you to do just the opposite: keep the thought to yourself. Eventually you'll be able to tell the difference between the real realities, and those produced by anxiety." *Gestalt.*

And so I didn't tell Kennedy about how it had all ended that day in Dr. P's office. How when I woke, I found I had been admitted to the hospital, under the care of Dr. P himself. He told me he had been trying to explain some routine testing they'd done on mother and I'd begun having a delusional episode, speaking incomprehensibly about "Bessie" and "the red room," and "falling sick with crying," and not looking at him at all, and then I became violent, throwing things from his desk, kicking at him when he tried to help me. Those words rang familiar: *Jane Eyre,* they were from.

My instinct was not to trust him; it had all felt so real. But his own words assured me I would think this, and I didn't dare utter a word of my suspicion. Why would he lie? Or was this a technique, a tricky way to get me to work out what this gestalt was all about for myself? So he could separate out those who had the magic touch and didn't? I let it go. What choice did I have if I wanted out of here?

My stay was short. I'd reached a crisis point, and this was how my brain shut down for a reboot. I needed some drugs to stabilize my field perception—determine what was real, and a prescription to begin therapy, and I was on my way.

Later, throughout my outpatient therapy at a local psychologist, Dr. Samuels, we unpacked everything that happened on that day, and everything that had led to it, in welcome absolutes: I'd imagined the whole thing; not an uncommon occurrence after a period of such extreme stress, not to mention abandonment. Still, while it was happening, the experience was so real: I was *in* the world of *Jane Eyre*.

It was no surprise why it was this particular passage I'd been transported to: the four hands carrying me up to the red room. I was Jane Eyre as a child, after Master John had struck her. God, how I'd responded to that opening scene. She was ten, the age I was when my parents split. Her mistress "regretted the necessity of keeping [her] at a distance," the girl who was excluded from privileges, who "was like nobody there," and felt "resolved in [her] desperation to go to all lengths."

I lost myself in her misery, my misery, relished the company, the words that expressed my loneliness at home, my failures and isolation. And then there I was, telling Bessie she needn't use her stays to tie me in a chair, alone in the room. Jane was me; I was her—asking *why could I never please?* To feel this deep empathy was everything. It's why I'd read that scene over and over.

I loved the idea that one could "fall sick with crying," as Jane did. And I felt myself do so, the physical manifestation of my suffering I had always hoped for. It was rich, delicious, and then sickening, when the paltry gestures of tenderness of Jane's visiting physician—rather than the people who should have cared for me—made my heart sing.

The beauty my pain transformed into was meaningful, soul-nourishing, inspiring as I'd always wished it could be. I felt power zing through every bit of my body, which both was and was not a pale, frail ten-year-old. I was proud to be a "noxious thing; and did not shy away from it."

But had I dreamed, imagined, hallucinated it all? Or was I in the dimension created by my mind's interaction with *Jane Eyre*? It felt so real. Sometimes I truly didn't know.

To this day, I can see the crimsons of the room—damask and heavy velvet, the slight covering of dust over the mirror, the darkness, the strange light, the careening of Jane/my mind in directions I couldn't discern as real or imagined, the terror, the screams that ripped and shredded me, the ensuing comfort, "however meagre or resented," from the nursemaid and servant, the physician.

It was at once an experience I'd known, but felt in a new, beautiful, haunting way, that could touch one's soul, that did touch my own soul. I felt the warmth and caress that in real life I never got as a child. It had fed my needy soul and strengthened me for what I needed to do: care for myself, as both Jane and I understood that no one else would.

Sometimes, afterward, words would come to me—dreaming or conscious. And this was no delusion: suprarational, preconscious. I would see them, like words on a page, before my face, telling me that in this conversation with Dr. Pinocchio, he had been telling me that magical things had happened; it wasn't just a delusion. But Dr. Samuels explained this can be the way with delusional episodes—we can find meaning where we want to, though it isn't really there. I wanted so badly to believe him. That way lay answers, solutions.

I learned to take pills and ignore them, ignore the little girl with her family through the window of the ice cream shop. The limping version of myself, holding on tightly to the handrail. *Laugh at the intrusive thoughts,* my therapist instructed. And I learned to.

For the same reason, I never told Kennedy the strange

shards of memory about what I'd buried in the garden. Despite my work with Dr. Samuels, and my increasing power to laugh at intrusive thoughts, I wasn't always sure. I admit my stomach swirled with terror sometimes.

Mother had disappeared for good. And I hated her by then. I'd found myself in the garden more than once, dirt under my nails. But if I'd done something terrible, wouldn't I remember? After a couple weeks of particularly painful mind-grinding on the subject, I confessed my worst fears to my therapist.

"My dear, I have no doubt you are nothing but the lovely young woman I see before me," Dr. Samuel's had assured me. I'd written his words down, so I could stop asking him to repeat them.

"Survivor's guilt. That's what you have. Unethical. That's how I'd classify the medical treatment of your mother. Psychiatric patients should not be used as guinea pigs. Science has already made these mistakes. There's plenty written on the subject. And as for you, don't you think the police would have found something if you'd buried her back there?"

I had certainly entertained the question on many a terrifying day after Mother's disappearance. But luckily, my worst fears hadn't been realized.

"You, my dear," Dr. Samuels said, "have suffered a great deal, and it's time to forgive yourself of however it is you think you've mistreated your mother and begin your life. It sounds like no one's ever really taken an interest in that before. It was never about you—especially in the formative years, when that's all it should have been."

Of course, the therapist never believed any of the stuff about the book realm. And that's why I liked him and chose to believe him.

So, in the version I told Kennedy, there was no dirt on my fingernails, no blackouts. Leaving those parts out reassured me these were insignificant anxieties, something to laugh at. Even more so because when I went to grab for the threads of the story, those bits felt like confessions, and Dr. Samuels had warned me off of those, and this was proof that they were nothing but intrusive thoughts I needed to laugh off. It felt so right—like the happiness people were always after. Dr. Samuels praised my progress. Surely, I'd followed the right path, I told myself.

Still, in my omission, I hadn't been completely honest with Kennedy, and there were days when I felt the weight of the untruth between us.

And he'd been keeping the Big C from me. Did the weight bear down on him too? Wouldn't it be so much simpler if we could unburden ourselves and get it all out there? Life was always looking that way—so simple if only...But we both knew no simplicities lie in that direction.

10

MILLIE

A FEW MORNINGS AFTER ANGIE'S VISIT IT'S FINALLY KENNEDY'S test day, and I'm mixing Rose's hot cereal (oakmeal, she calls it) with raisins (not too many raisins, lots of almond slivers, extra cinnamon sugar), pretending I don't know why Kennedy's got a late start this morning (10 a.m. appointment at the Kancer Doctor). Or why his knee is bobbing up and down and rattling the kitchen table when I look out at the relentless survivors of Mother's garden, for I never did manage to grow anything on my first attempt, and didn't have the heart for a second go at it.

Today, the first slants of morning light catch the fronds, illuminating petal tips that were not there this time yesterday. Is it possible they are more beautiful because of the visions of death surrounding them?

"Coffee?" I ask, shocked at the way ordinary tasks shelter us this morning.

"Nah. Trying to skip caffeine today. Didn't sleep so well last night." His lie slips out so naturally, it frightens me. You can't eat or drink before these blood tests you're having and we both fucking know it.

But it's Kennedy's chapter, David Duchovny Goes to the

Oncologist, is how my mind frames it—a product, I suppose, of growing up on *The X Files* and of lately reading too many children's books. I've been trying to cast it at a safe distance, and I try to give him the benefit of the doubt if he feels right that it should be handled this way. Which means I'm clenching my fists behind my back and trying very hard not to flare my nostrils. I don't know how things will turn out, but I tell myself that somehow everything will come together—if it doesn't concertina on itself. Either way, if I can't work it out, a natural progression will take over, for better or worse.

An hour and a half later, I follow Kennedy, about six cars behind, having caught up with him just as he's lifting Rose out of her car seat with all her glitter pots and an assortment of pastas in individual Ziplocs, non-toxic glue, drawing utensils, and Q-tips, outside Richard Segal's, where she'll be spending the day oblivious to the forces in action across the bridge.

I park clandestinely inside a church lot across the street. In the Segals' driveway, Richard and his wife fawn over our daughter as if it's the only thing that could possibly unite them.

I quickly U-turn and wait along the curb of the main street, and in moments, catch up with Kennedy, following him onto the highway eastbound to Manhattan. Is following him worse than approaching him? Could this be—as I'd told myself—a better way to respect his needs? It isn't so clear as things get into motion. I only know I can't do nothing. I tell myself I've distanced myself enough that Kennedy won't have to worry about me breathing down his neck, forcing my point of view. If anything, he's forcing this upon me. It's all I can do to follow along.

There is a roughed-up Ford Focus, a Toyota Corolla, and a bright yellow Mini between us. I am counting on Kennedy's tunnel vision, his obliviousness to surroundings when something key is at hand. At the wheel, I rub my mother's necklace along my lower lip with my thumb and forefinger—just the way Rose does with her charm. I laugh out loud.

Kennedy seems glued to the destination. I see no movement but his arm reaching for the radio tuner now and again. God, the way he can use a radio to avoid things. Just when I think it's impossible he's listening, he'll come out with an outraged comment—no matter what the content, from his point of view everyone is quite convincingly an imbecile. My assessment of the world has certainly deteriorated over the course of our marriage.

The tunnel swallows him first, then the Focus, the Corolla, the Mini, then me, as in my head I settle on one thing for sure: if this had been a chapter in a book, my mother wouldn't have let me skip over it. She didn't believe in that kind of thing.

If Hansel and Gretel were meant to burned in an oven, I read every word, looked in detail at the illustrations and the terror in their eyes. See how his shoelace is artfully dangling from the corner of the cell there? If Bambi's mother was murdered, we read over it twice to make sure I understood she wasn't coming back.

There's plenty of traffic on Second Avenue, though it's the middle of the day, and there's no apparent jam-up or construction zone. The sky is bright and the sun dazzles off the mirrored skyscraper glass.

I imagine Kennedy checking the dashboard clock every two minutes, increasing the suspense. This vulnerable gesture would reunite us if we were in that car together—him from his news radio escape and me from my analogical one—so that by the time we'd have left the parking garage and approached the medical office lobby, we'd be huddled together and moving as a single, though conflicted, mass.

As things stand, I circle the block while Kennedy hands over his car keys to the attendee. When I see him exit, I do the same and head to the building bearing the address I will never forget.

He must have stopped for a drink because I catch him ascending the top tiers of the wide brick staircase up to the row of glass lobby doors just as I'm approaching the base of said staircase.

Inside, I hate the way Kennedy moves past the giant board of suite numbers and sails directly to the elevator that goes to the 12th floor, selecting from four identical banks on opposite corners.

Dr. Leonard Kramer, Oncologist

At the sight of the name at this place globally connected with Kancer and the receipt and yesterday's faxed confirmation that yes, my worst fears have been realized. Kennedy's been getting treated for Non-Hodgkins Lymphoma for nearly five years. My brain flashes back, vainly trying to whirl us to the time before this name and this place and its ugly consonants and poorly-named disease (if it's a Non, then it should be named what it is) weighed heavily on our lives.

I know there's a way to do so. Mother's done it, and though I never admitted it to myself, I did too—with my incomprehensibly healed ankle all those years ago. It's to do with what you've read—meaningfully—and where you've read it, and Dr. P, and suprarationality and preconsciousness, and all the stuff I've been denying all this time.

Once Kennedy's elevator is safely past the second floor, I enter the neighboring one, watching the floor number display tick over. My doors open to the twelfth floor. He's out of sight, but I smell his cologne. And that's when I feel it. I've been here before. But when?

The sense memory is so strong, I can almost *see* myself here.

I walk as slowly as possible toward and then past Kramer's glass-fronted office where the receptionists—the detail upon which I'd gambled—both seemed overly familiar with Kennedy. Like most women, they can't help but beam at him. Right away, I can tell which one is Cindy, who, as her voice hinted, can't be older than twenty-five while the other's not a day under seventy. I instantly resent them. Get a hold of yourself, Millie, I think. Go downstairs and wait. This is where you part.

I allow myself one last look, scoff down a chocolate croissant at the lobby café and do my best to pass the time while pretending not to gawk at the elevator bank for his exit.

I suddenly feel ashamed. What is this semantic trick I've used to convince myself that tailing my husband around is better than facing him? This is so unlike me. And yet, all my actions are instinctive, accomplished, without hesitation.

Two endless hours (and another croissant) later, I see him. Instead of confronting him, the way I'd told myself I would, I raise my newspaper to cover most of my face. A wasted effort. His eyes are glued to the geometric carpet. He's pale. My heart sinks. The news isn't good. It isn't fucking good.

I should run to him, tackle him, force him to tell me. Make him kiss me because who knows how many more kisses I will get. But there are rules. And we've both somehow made a mockery of them.

I stand and follow as he walks through the door and makes his way back to the garage. Staying a block behind, I trail, then wait, browsing in a souvenir shop to waste the time I imagine it will take him to retrieve his car.

As I wait at the shop's door, I see his Range Rover turn north toward his store, and I run to get my car. It takes a long time. I cannot understand what the holdup is, I say rudely to the Pakistani man who has no idea what I'm saying, just trying to man the booth like his partner instructed him, smiling tightly and saying, "Car is coming, Miss Lady."

"A person can get a cancer removed from their body quicker than this!" I yell. "This is not an important thing you are doing here!" This I also yell, sounding like someone I would hate, because this is the only person I can scream at. There are rules, I pointlessly remind myself. "Won't you say anything?" I scream.

He smiles. It is a kind smile this time, with two horribly twisted teeth top right—the kind of smile I do not deserve.

There's traffic on Madison; there's always traffic on Madison. I try to relax my fingers, my posture. There's no rush now. He'll be at the store all day.

I pull up across the street from Kennedy's shop and look for his car. I don't see it. But there is a conspicuous space right in front. I try to look calm as I enter the store. Seb's hair is lime green and black, swept to the side, somehow affixed in a surprisingly elegant swoop with gel, or spray. He looks surprised to see me. "*Quelque Chose*," he says. It's our little joke.

I came here some time ago, before meeting Kennedy, pulled by intuition. I found the cutest stationary I could make notes on that read *Quelque Chose* across the top. I guess that's how he remembers me, besides being his boss's wife.

"Quelque Chose," I say. "So, where's that wonderful husband of mine?"

"I'm afraid you've just missed him, Mon Cherie. He's dashed out a second ago to see a salesman in New Jersey."

New Jersey? Why wouldn't the salesman come to him? I voice my curiosity.

"Good question," Seb says. "I was just so glad for the opportunity for an afternoon of slacking off, I didn't think of it."

"Perspective," I say. "It's a killer."

"Quelque Chose," he signs off.

I shouldn't be following him anyway, I tell myself as I get into the car. I feel my body start to relax, as if it's just finished a big job. No sooner do the muscles start sliding down my shoulders than the panic sets in. It is unlikely that Kennedy would go to Jersey to see a client—especially after his appointment. More likely, this is an excuse when really he's going to see some specialist radiographer or something. So now what?

I pull out, turn a right across town so that I can make my way back to the FDR Expressway. At a red light between Park and Third Avenues, I see him heading in the opposite direction. Is he going to Jersey? My muscles pop back up. I rearrange myself, more erect, in my seat.

When the light changes, I take an unplanned illegal left and follow Kennedy. When I get going in the right direction, he's nowhere to be found. The lights are not in my favor. But I know the way to Jersey (of course, I do!) and hope I can catch up with him before he reaches the West Side Highway.

Once I get onto the Jersey Turnpike, the ride goes smoothly. Somewhere up ahead, first he, then I pass the Clara Barton rest stop, the Walt Whitman rest stop. I spot him going slowly in the left lane about five cars between us—something he hates; he's distracted.

My throat goes dry and I start to gag. I grab for a bottle of water floating around on the passenger seat. The gagging turns to choking and I can't get the damned bottle open. One-handed, my driving isn't great. There are honks. Shit. I don't want to draw attention to myself. I look up to see if Kennedy's turned around. It looks like he's checking his rearview. I feel like he's looking right at me. My chest goes cold. But then he looks down and continues straight ahead, doesn't change his speed or anything.

I finally get a sip of water and that starts me choking again. Water's spurted everywhere. How come this never happens to Miss Marple? My cell phone rings. Oh god. It's him. I should ignore it. If I answer it, and he hears a background noise that is also going off where he is, he will know where I am.

"Hey," I say.

"Hey."

I watch his back, which gives me nothing. He's got himself organized with some kind of hands-free device, so there's no fumbling with a handset, risking an accident the way I'm doing.

"Where are you?" I ask.

"Where do you think?"

"Work?"

"Yeah, work," he says.

Does he know? Does he see me? Why did I ask where he was?

"Everything all right?" I ask.

"Seb told me you stopped by looking for me, so I wanted to ask you that question."

"Right," I say. "Yeah, fine. Got a lot done. Thanks for taking Rose to the Segals'." I'm lying and he's lying and it feels like we both know it but can't stop ourselves. I'm going to say something. The next word I utter will be the truth. But a truck horn sounds and a second later it's echoed on the line, then after a long, bizarre silence, the reception goes spotty and the connection cuts out. Neither of us calls back.

He takes the New Jersey General ramp, and I switch onto autopilot, flicking on my blinker as we exit and approach a parking lot. I shake my head at Kennedy not using his. And it comes heavy and sudden then, that I feel the years since Mother's disappearance. Is this where he's going, to the hospital, her hospital?

When the light changes, he continues straight. Someone honks at me from behind. As I thumb off my indicator, I look up to see if Kennedy noticed me. There are three cars between us. I swear he's looking in his rearview. I swear our eyes lock. But he keeps driving, as if he hasn't noticed a thing.

The hospital disappears from site as we make our way down the main drag. Where is he going? Maybe it is a salesman. I should turn around right now. But I can't. Soon enough, my daughter may not have a father. The least I can do is see this, whatever it is, through.

I catch every light going on red, praying as we approach that he doesn't sail through. Once, twice, and we aren't separated. The third time I get caught. Kennedy races on without me. My heart sinks as he continues down the road and out of sight. It must be the longest light cycle in history. I feel my face flush, my jaw tense.

When the signal turns green I can see it's pointless. He's gone. I can't see him anywhere. What had I been thinking? I drive for six blocks until I come to the gourmet supermarket, Walker's, where I often stopped after visiting Mother; a place I for so long associated with thoughtful cups of coffee and lots of time connecting the dots.

Now, however, it reminds me that Mother's disappearance was not something I should have put behind me, that I let myself be persuaded to let that go because it was too hard. But I seem foolishly to be trying to make up for that behavior now with Kennedy.

The lot is nearly full. I steer slowly down two parking rows, and halfway down the third, I see Kennedy's Range Rover. I look around but don't see him anywhere. Let the man have his lunch meeting! But I don't. I park at the farthest corner and run as fast as my belly will allow, holding the small bump to prevent that awful bouncing sensation.

Inside, I wheel a cart around and pretend to inspect the wide aisles. On any other occasion, I would have been gaping longingly at the Listeria-laden salamis, the mercurial mussels in their netted bags. But today, I've got bigger problems.

I have no plan, no way of finding him except to scour the capacious prepared foods area, which is popular with the lunch crowd. Sharply through the fresh bread cloud, a whiff of garlic beckons as I beeline toward the expensive, inauthentic ethnic foods buffet. Immediately, I spot my father, the man I never hoped to see again, stiffly fingering tongs to pinch a generous helping of high-gloss chicken wings onto a Styrofoam tray.

I stand frozen, hands on cart, my father at three o'clock, tonging himself more chicken wings smothered in an unnatural hue of glaze, and then some dumplings, into the container, his kids pointing along at the chafing dishes. One of them looks about Rose's age. The other a few years older, much taller anyway. I can't turn away. My chest thuds. Beneath the tempo, an exquisite heartache blooms. Stop feeling sorry for yourself, Millie! Think, think. Are Kennedy and Father here meeting each other? And if so, why?

I scan the rows of chafing dishes under incredibly peppy illustrated signs. I spot Kennedy at a French bakery counter, pointing out a nice-looking baguette sandwich, ruffled lettuce peeking out bright as anything.

Suddenly, I'm in motion, careening around a taco chip display at the end of the aisle in an attempt to conceal myself. I pick up one of the organic styled paper sacks as if to inspect the ingredients, and watch Kennedy's sandwich get nimbly wrapped. He points to one of the fancy soda bottles in the refrigerator case and the woman in the white apron retrieves it, and tucks both of his items, along with a wad of napkins and two straws, into a rustic paper bag with the Watson's logo. That should be my straw. Talk about grasping at...

I cannot believe what I'm seeing. Kennedy makes his way to my father, who is just palming his change at the buffet register, balancing on his tray an assortment of fountain sodas beside the hulking Styrofoam container. His pitiably named boys— Leonardo and DaVinci—are already gnawing on a wing apiece, the high-pigment sauces clowning their mouths. My father looks up and Kennedy catches his eye, indicating toward an empty table with six swivel chairs.

My father corrals the boys to the table and they all sit, Kennedy alone on his side, the three Burns men on the other side. Kennedy is gracious and at ease, asking the boys questions that make them squirm and smile. My father cocks his head and folds his hands in a prayer position as if getting down to business. What is the business? Judging from where Kennedy has just come from, it can't be good. Why else would he go to this extreme? We don't see my father. There was the one time at our wedding. And of course, Mother's body-less funeral.

I put the chips down and pick up another bag as if this identical one is more to my liking. Across the way, Kennedy ignores his sandwich and digs inside his jacket pocket, pulling out a leather envelope (we have eight of these from the original design samples sent to his store). I fumble for my bag's zipper, as if simultaneously holding my own leather envelope will somehow bridge the gap.

From his, he slides out photographs. Even from here, I can tell they are of Rose as Kennedy looks and then rotates them around for my father and the boys to see. Who are they telling these boys Rose is? More photos with Rose "writing" her name, Rose taking her first no-hands goosesteps, and Rose in her first red, shocking, hour of life, swaddled and tight-lidded between my swollen breasts, my robe barely covering a thing.

That's as much as I can take. I return my attention to the taco chips, putting this second bag down, clumsily, unevenly. As I circle my cart to escape, that row of chip bags topples over onto a woman in a rabbit fur vest who takes the opportunity to draw attention to her expensive blow dry by yelling as if she'd been stabbed.

Everyone looks, but there's only one person whose reaction I check. Kennedy turns and our eyes lock. He's got the birth photo in his hands and we both look to it before he excuses himself and comes chasing after me. I run, leaning into the cart to pick up the pace.

In the obscurity of the next aisle, I stake out a hiding spot by the gourmet cheese case. A corpulent man in an elongated chef's hat approaches from the other side of the counter.

"Yes, ma'am! What can I get for you today?"

I notice his delicate smile—tight lips and miniscule teeth—as he hands me a toothpick-speared chunk of Munster with the one telltale corrugated orange side. In my panic I decide I must purchase something. I know it's important what I buy, symbols being what they are, and my mind reels. This is when things get tricky.

It's all well and good to have an idea, but I've been chasing the ghosts of these ideas my whole life. This time it has to be put into action. Kennedy has seen me and I can't pretend anymore.

The cheese monger must sense I'm overwhelmed because he dips a knife into a giant wheel in front of me, even though I haven't even bitten the Munster, and says, "Try this." This gentle man holds out the cheese-skewered tip, winking like he's about to let me in on his best secret, and this—ridiculously—soothes me. There is always cheese.

I reach over a basket of water crackers for the hunk he's lopped off. It's creamy and melts on my tongue, pooling at the sides and back, going pungent, then smooth, hitting all the right buds. I'm sure I'm not supposed to eat this. Anything this good has to be forbidden for pregnant women.

I hear tight, determined footsteps that I could identify anywhere as my husband's.

"A California brie," the cheese man says. "Small boutique creamery. People kill for this stuff. The town it's made in, the locals tear the sign down all the time. They're sick of the tourists." The taste is divine, and I try hard to concentrate on what he's saying as if working this out could save me—killing for cheese, tearing down signs.

"A cheese with a story," I say, mostly to myself.

Kennedy is behind me. Any second he is going to place a hand on my shoulder, and then what? Will I melt into a puddle, which will disappear in a cloud of green smoke? I wish for an escape like during that time at Pinocchio's office.

"Everything's got a story these days. Without a story you've got nothing. Boy or girl?" the guy asks, passing me the tiniest disk of baguette. People are just starting to notice. That man hamfisting a Day-Glo chicken wing one aisle over is going to be a grandfather. Again. Leonardo and Davinci will twice be uncles. Mother is dead, or gone, or—

On my shoulder, the hand falls, not exactly gently, in its place. I watch the cheese monger's eyes work out our equation.

"I'm having a boy," I say, acknowledging the fact grounds me.

"Really?" Kennedy says. "A son? Why didn't you tell me?"

Why did I say that? Kennedy didn't want to know. But I did. And I wanted to know about Kancer but he wouldn't tell me. And apparently, he thought my father should know first. Nanny nanny pooh pooh. Beneath the compulsory adult considerations, I'm just a child.

"You have to be careful what you reveal these days," I say further proving my immaturity. Shut up, Millie. Shut the frig up. "Did you know people kill for cheese?" I say to my husband. What was the point of all the sucking it up if I was going to do this? Fuck, I hate myself. And I hate how suspicious and distant I feel from the man I love.

After we stay silent another few seconds, the cheese man

turns and smiles at the next woman, a dip of the chin begging her patience.

"I'll take a quarter pound," I say, desperately buying myself another minute. This man doesn't know, but neither of us likes scenes.

"Here you go," he says, and hands over my butcher paper package of cheese people kill for, hide the signs for—the secret cheese. Kennedy reaches out for it. We're both complicit, the gesture seems to say.

My husband escorts me to the checkout. I don't know what he's said to my father, but he's nowhere in sight. He never liked scenes either. I didn't see him shed a tear at the funeral. In fact, he looked disgusted with me, as if hugging me were a task too distasteful. I fumble for the change and Kennedy hands it over before I have the chance. The gesture makes me sheepish.

He tucks the bag under his arm and leads me by the waist to his car, opens my door then walks around, sliding into the passenger side. Sighing, Kennedy allows his jaw to drop slightly before he self-corrects. I look to his hands, to the radio buttons he touched on his journey, the rearview where I caught his eyes.

"Anything to say, Mill?" His gaze is trained straight ahead—to the air balloon advertising a discount carwash. God, I wouldn't mind soaring up on one of those right now.

"Yeah, sure. Crazy seeing you here! And with my father! Why don't we go around the corner and visit his lovely wife, Tennessee? While we're skipping down memory lane, maybe that lady who used to talk about all the army wife sluts with VD is still at the Cuckoo Bird Hut; we should check it out. That would be a hoot. Visiting hours are only forty minutes away." God, why is anger always the lowest hanging fruit?

He turns to me, and this is worse than the not looking; it's disarming. Even at this juncture he looks so self-contained. I almost believe he could tell Kancer to fuck off.

"Cut the shit, Millie. I know you followed me. I don't know how you know, or exactly what you know, but you do know where I went this morning and a bit more than that. And it really shits me. So it looks like we're both going to have to face up to something in a way we don't approve of."

"I don't know what you're talking about, Kennedy." I say it without cadence or emotion. It's a retreat, a chance for him to go back to pretending if he thinks that's best, because now I've got what I want, I'm worried I didn't really want it after all. I feel more separate, on different teams.

He searches my face. I try to remain steely. This man appears fine. What his look is saying, as far as my mind goes, is this could all still go away, just like this. If he knocked down the signs like the cheese people, maybe I wasn't meant to go there after all. I'm just thinking how lovely that would be when I realize it's as if he has blurred the lines of fact and fiction, too. Kennedy, being literary! Imagine that. I wouldn't dare say it.

In the distance, like a mirage, I see my father corral the kids into a Ford SUV, and I know I'm kidding myself. Not only can't we go back, we shouldn't. What's known can't be unknown. What's unknown should probably fucking stay that way. I shiver. What kind of wisdom can we expect to gain from a move like the one I made today?

He looks at me so long, his finger at his lip, my eye twitches where it feels watched.

Finally, he speaks. "Right, of course you don't know. Maybe I was confused—" The bridge between the words and the truth stretches for miles. It's too long for a bridge and I know it.

"Stop. No, obviously I know, Kennedy. I know you've been seeing an—" I find it's one thing reading the word, and it's something infinitely uglier to utter it, "—an oncologist."

From the tightening at his features, the pinch of his shoulders, it doesn't sound so great on the receiving end either.

He strokes my hair, the way he does with Rose, pulls it tight from my forehead. Are there hard C cells just beneath his skin attacking—beneath those fingers that are touching me? He smiles. "I did have it all under control, Millie."

"*Did*? *What* did you have under control?" I ask, terrified, getting it out before it's too late. There's a foreign, practiced tone to his voice. How often had I imagined him on his merry way, driving to work, when all the while he was rehearsing this tone, getting the slow cadence, the unspeak-overable volume just perfect?

This erstwhile solid man of ease, with his sloppy give—his stroking of his palm so rapidly, I know he isn't aware he's doing it —is the anti-Kennedy. This soothes me slightly, as if I can pretend it's someone else we're talking about.

"That's what I'm getting at, but first I want to explain about your father." He pauses, his chest shaking out the exhale.

"What's to explain? You were having lunch with a man who's basically a stranger to you, who doesn't know your daughter, who abandoned your wife, likely because you think you're dying and want us to have my family in your place. It's all very sensible to me." Too late, I clamp my hand over my mouth.

He opens his mouth and then shuts it. He looks at me for a long moment. "Are you done with that?"

I nod.

He lowers his gaze until I meet his. In it, I'm trained to see all the male things that Mother had claimed our enemy. Are all men this powerful, or just this one? Either way, I'm so obscured I can't tell where one of us ends and the other begins. Who's got the Kancer? Which of us has to sit up on the noisy hygienic paper? However he frames it, however self-sufficient he forces himself to be, he is about to smash my world.

"I know it looks fucked up, Millie, but I want to do what's best for you. Sometimes, though, means I don't always know what that means. That was my thinking. Has been my thinking all along.

"And you know the truth is I'd rather do this on my own. You know me, and I don't have to explain that to you. That's thanks to what we've built, and I believe it's something—excuse the frou-frou language—magical. I believe it's what's helped me all this time."

All this time? All this time? All this time I've been enjoying his parental concern without really considering the burden of it. Suddenly my life of novels and mothering and blocking out my own mother's mothering seems an indulgence while the real people are off working, protecting their family from the Hard Cs. I can't believe Kennedy had to get Kancer in order for me to recognize the mountains we've erected between us.

Perhaps all our lives are a fiction.

I feel my chin wobble. Oh, stop it. What will crying do? He squeezes tighter and this pushes out the tears. However fucked up our expectations, he is my life. How could I have wound up here—with everything to lose again?

Because it doesn't matter. It doesn't matter even what you think you know. It's rubbish. This is love. We're helpless against it. We expect the impossible from it. With each reading we come away with something different. And the truth is, there's no point to any of the rest without it. The question is, how far are Kennedy and I willing to go in the name of it?

"I wanted to tell you. But how could I? I come home and there you are with Rose and your growing belly—all this fucking unbelievable life that's everything." He stops speaking just when I want to tell him to stop fucking speaking. He fears he will crack. I see it in the twitch of his left nostril. But he won't allow it. He fixes the line of his sight directly on mine.

When did those lines etch the skin above his brow? I want to press my fingers there, smooth them out. I want to have never seen those words on that page. I can't imagine how many receipts I've washed since I stopped looking. And this is exactly what I'm aching for now—complete denial.

And then, all the bits of the car around me are suddenly so hyper-vivid, I have to shield my eyes. There's a sort of halo around everything. I close my eyes to shut it out, but then the images in my mind are just as brilliant. Some are memories—there's me and Rose on the swings the other day, and some are from books—the scenes flash so quickly, but I identify that *Jane Eyre* scene I felt I "lived" that day in Pinocchio's office all those years ago—the hands carrying me, the deep, almost triumphant connection in pain. There's another one, a dark-haired man riding a horse, a rock lifted in my hand that I feel myself push away as an *intrusive thought*. I have to hold on from the dizzying effect.

Seeing myself with the rock is terrifying, not knowing what I'd done, who I'd been with, or whether it was real even. It is not a good sign that this is coming back to me again. Or that I feel a blackout coming on after so many years. I recall my therapist's words: it's a defense mechanism. My brain's way of reacting to stress. Not unlike a panic attack, only a lesser known manifestation of the stress. That's all this is. There is no "book world." There's just me, losing moments here, in this car where my world is crashing in on me.

"I want to know what's wrong with you," I say, though I'm trembling, certain the exact opposite is true. "You've been found out. You can't go on pretending you haven't. I deserve to know what's going on."

He droops slightly. "Obviously, you're right."

"And there are things I need to tell you." My words terrify me even though I know he can't possibly know what those things are. "Listen, why don't we go home first?" I say, still buying time, hoping the car ride will allow us to consider our positions, make this trembling go away, ground me in reality before it slips completely out from beneath me.

Over the two bridges and the now slowing early rush hour traffic, I must drive my car home, as Kennedy leads the way in his, but I can't recall a moment of it. Instead, when I pull in the driveway, I can think only of where my mind travelled: I found it easy, comfortable to give in to what I'd fought all these years. First, I focused on one concrete image: the metal box in the yard. The one Pinocchio gave me when Mother disappeared for good. I buried it in the garden without looking. I did not want proof that it was all real. But now I do. Now I am desperate for it.

If the book world is real, I am going to do it for Kennedy, for all of us.

I am going to alter reality so he does not have Kancer.

I am going to dig it up. I am going to see what is in there. I can no longer pretend it isn't important. I can no longer pretend I don't want or need to go where Mother has gone. Even if the possibility is incredibly destabilizing.

I must have been driving, but all I can recall is thinking of the box, its incredible relics, of going over in my mind Mother's mysterious disappearance.

Words I'd forgotten from Dr. P's office that day came to me. "If I spoke," he said, "Emily would turn as if she were listening to me. And if I asked a direct question, say, 'What year did The Great War start?' Half the time, she did answer. With words. 'Nineteen fourteen,' she'd say. 'The War to End all Wars.' And then wouldn't say anything again for weeks on end. You see what I mean? She could speak. She chose not to." Had he said those things as I blacked out in his office/felt myself carried away as Jane Eyre in the terrifying upstairs room? What did it mean if Mother *could* speak? Were those words giving me a clue, and if so, what?

11

MILLIE

"RIGHT," I SAY TWO HOURS LATER, HEADING FROM THE FRIDGE TO the table. Inspecting the bowls Kennedy and I had eaten clean, the careful spoon drag lines in the dregs of tomato sauce. I'm surprised at our appetites. Aren't people supposed to feel sick at the sight of food under such conditions? When I grasp my fingers around my bowl, I have every intention of restarting the conversation from the car, but he seems to have forgotten all about it.

Apparently I'd fallen asleep in my car after I pulled into the drive and he'd carried me to my room. I don't remember any of that, and since I woke, I've been stuck with a feeling of disharmony, the way I imagine a painter would when he discovers what he assumed would occupy the top left corner of his canvas in reality doesn't feel *right*.

With the concentration and restraint of a prima ballerina tuning everything else out, I plug the drain, begin to fill the sink, squeeze out the dish soap. Now. Now. All that needs to happen is for Kennedy to speak. *Speak, speak! I charge thee, speak!* But this isn't Hamlet.

I drop the dishes and silverware into the soapy water, one at a time, plunk, plunk, as if drawing out the process will slow the beating in my heart. One. Two. Three. Outside, some matter of feet away, under the earth, is Pinocchio's box. Yes, I'd been thinking of that when I passed out in the car. The idea of digging it up tonight registers more like a déjà vu than a plan. I shift my view to the sink, waiting, sensing, moving in time toward the inevitable.

Kennedy's hand emerges from behind. He lowers the bowl from my hands and into the soapy water, turns off the taps, takes the sponge from my grip, and pulls me to our seats at the table. Once I realize the moment's here, I feel absolutely nothing, like I'm drifting off to sleep. I can't look at him. Still, I check the clock, watch the tap drip, the condensation fogging the window over the sink.

Mom The Dog jumps up on Kennedy's lap. His hands slip from mine to Mom's rump, which she wiggles in closer to his chest, as if she feels the same way I do. He sits up very straight in his chair. Without looking up, Mom shimmies in even closer, then lets out a big breath.

His gaze on a smoke break, my husband inspects the faucet as he speaks. "I was in remission," he says, letting this clinical, odd word soak in. But it doesn't. What could it possibly have to do with us? It sounds like a sales word for a second commission. Johnny here did so great with the Albany team, he earned us a remission, I'd probably crack the joke if we'd heard the husband character say the word in a Diane Keaton film. Too slowly the most important word registers: was.

"That time, when we were first together, and I fell off the radar, that was the initial detection—" He gets up, fiddles with the joint where the faucet threads through the countertop.

"What?" It's not the last time I'll clamp my hand over my mouth during this conversation. All this time.

Homing in on something loose sounding, he crouches down

to look under the sink. "...the non-Hodgkin's lymphoma. If it didn't look better, I was never going to call you again. I was clear on that."

It's impossible to picture Kennedy in the scenario he goes on to describe. Scans and partial biopsies, outpatient clinics and noisy scan capsules—all this apparently unfolding as I imagined myself deserted for a wild fuck with Primavera (the name I came up with for the slut he'd left me for) on every surface of his kitchen.

My brain seems unable, unwilling to connect me to this story. I see it the way Mother would—the words pointing me to a line from our favorite (because it was her choice) children's book, *Snugglepot and Cuddliepie*. "What strange birds!" we'd sing.

This book and the irresistible bits of Mother are inextricably entwined. The next second a thought flickers: I am doing exactly what Mother always meant for me to do. But just as quickly it's gone. Replaced by the halos, the incredible illumination of everything around me. I have to grab onto the table edge to keep my breath coming.

I'm sure Kennedy can't tell what I see: Mom the Dog is technicolor, a laser light show distracting me, pulling me inward, toward other connections. I try to make them out in the chaos of the flashing images. They're so familiar. Books I've read, I know, but there are so many, it's like an inextricable cluster of traffic noises. I try to concentrate on my breath, what Kennedy is saying, force the images to slow the way I was taught with these anxiety manifestations. They can be there, but don't attend to them. You can't concentrate on two things at once.

"I'm sorry, Millie. I'm so sorry."

It starts to work. The images slow. I pick one out. It's *Robinson Crusoe*, definitely. I remember the way I pictured his hair, like a member of Kiss. It's unclear how I'm him and he's me, but that's the way it appears. Perhaps I'm getting there just when I need to.

Perhaps I can help Kennedy. Perhaps I should believe. What other option do I have in this situation where I'm completely powerless? Thankfully, Kennedy sits again, lifting Mom onto his lap in a position so perfect, she doesn't adjust a thing before sighing and lowering her snout onto his thigh. I take it as a sign. I lose the *Crusoe* image. This is a success, the episode staved off, but it doesn't feel that way.

Kennedy must feel the reality of it all now that he's said it out loud. He's sobbing. My hand hesitates before it goes to him. When it does, he flinches. Something—if I had to guess, guilt—angers this coolest of men enough for him to hurl his mug at the backsplash behind the sink.

Mom jolts, turns her gaze to Kennedy, shocked enough for everyone. Though I didn't see that coming, I don't wince. It's an imaginary cup in an imaginary scene. There really is the feeling of unreality to this scene—like maybe it was *Crusoe* that was real. In this story David Duchovny barely helps make it digestible. You know there's something really wrong if even David Duchovny can't add a spoonful of sugar to a scene. We watch in silence as the milky tea runs down the grout lines. A half-circle of porcelain handle has landed in the soap dish, artfully.

"I'm sorry," he says again after a moment, looking slightly more like himself, which makes me look away again. "It's one of the reasons I didn't want to tell you. When I think about you knowing, I get so angry. I've made a terrible mistake. A terrible mistake. I shouldn't keep things from you."

Things, plural? I spot shards on the wood floor. I don't want Rose to get cut on one of them. Suddenly danger is everywhere.

He's quite for a long moment.

"I'm so sorry, Millie. I lie there on that bed and thought of you when we met—walking every day to Three Guys, your crazy hats, your pretty stockings, that smile plastered to your face because you forced it there. That meeting was your destiny. And I didn't want to wreck that. I had to give you this life, at any cost."

At any cost?

"I was struck with how hard you've had to work to care for the people you love. I promised myself I would never do that to you. And besides, I think, deep down, you didn't want to know." He catches his breath as if he had to get that out all in one go or he wouldn't. Every word is true. But that's not all. He's leaving something out. Something doesn't add up. *Your destiny.* Not his? It's a strange word choice.

My eyes close against the tears. He's right about one thing: sometimes all the signs are there, but we suspend our sense of observation, self-editing where we want, getting caught up in hope. What I need to know is whether it's wrong to want things to stay the same when it's inevitable that the story will change. Our beginning felt right. It felt perfect; can it be that it wasn't? I can feel its oblivion pulling me even now. If we could just get back there... Can it still be wonderful with us, though from here it all looks fucked up? Because that's how it feels—both doomed and perfect.

Of all the emotions bobbing inside my head, rage wins out. I'm not sure who it's directed at. "Fuck you, Kennedy. I'm not frail. I'm the opposite of frail. I'm...I'm that glue from that television commercial—the one that holds the construction worker by his hard hat onto a steel beam. And those hats of mine are not crazy. They're couture. You call yourself a fashionable luggage salesman!"

He rolls his eyes. It's such a normal reaction, for a second my heart sings.

"Don't you think I know that—about your strength?" he says. "Can't I still want to protect you? You're making jokes and missing the point."

That's right. I didn't work alone in burying my head in the

sand. It was a conspiracy. The both of us were in on it. It's wonderful and terrible. "No, you're missing the point! You don't marry someone without telling them you have cancer. No jokes to be made about that."

He holds his head in his hands and I don't like the bouncing of his rounded shoulders. I don't like the idea that a man tells his wife he has cancer and she screams at him and then he cries ugly sobs he will hate himself for. And yet, here we are. To his crotch he says, "Sure, it sounds bad when you put it that way."

"That's the way it is, Kennedy!" Why am I forcing this when I know damned well what his point is? I know what I am.

Fact, fiction. Would it have made a lick of difference if I'd known? I'd have married him no matter what. I think, in the silence, of a kinder, more dignified tack I might scramble onto. But the images are picking up a dizzying speed again. The tremors are spreading. I'm nauseous with the motion.

"Kennedy, we're in this together. You're a noble man. No one knows that better than me. But you can't protect me from life. No matter what we convince ourselves of, no one can do that—for anyone."

His head jerks at that.

He looks at me as if *I'm* the stranger.

"I am noble," he says, strangely.

I nod because I can't quite manage to verbalize my reaction to that. I close my eyes to keep from falling. The image flashes are gaining intensity: *Jane Eyre*, the unidentified man on the horse, the rock, *Robinson Crusoe*.

I drop my head between my legs and breathe.

Even ostriches don't really bury their heads in the sand, it just looks that way when they're turning their eggs over, caring for their young. Imagining you can avoid your own fate is madness. I'm so absorbed in all of them—Mother, Rose, Kennedy, do I even know who Millie is anymore? My face burns.

He stands, pours us both glasses of ice water from a pitcher in the fridge. I manage to straighten up as he hands me mine, then backs up against the sink.

"Are you okay?" he asks. "You're shaking like crazy."

At least I know that part is real. I nod and though he looks skeptical, he continues on.

"I can tell you why I didn't tell you from the beginning. Do you know what I saw when I went to that doctor's office?" He takes a sip, looks above the old phone to the photo of the three of us by the beach last summer, my hair blowing so wildly it seems to wrap around both of their heads.

"The men were fine with their diagnoses—this thing, this Non-Hodgkins Lymphoma is something that happens a lot to younger guys—but the wives, they were hysterical. You've never seen anything so sad. And the husbands, every one of them just sat there helpless. I wasn't going to be helpless, and I certainly wasn't going to do that to you. Be honest with yourself, Millie. What would you have done in my shoes?"

In a way, I'm at a disadvantage. Do I want to give my husband, who has cancer, something more to worry about? Look at what I've been keeping from him. Still, it feels important to speak my mind. "Look, I can't claim to be an expert on men's roles in the family, but I do know this: I would never keep something like that from you." I'm lying. Every word is a lie, but I can't seem to stop. My secrets. They're the cause of all this. I'm to blame.

"And now?" I ask, though I'm terrified.

"And now it's back, and the test results look bad. The doctors put me on some drugs while we wait for the re-test. He said in a small percentage of cases there can be a false-positive. He doesn't want me to get my hopes up, but he has to make sure."

At some point we have sex, we fight, nearly physically—I throw a pillow, followed by a glass frame containing a picture of Mother pregnant with me that's always meant a lot to me. We've come to the edge of losing it all. It must be the longest day on record. I can see the sun coming up over the trees.

"So how did you know something was wrong?" I ask, suddenly unable to look at him as if he isn't who I thought he was, but instead this new character who I've got to get to know—like it or not.

He looks with mild distaste to the place where the wall and ceiling meet. He continues the story the way he began, as if it's the only way he can tell it, as if he isn't ready for critiques. "I was changing after work to come here for dinner. It was when you were doing all those, what did you call them? 'winter-warmer one-pot dishes.'" He smiles—and there he is, the old him. This is a good memory—our beginning. At least it *was*. "I think you were doing an Italian white bean and pancetta stew." Kennedy stops.

"It was a good one," I say with a shrug that feels as if it's hijacked my shoulders. We both pretend I'm not sitting on my hand to steady it. "The sage."

Kennedy strokes my hand. He's trying to get me to look at him. In truth, I'm dying to. For a moment, I can imagine we're sitting in these exact seats where three and a half years earlier we were spooning our white bean and fancy bacon stew. The taste was both bright and rich, but the texture was wrong—like congealed pasta. In the muddle of what he was dealing with, Kennedy must have lost this detail. Or he never noticed. Funny, what we take away.

Looking at our hands now, Kennedy continues. "I turned down my collar and bumped my hand against my shoulder blade—ever so slightly. I remember this is what freaked me about it—and pow! It was the worst pain. I felt around and noticed a lump—nothing you could see. I went to a doctor I knew from the store and he sliced a bit off for a biopsy. But he knew right away. It was textbook."

I think back to that night. How many times I'd replayed and dissected it! The last night I'd seen Kennedy before he disappeared for a whole month. How could I have missed it? There was barely a moment I couldn't recall even now—the way he'd paced while I did the dishes until I let him dry. And then his sudden exit. His rejection of coffee and Italian pastries, his tender goodbye belly rub for Mom.

"So where did you go?" I ask.

"I was at Sloane Kettering, only as an outpatient, getting radiation treatments."

"Did you have anyone with you?" I'm unsure which answer would be worse.

Kennedy stands, pacing the way he had on that white bean and pancetta stew night, rubbing at the front of his hair. When he speaks it's almost theatrical, like the only way he can bring himself to say this is to be someone else. Perhaps he has David Duchovny in mind too. While he inspects a half-melted candle, Kennedy tells me his parents knew, that he'd sworn them to secrecy, and that every time we were at their place he was afraid they'd slip up, that they'd begged him to tell me.

In my mind, the deception grows to elaborate proportions. The horse rider image is suddenly overtaking the moment. I know that rider. It's...it's freaking Heathcliffe from *Wuthering Heights*. And there I am, the rock in my hand. There's blood on it. No. Not that. I can't handle that now. *Go away intrusive thought.*

"Kennedy, I just don't know what to say. It's as if everything we were is a lie." I didn't know I was going to say it, but after it's out, I realize I didn't say the other part, that I want to patch the holes.

"Oh, don't be so melodramatic, Millie. What would you have done? I ask you again." He doesn't sound like Kennedy. Kennedy doesn't say things like that.

I would have had you there with me, but I'm not going to say it because what is the point of arguing about this anymore? I would have done it because that's what people do, Kennedy.

"I don't know," I say finally.

Silent, slowly nodding, he seems satisfied with that.

I switch to practicalities. "But what's changed? Why are you suddenly in danger?"

"I go in every six months to check things out. And this is the first time something's been bad."

Six months. That's eight times since we've been together. Are we even telling the same story?

"It's really bad, Millie. I'm probably going to die."

"You're probably going to die." Now, I'm as desperate as he must have been. What wouldn't I do?

He grabs my hands. "Eight times healthy, all clear. Millie, I would do the same thing again. It was the best thing to do. Look at you. Do you even see how you've let yourself be you?" He's controlling the narrative, and maybe I prefer it that way. I like the me he sees.

I'm suddenly weak. The pressure is incredible. I drop my head onto the table. We must look like we've been beaten by an intruder. Perhaps we have.

"Kennedy." Without lifting my head, I reach for his hand. Squeeze it. Mine's shaking terribly. He's looking at it. There's Jane/me, and then Heathcliffe on the horse, the rock in my hand. And then everything goes blank.

12

MILLIE

I LOVE HIM SO MUCH IS THE LAST THOUGHT I HAVE AS I GIVE INTO the black out. It's *Gatsby* this time that takes me there.

I'm Daisy, of course, in the early parts of the story, where one can and will still want to be her. I'm in Louisville, in my white coupe, basking in the glowing awe of my line of soldier suitors. To be wanted, desired, without trying.

I could feel Gatsby's lips, but I recognized this feeling. Kennedy and I had a love like this, passion like this. It might also end in disaster. But I could enjoy it now, couldn't I? I, Daisy, I feel Gatsby's/Kennedy's lips on mine.

It's like in the beginning, when we believed we could be saved by each other. The sun is bright on my shoulders. I'm wearing white, as I remember from the text—the image of Daisy always this particular one in my mind—but what happens next is unfamiliar. I don't think it was in the text at all.

I'm writing my own story, a fantasy, I guess. I don't think they would have taken things this far—at that time and in that culture—but we do. We are on a beautiful woven blanket, beneath a tree, near a stream. There's no one in sight. We seem to know that no one will come. It is our story, after all.

There is some familiarity to the rhythm of our kisses and grasping hands. Our first time—Kennedy and I—is being played out here, amidst this glorious, iconic backdrop. We are beautiful, Adam and Eve about to fall from grace for everyone to see. It isn't a memory. It isn't an illusion. It's happening. I feel it.

"I'm going to come," I hear myself whisper in his ear. He groans. And I do as I'd promised, just as he does. We lie in the warmth of the sunlight, his hands on me, completely satisfied. Our best moments, here, alive, to *live again*. It's the most amazing gift—the good old days. If it could only be like that again. Well, it fucking can.

And I wake to the morning light in my window. I know something's different.

13

MILLIE

"WHERE ARE WE—GOING?" I ASK, ADDING THE LAST WORD because something tells me not to show my disorientation. My hands, arms, all the way up to my elbows are trembling. The old anxiety settles in like it never left. Guilt. What have I done? I don't know. I don't want to know. I struggle to recall what we'd been doing before my blackout.

We were in...in...the kitchen! Yes. I remember. Relief floods, but it's quickly chased away. The Kancer. We were talking about the fucking hard C. I suddenly don't like that phrase.

"Patience, my darling." Kennedy has settled me on the cozy chair in the study. He's at the shelf, flicking his finger along the spines of our photo albums. I suddenly have loads of energy, like I've woken after a long sleep. He seems to, also. I'm not sure how much time I've lost, but Kennedy looks different—brighter. He doesn't say anything about my absence.

"What are you looking for?" Punch-drunk, there's a hysterical lilt to my voice.

He clears his throat and holds up his forefinger.

My knee bobs.

"Aha!" he exclaims, a character in a harebrained mystery

film. I'm struck by how much I love him. There is the image of us making love in the grass. But it's more than an image. It's here with us. Lending a sensuality to the moment. Are we some-where, still lying there together in the grass?

I feel my chin quiver. *Keep it together, Millie.* He's beautiful, perhaps more beautiful than ever—his determination, strength, the silhouette of his body against the bookshelves as he flips through a few more pages I can't see from here. He's mine, but he's out of reach, too. I feel glued to my chair with all the shaking.

"Look," he sits on the chair arm, hooks one arm around my back. With the other, he shifts the album over to rest on my knees. These are photos from when he first began to spend time with me. I barely remember posing for these.

No. It's more than that. I don't recognize the restaurant in the photo we're in. The way I'm wearing my hair. When did I have bangs? I reach up instinctively. Did Rose get crazy with the scis-sors again and cut my hair while I was asleep? Because sure enough, my hair on my forehead comes to thick points over my eyebrows. I make my way to the mirror.

"Do you like my hair this way?"

"What way? It's the same as always. And yes, I love it. Don't ever change it."

"Where's this picture taken?"

"This picture? You're kidding, right?"

I shrug.

"Look at that dress you kept complaining about. Ring any bells?"

The fussy floral pattern is certainly not something I would pick out myself. But why would I buy a dress I didn't like? "Nope, nothing."

"Your best friend's wedding? Are you okay?"

"Angie's wedding? Are *you* okay? Angie is just getting married to Pete—maybe! If she doesn't back out."

"Millie, either those IVF hormones are making you loopy, or you're playing an incredible trick on me."

"IVF? What are you talking about?" This isn't right. Am I just exhausted? Or is it happening again? The lost time from the blackout is terrifying. Clearly time has passed here while I was in that other world with Kennedy/Gatsby having a grand old time. But things are different here than when I left.

"Millie, I think you need to rest. You aren't yourself with all the hormones. I told you, I don't think they're the best idea for someone with your history."

He looks earnest, honestly worried. But how can that be? Just the other night we were talking about that *Culture of Motherhood* book as my palm circled my swollen stomach. He made the inappropriate comment about Charlene, Jemima's mother at preschool. I followed him into the city, saw him at the doctor's office. And what did he mean by *your history*? Have I told him everything?

I don't want to look down at my stomach, in case it's true that I'm no longer pregnant. But I force myself. It's the only way to know the facts.

I take a deep breath and drag my hand down the front of my shirt. My belly is perfectly flat.

"Were we talking about cancer just now?" I ask, terrified of the answer.

He looks up, as if shocked at my knowledge, which previous to the blackout, we'd been discussing for over eighteen hours.

"What do you know?" he asks.

I don't know. Nothing is as I remember.

14

MILLIE'S PRETENDING SHE ISN'T SCARED TO DEATH AND I'M
pretending I'm not pretending that I'm not scared to death. It's
the day after that terrible appointment going over the details
and prognosis of the original test results, sitting through them
all again, only to follow that up by betraying my wife by meeting
with her father, and then breaking everyone's hearts further by
Millie telling me she knows about the cancer. Seb is manning
the front while I shut myself in the back office.

That was my moment with Millie to get everything out in the
open, but I didn't. I didn't, and still don't see the point of hurting
her even more deeply. She's been so happy until now. What does
it matter if she believes some things that aren't exactly true? Isn't
it better than the alternative?

Piled on top of all that deception, I'm still pretending
nothing strange is going on with *her*. That her hand isn't twitch-
ing. That she isn't blacking out, speaking jibberish to no one,
and losing hours. We're both pretending the security of our
daughter isn't threatened because of all that has remained
unspoken.

And so it's my fault she lost the baby. Of course. What did I expect of such a shock? I didn't mean for the lie about the IVF to come out, but how would she cope with the loss of a baby amidst all this? If she doesn't know about the baby, then things will be that much easier on her. And she needs a break if she's going to get through this. I owe her that much.

I keep waiting for her to say something, but she doesn't. I'm not sure whether we have reached an agreement to keep the rest of our secrets to ourselves, or a clinical state of denial. Part of me hopes the cancer tests will turn out to be negative this second time around and that dealing with this domestic fall out will be the largest of our problems. In that context, a few omissions and lies don't seem so bad. The bangs and the touched-up photo were tricky, but have definitely helped to convince her she's disoriented enough to be wrong about being pregnant. And the lie about angie? I'm not sure how I'll handle that. I'll cross that bridge when I get to it.

I pull the plane tickets out of the drawer and think about when I'll hand them over, about the three of us in the executive airport lounge, Rose drinking too many sugary apple juices because they're free. She doesn't even know what that means; she just says "they're free," like that's a flavor, or a brand. I bought them before this round of testing and something about them seems like a charm, a talisman, that says, you'll be fine, and you *will* go on this trip as planned.

I will make up to my beautiful daughter for having her lie to her mother. I appealed to her constant need to be a big girl. I told rose that the book was upsetting Mommy, so we needed to pretend she didn't have it. No matter what Mommy said, she was to say she didn't have it. "I will help Mommy, like a big girl," she said. I was very proud of her. And I was. She helped me to maintain control of the situation, and that was best for all of us.

Before I leave the store for the weekend, I need to update the calendar so Seb will see when he has to man the store next week. *Thursday Test Results*. How can three innocent looking words mean what they do? I hate the guy who wrote that.

After a few too many scotches last night, I woke early this morning, forgetting long enough to enjoy one unencumbered moment of viewing my naked wife in our bed, the beautiful upturn of her breast. I tried to ignore the slight remaining swell of her stomach. But I couldn't. So, I placed her hand on my own swell and watched, enchanted as her nostrils flared, her eyelids squeezed and shuttered, and finally, an undainty yawn snuck from her closed mouth, her hand caressing me.

"Fuck me," I said, feeling powerful. I had already begun to believe this version of events I'd created for Millie, Rose and myself.

Her eyes came to life. It was like she was someone else, so passionate and sensitive to my touch; there's no underestimating the effect this had on me, and it seemed to reinforce that I'd done the right thing.

"Jay," I thought she called out to me, but in the intensity of the moment, I couldn't be sure. *The Great Gatsby* lay open on her bedside table, and if she did enjoy an overlay of fantasy to the moment, well, who could blame her? We all need to write our own narratives. I certainly understand that. Besides, her other-worldliness has always appealed to me anyway; I could not divest her of it now.

My wife is extraordinary. And I am going to die, and leave her alone; fantasy is all she will have. Why would I take that from her?

I lifted her into a straddle over me, and turned her slightly, to face the mirror.

"Watch," I said.

As she lost herself in me, let her guard down like no woman I've ever known, I watched her in the mirror, her bangs parted almost sculpturally over her left eyebrow. The style suited her. I could almost believe she'd always worn it that way. She came in a stutter and that's what sent me off. I clutched her hair, kissed her breast. I ignored that shoulder pain that may be the end of our plans, the secrets that could end it along the wrong path. I did what I had to, I told myself. I have always done what I had to do. For her. Everything I've done has been for Millie.

I kissed her beneath her ear and got up quickly like a man with better things to do. If I laid there, we'd start talking. And that meant more lies that I didn't want to tell.

"Stay," she said, clutching my wrist, trembling. It's all I wanted.

"I can't."

15

MILLIE

WHY WOULD KENNEDY BE PLAYING A TRICK ON ME? AND HOW could he possibly play anything that would involve removing my baby from my stomach with absolutely no residual pain or symptoms? If this were a horror film and Kennedy was a bad guy, perhaps he'd have put me into an induced coma until I recovered from all the aftereffects of the pregnancy.

But a quick look at the calendar on my computer confirms I haven't lost much time. Which is a relief. It means this is real. I'm paging-in, crossing over into the book world. It's the only answer. Otherwise how could everything have changed so incomprehensibly in such a short time?

Then I realize what an incredible line of thinking I had been following before the blackout. Kennedy is a good guy. *The* good guy. I know that. I'm just so confused. Because he had been keeping a great big lie—the fact that he has cancer—during our entire marriage.

After Kennedy left, I lay in bed, remembering our lovemaking in the grass. Wait, no. That was Daisy in the other world. But we made love just now, and I'd called him Jay. *Was* he Jay? I'd forgotten this—how difficult it was to keep the worlds apart.

When I used to have trouble, I'd come back to that term of Dr. P's: Gestalt. Working it into the techniques Dr. Samuels had taught me, I had boiled it down to this mantra—decide which is the significant reality. Trust your instincts. I'd force myself into a knee-jerk reaction: which bits were real? In that moment, I went through the drill: I could cross over into another world that is made of the books I have read, processed in a specialized way that Mother turned me onto. After a long time of not doing this, I am once again doing it. Whether it is a question of capability or will, I am unsure.

"Mum!"

Rose! Yes! She will surely know if I've been pregnant. I scoop her up in my arms and squeeze tightly around her "silky" Peppa Pig nightgown. She squeezes back. Rose is a world-class hugger. I've seen people reduced to tears from her embrace. I fight them from falling for her sake. I need to keep it together. I know the dangers of mothers who can't.

"What do you need, darling? You had a nice, long sleep."

"I was thinking about how we saw that *Magic Charm Book* at the shop. I should have chosen it instead of the blocks. I keep thinking of it. I can't sleep thinking about it so much."

"But honey, you *have* that book." As soon as the words are out, she throws a fit.

"I do *not* have that book. And I must. I must have that book. It's calling to me."

"Calm down. Next time we go to the toy shop, you can pick out that book. Okay? How about that?"

"No. No, I can't wait. I need it now."

"The stores aren't open now. Shhhh." I try to hold her to my chest but she's not having it. Her feet start stamping. My mind is spinning, looking for an explanation. What is happening? And then I get it. My foray into the book world has changed this bit of the real world, too. It's just like Dr. P was saying that day—

gestalt, everything connected, change one thing and it's all changed. Even something as seemingly insignificant as Rose's book choice; it's different now. My power frightens me. How can I control it? If I've lost my unborn child, what's to say I can't lose Rose, too?

"I'm supposed to have it. And now I've ruined everything."

I sit on the floor and pull her onto my lap. "Listen. I know what's happening here."

"You do?"

"Yes, you've had a bad dream." Simple answers are best for kids; not the kind of open-ended bullshit Mother always fed me —if she bothered to answer at all.

"No!"

"Yes, and do you know what we can do about that?"

"What?"

"We can get you a dream catcher. It catches all the bad dreams so you only have good ones." If only I had something like that. Right now everything seems like a nightmare. It's so difficult to know what's real. Just like Mother was always getting at.

She seems to like the idea, though she still looks unsure. "A dream catcher?"

"Yes. How about we go and pick one out tomorrow? In the meantime, you can come and sleep with me and Dad."

She nods. I scoop her up in my arms and start walking the hallway. Then I stop. "Rose, does Mummy's belly look smaller than yesterday?"

She pulls her head back, tightens her brow. "Let me see." She climbs down, lifts my shirt, rubs her palm up and down. "Bigger, Mum. You probably shouldn't have eaten that bagel, like you said."

"Right."

Sleeping in our room does the trick for Rose. I watch her and Kennedy the whole night, wondering what's happening to my relationship with reality. Perhaps I need a dream catcher. Could it be that Rose never had the *Magic Charm* book? That I've, I don't know, hallucinated this scenario about her misplacing it, gone back to my old dissociative thinking? Could it be that my belly just doesn't look that different because I've only just lost the baby? But wouldn't I remember some of that? *Listen to your instinct.* I shut my eyes and force an answer: *Magic. You're going into the book world.* It's the only answer that makes sense.

I think of the sex in the grass. Yes. I've done it. I'm a Reader. "I want you to be a Reader with a capital 'R,'" Mother used to say. I've worked out what all your blackboards and your notes and piles of books meant. But would that mean that what I "dreamed" I did to Mother was real, too? No. No, I've put that all to bed long ago. I feel the need to confess about my fears of what I may have done to mother, and as uncomfortable as that is it's reassuring. I know what to do with that. Laugh at it, as Dr. Samuels taught me. I have that written down to prove it to myself. But even this leads me into unanswerable, circular thinking. If Dr. Samuels was right about that, then wouldn't he have been right that going into the book world was just a delusional manifestation of my anxiety, too? And if that's true, then how did I lose the baby without knowing? How did Rose never have that necklace? And what about my hair? Angie's marriage? How else could reality have changed so much without my knowledge?

How can I get a handle on all of this? It comes over me in a shiver. I should come clean about everything, and make Kennedy understand it isn't just IVF hormones weirding me out. Fill in the blanks of my story—past and present. Explain that in fact, I don't even remember starting IVF, or most anything that's apparently going on, that I may have killed my own mother. Kennedy will help me, won't he? Right now, the lies and secrets are working against us. We need to get back to being a team. That will help us to fix whatever it is that's happening. So why can't I just say it?

I think again of my conversation with Pinocchio. My *Gatsby* experience, my *Jane* experience. That must be it. I'm changing the world. The Butterfly Effect. How exactly I did it, I don't know. *Preconscious. Suprarational.* I have to speak to Pinocchio. *Dr. Pee?* Yes. If that's what's happening to me, he's the only one who can explain it. I know he can.

16

MILLIE

I WAKE THE NEXT MORNING AND MY BELLY LOOKS SLIGHTLY MORE swollen to me. Or maybe it doesn't. Fifteen minutes of staring at it and forcing my instinct to come up with an answer has produced unclear results. Kennedy is ill from the Kancer pills, which is about the only thing that's out in the open with us, and I'm setting up an experiment. I'm crazy, or there's suprarational stuff, inexplicable stuff, at play here.

I believe Rose has crossed over, too. That has to be the explanation for the discrepancy: her losing the necklace, and then claiming she never had it in the first place. Likely she thinks it's a dream. The magical is part of the everyday life of a child. I'm going to make it very easy for her to do it again. I've given her one of the spare magic charm books, and propped her on the same couch where she always reads the book. I've put on *Sesame Street* for background noise. *Ground your book in reality,* Mother always said. And now I know why.

After morning snack, she's fingering the necklace, telling me what the story says, excited like she's just seeing it for the first time. She actually believes she is, which I can understand, if she too, is going to the book world, making changes to reality and then returning to an unrecognizable world, the way I have been. I can see her eyes widen as she imagines experiencing the winter wonderland ice skating contest herself. She has a special talent for imagination, though children in general are excellent at it. I bet she's better than I ever was.

There are questions: what if she can't come back? What might change when she does? I don't know how it works. I collapse into a kitchen chair just outside the family room, when suddenly, I feel a kind of déjà vu. Here I was on this chair, but Kennedy's cancer was just a scare—a product of an annual check and my imagination. He was totally healthy. If I'm going mad and a healthy Kennedy is the outcome, that would be worth it, wouldn't it? Is there another reality I can reach through the book world, in which Kennedy is not sick? It feels like a possibility within my grasp.

I clasp my strangely empty belly. Look at the prescription bottle of Clomid with my name on it. These things are real now, I tell myself. However I got here, I must keep it together for my child. That is the most important thing. I try to catalog the events of the past week: the receipt, the strange day of tailing Kennedy, catching him with my father, the miscarriage I don't recall, the incredible Gatsby sex, Rose's mix-up with The Magic Charm Book. *Did all of that actually happen? Some of it?* It was so surreal and impossible to pick apart.

For a second, I'm unsure. *What does your instinct tell you, Millie?* I close my eyes and distinctly remember the cheese man talking about the town that takes down its sign. Of course, it happened. And so did the *Gatsby* sex and the conversation with the photographs.

I return through the doorway to the sitting room and lift Rose on my lap, open the book, tell my daughter the truest thing I've ever said. "Mommy loves you more than anything in this world."

I turn and allow her to head back to the floor, where she's struggling to go, as a branch scrapes the window pane. I don't know how long I'm staring at it. Again I'm watching Heathcliffe. I've got the bloodied rock in my hand. I see something more—a body, a woman's body. I yell out "what have I done?" And suddenly I'm back on the couch, looking at the branch, which is still scratching its hypnotic sound. But when I turn Rose is gone. The necklace is stretched out over the pillow, a perfect vertical, in her place. It's exactly how I remember seeing it the last time. She's gone into the book world. It must be.

I barrel to the sofa and grab it, stroke it as if it has the answers.

"Rose? Rose! Where did you run off to?" I look all over, screaming her name and shaking. I'm panicked.

And then it hits me. *What does your instinct tell you, Millie?* Yes. She's inside The Magic Charm Book.

My daughter is by herself. Sure, she's in a world where candy canes hang from trees and everyone is wearing pink, but she's *alone*.

Eventually, though, the panic begins to recede. In its place is something akin to wonder. She's there, that impossible there. She's there and I was there.

I know what I know. I know that's where she's at, and it's not just because the necklace has landed exactly as I recall. But I don't want to know because if I know that, I know what I did to Mother was a real thing. A crime. And I don't deserve anything good in my life. I feel it all slipping from me.

I shake it off and return to the matter at hand: Rose, in the storybook. Everything is so wondrous to kids. Does she even notice how she's not *imagining* the skating rink's surface turning pink, not *imagining* she's Kelly, winning the contest, but actually *is* Kelly winning the contest?

So, that's where we would be, at the Woodside Rink, and it's the first snowfall of the season. Could she imagine Kennedy there so strongly that in a manner, he goes too? Could he "leave" his cancer there and come back healthy, the way my ankle healed? It seems too simplistic for it to work that way. And yet, it's beautiful, and meaningful, and would make for such a significant reality.

I sit, silently, next to the spot where Rose disappeared. For a while, I hold my arms out for her, staring at the book, just in case she tumbles out violently the way I always imagined Mother doing. But nothing happens. I catch my reflection in the window pane. I look crazy. I tried so hard to leave this part of my life behind. And yet here I am. And I'm trembling, this time, my legs shake too.

The hyper colors wash over the room, the noise, the pulsing in my head. And then I black out.

17

KENNEDY

"Sir, I want to apologize for Millie showing up the other day. I know it must have been upsetting for you." I'm at my wife's father's house.

"Nothing to apologize for, Kennedy. I have no relationship with my daughter. Whose fault could that be but mine? I fucked it up with her. Did it hurt to have that right in my face after all these years? You bet. But it made me realize something. I can't go behind her back anymore. I have to come out with it. She deserves to know the truth."

"But, sir."

"Please stop fucking calling me *sir*. I'm not in the damned military. Never did an honorable thing in my life. But I will now."

"But, Greg."

"Don't 'but Greg' me either. I'm telling her and that's that."

"I'm dying."

Finally, something to silence him. It's powerful, this, strange as that sounds. I will not be embarrassed for using it.

"You're going to leave her?"

"That's a strange way to put it."

Mr. Burns shrugs.

"You know where I stand on Millie's need to know when it comes to Emily," I say.

"Yes, I do. That's what you were against. Found the need to come here and make me swear never to tell Millie the truth, even though I already had no relationship with my daughter. You told me you'd care for her. And now you're leaving her."

He was right. What could I say to that?

"Let me guess, now that you're at the bottom of the barrel, things look a bit different, am I right? You're a real schmuck, Kennedy, you know that? And I'm a schmuck for ever listening to you in the first place. I should have told the truth."

"You believe what you believe, sir." He doesn't verbally correct me this time, instead just shakes his head.

"You do what you've gotta do, Kennedy. Not that anyone could ever tell you what to do. But I'm telling my daughter the truth. She deserves to know."

What's Millie going to do when she finds out the truth? She's going to fucking hate me, that's what. And she's not going to cope. And despite every ugly thing I've done, every lie I've told, I love her more than life itself. And that makes it right. I'll have to come up with something.

18

MILLIE

AN HOUR AND A HALF LATER, I'M CONSCIOUS AGAIN. THIS TIME, I feel for my belly right away. It's still indeterminate, but there's a distrust in my craw. I know there is reason to question. Everything.

"Rose! Rose!" I yell all around the house, outside, down the block and back. She's still gone. The necklace is where she left it. Can she still be in the book world? I'm sick with panic. Rose hasn't returned and Kennedy is due home any minute. How will I explain this? Our child is missing.

He'll want to call the police. Of course, he will. But I can't let him. She's fine. She's in the book world. Still, there's the echo, deep down in my bones, *things are not right.* I recall the last period of blackouts and paranoia, and the extremes I drove myself to; I see the rock, and the things that must have happened at my hand with it, and I try to shut it out. *You are nothing but the lovely woman I see before me.*

I pace the living room, holding the necklace in one hand and my not-pregnant abdomen in the other. *Please come back, Rose. Please come back.* The book's splayed out on the floor like an inanimate object. Its dreamy drawings designed to attract young girls to the wonders of make-believe. All so innocent. Surely, it's me who's the dangerous one.

19

I SIT IN THE CAR FOR TEN MINUTES. I DON'T KNOW WHAT TO expect inside the house. The lights are on in the family room, which means Rose and Millie are in there, or Rose is in there, watching Sesame Street while Millie cooks us dinner, worrying that I'm dying, and most likely busting to work out how to cross over into her "book world" to cure me, all the while worrying why reality keeps changing on her, and whether I'll think she's crazy.

And she doesn't even know the worst of it, my involvement, my deception. Unless her father has already called and told her. Days ago, our lives were perfect. Happy, healthy, in love, awaiting our second child. Now look at us. And that's because it was all built on lies. But she's not going to hate me. She will see this is right. It's even beginning to feel true, the IVF, the bottle of Clomid I mocked up with some sugar pills. Why couldn't it be?

The door is unlocked and I open onto a scene of fright. Millie is pacing along the couch. She's holding that same junky kid's necklace I told Rose to pretend never existed like it's a magical charm. She's big on symbols, my wife. Piles loads onto them. She must have had some backup necklaces though; this is the woman her father believes is a danger. I have to feel her out so I know how to play it.

"What's wrong? Where's Rose?"

Millie opens her mouth, but nothing comes out.

"Come here." I lead her to the couch. "Sit down and tell me what happened."

She sits and stares at Elmo, who's muted, carrying lots of things too heavy for a puppet to lift.

"Rose is gone." Then she looks at me, her expression pure terror. Oh no. I've made a misstep already.

"Are you sure she isn't just having a nap?"

"What do you mean? I just said our daughter is missing."

"Where do you think she is?"

"Where do *you* think she is?"

We stare each other down, neither speaking.

Then, finally, she spits out a lot of stuff that's spot on about not remembering anything about starting IVF, about her haircut, and then mixes it up with an incomprehensible story about Rose. The trigger word that gets me terrified is *book*. When Millie starts talking about books, looking this distressed, I know she's in trouble.

"Is Rose okay?" I ask. Oh god, oh god, Mr. Burns was right. Why have I allowed this to go on so long?

At that moment, I hear Rose shout from upstairs. "Help!" she yells. "I can't open my door.

Millie and I start, turn to each other, eyes bulging. I run first, she follows. Please let her be okay, I think. Please. At the top of the landing I see a strange sight. Millie's barricaded Rose inside her room. There are at least half a dozen items shoved up against the door. There's the chair from our bedroom, the sideboard, an ottoman, one of Emily's giant blackboards, and on top of that, a pile of immense hardcover books.

I pull them all away and open the door. There's Rose, crying. Millie runs to her and squeezes her arms around her, rubs her hands up and down Rose's arms.

"Mum! Why didn't you come and answer me? I was calling you and calling you? Mum, give me my necklace! Why are you holding it?" She grabs it from Millie, who is looking over Rose's shoulder trying to silence her sobs because she doesn't want her daughter to see her crying.

"Daddy!" Rose breaks free and runs into my arms. Millie is facing away, toward the kitchen, trying to wipe her tears. Has her father called already? If so, what has he said? Is that why she locked Rose up, to protect her?

Rose settles quickly with crayons and a coloring book in the kitchen. "I have no idea what I did," Millie whispers to me when I come to her in the living room.

20

MILLIE

It's been two glorious Indian summer days since Rose's "disappearance." We have five days until Kennedy's test results are back. I try to continue on with the laundry, the dinner, with Rose's somewhat art nouveau attempt at paper lunch sack puppets. But nothing is right.

I spilt grape juice on the one puppet she didn't dismember—the merman—and spent the night dabbing the stain, blow-drying tissue paper ovals, and when that failed, re-creating Rose's efforts with just the right amount of felt-tip marker pressure and shaky safety scissor cuts, while in my mind. This puppet, at least, I can fix.

In our new arrangement, neither Kennedy nor I say a word about anything important. I can feel the miles stretching between us. Did he know that Rose had crossed over into the book world and that's the only explanation for why she was so inexplicably barricaded? Or did he think I did it? That I locked our own daughter in her room? And if he does know about Rose and my special abilities, what else does he know? All his disdainful comments about Mother, all his sarcasm and appealing whitewashing. I'd welcomed it without thinking. It had been so easy. Too easy.

Amongst all the strange inconsistencies, there's one thing I know for sure, now that I've experienced Rose's disappearance into a book, I will do everything I can to stop my daughter crossing over. What if, like Mother, she never comes back? What if she needs me and can't get me? What might we lose along the way? *Dr. P.* All roads point to him.

I wish we could have put it off longer, but she's a natural Reader, it's clear and she took to it with very little instruction. We all read differently.

"Reality is fluid," I'm telling her when Kennedy enters the kitchen. "Stories are fluid, dependent entirely upon our engagement with them, which is dependent on our histories, our openness, our imaginations, our environment, in short, everything we've ever done, everyone we've ever been, and everything in the moment of reading."

He clears his throat, like I've said something wrong. "Why don't you go play outside?" he says. She pushes her chair back with a screech on the tile.

"No, I'd rather read." Neither of us says, but I know an understanding has passed between us.

Her footsteps lead up the stairs, around her bed, and then the springs groan.

Kennedy starts talking about dinner.

Later, I wait until Kennedy drifts off to sleep in his characteristic jerks and surprised breaths, then wait another twenty minutes until he seems deep enough into whatever he's dreaming about not to be startled by the unavoidable creaks in the plank floor, and only then do I go out to the garden, to grab a spade from the shed.

To think I was so worried about disturbing Mother's overgrown garden. Today it's insignificant. Today it might just magic into place, or magic into something completely different—a gazebo, or a jungle gym. I don't know what to expect.

I have to clear about ten years of cobwebs off the spade, which I do after slipping on Mother's garden gloves—the red polka dotted ones—only to have a mouse scurry out from the corner where the gloves have been sitting, waiting hand over hand all this time. I watched it race to a far corner draped with a dirty blue tarp. It seems there's an entire civilization in my yard that I have no part in.

Following the mouse, I pull back the tarp and there is secreted a pile of books. Had Mother put them there after the night she'd found me with her copy of *Truth and Art*? How strange to find this on a day when Rose herself has discovered the truth about art in the same way Mother had.

I recall with Mother, the way she inexplicably appeared locked in a room, banging and yelling to get out—the same way Rose had today. When I pulled aside the furnishings that had barricaded her in, I could tell from the way her hair was mussed, and her heavy breathing that she had just come tumbling, literally tumbling from the open book, the page she'd been on marked with a paper scrap. I read those words she'd underlined: *something not art, not life, but a new entity: a combination of the two.*

"Why won't you tell me how you do it?" I yelled. I recall shaking her by the shoulders, the bruising.

She didn't answer. It was during her silent time.

"I know why you don't want to talk," I said. I'd become bold in the silence she'd opened up, having fallen into the habit of expressing my inner dialogue as if alone. "You don't want to tell me how to do it. You want to save it for yourself." I stopped myself before I could say *because you don't care about me.* But I believe we both knew that by then.

She grabbed the book from my hands, the scrap I'd torn secreted in my fist, and threw it at me, a page slicing the flesh of my inner arm, drawing blood. It was a diversion. She ran out of the house, like she was afraid. Imagine her being afraid of me! But revisiting that experience with Dr. Samuels, I was taught that memory had been enhanced by my imagination. I worked his version of gestalt techniques. I trusted my gut. After a while, I barely thought about it.

Here, in the shed, atop of this pile of books is that copy of *Truth and Art*. I try to leaf through then realize I still have the gloves on. Before I realize what I've done, I have the dirty fingertips in my mouth, biting the thing off.

One thing at a time, I think, spitting, wiping at my mouth with my arm. I flick through to find the page really is ripped out. What do you make of that, Dr. Samuels?

Beneath it, the books are old and all different sizes; the smell musty and some of them have mold-mottled pages. I pick up the topmost volume, a hardback in orange fabric. *Baudelaire Theory*. I replace the book for later, saying the word out loud. *Later.* Then I quickly spin around. For what?

Isn't it obvious? To check if she'd emerge, now, when I need her. But she couldn't. I know that. Not anymore. Not after what I've done.

Unsurprisingly, all I see is a pile of dusty, smelly books. I shake my head. She won't show. I know why. And that's why I must dig right now. To know what's what. Once and for all. But my eye catches the spine of *Truth and Art*. I carefully slide it out from the middle of the pile, trying not to disturb the arrangement too much.

I leaf through until I come once again to the remnants of the torn page. I run my finger over the drops of my blood on the surrounding page edges. The old anger comes hurtling back. I think of how liberated I felt tearing her book. I think of her running away. It felt wonderful. Powerful. Her fear. It's when my plans first began to incubate.

I turn from the books to monitor our bedroom window for signs of Kennedy's waking. There's an ancient full-moon childhood nightlight of his in our bedroom, which I keep on in the evenings since Rose's early days. It casts hulking, but incredibly crisp shadows onto the walls and ceilings with every slight move in that room, and has been the source of many sleepless nights' soothing to watch, upon the ceiling, Kennedy's political shadow puppet program. From out here, it's a peeping tom's dream: movements to his dark silhouette are visible from even the slight motion of Kennedy's deep breath. If he's deceiving me, I should hate him, but I can't quite bring myself to. The thought of losing him to Kancer overpowers that instinct. He's my whole world. How many times has he said that! "I love being your whole world." And I loved it, too. But now it strikes me as an odd way to put it.

I retie my shorty robe over my bump and make my way to the rhododendron, where—in a self-preserving bout of psychologist-guided energy, I'd done my burying all those years ago. The lantern I use to light the way is old and heavy with D batteries. My father had bought it in the days when he tried to get Mother interested in things.

The earth is unrelenting. I never thought I'd go back to that time. If I did, I knew it would be the end for me, for this carefully constructed history I've written myself. This is the only way, I assure myself, and—ignoring the pounding in my chest—continue. But the dirt is solid, uncooperative, like unshakeable evidence. Turn away, it's saying. You are only asking for more trouble.

After five minutes of chipping away with little result, I pause to catch my breath and check over my shoulder at Kennedy's window. The circle flare of soft light is undisturbed. I eye the *rhodo*. Amazing how my mind retraces the path to Mother's nickname for the bush. The feel of the word shape in my mind transforms my perspective. Is my preconscious at play here? There was a time she was my whole world. When I treasured words like preconscious.

The bush is lopsided from the crash and has lost a fair amount of petals, but it's still sneering, putting me in my place. Within seconds I'm hunched over, retching from its root beer smell that could still catapult me back to Mother's bloodied suicide attempt in the Gremlin, and all that followed. *She was a terrible, selfish mother.*

When I regain composure, breathing as best I can through my mouth, I recall something. The smell. The garden. Mother always had those rhododendrons in her office. Vases full of them. I think for the first time in a long time of my *quelque chose* entries. *Rhodo*, I'd written on there.

I glove up and redouble my efforts, swinging with everything I have. Finally, the dry shards give way to softer, though packed, earth. And once I reach this threshold, my spade scoops seem to come from a force outside myself. The furrow grows. I look up at the bedroom, my heart beginning to race with the idea of being so close to uncovering the truth, after so much time.

The tip strikes something solid, the stunted energy jolting my joints. The sound of steel on steel. I kneel and use my gloved hands to rub clear a circle of the tackle box in which I'd buried Pinocchio's bag.

I set to digging at the dirt surrounding the box. My heart races. Looking around, guilty, I step onto the spade's base, and bearing down with all my weight, jump the tip into the earth. Inch by inch, I stamp the end of the shovel into the compressed dirt, bear down on the base, and then wedge the earth loose.

When the box begins to budge I kneel and hike it out with

two hands. The full moon of the bedroom nightlight shifts. Startled, I turn around to see the shadow of Kennedy's arms stretch, framed by the curtains. I have to leave it. Quick as I can, I lower the box back into the ground and frantically try to push the dirt in. Within minutes, the hole is plugged, but there is no covering the fact that the earth has been disturbed.

I think of covering the dark, loosened spot with a chair or a tarp, but decide that would just look more conspicuous and scurry to the shed and place the shovel beside the pile of books, behind the afghan. I bolt back to the kitchen, trying to appear natural at the sink, filling the kettle like I do on sleepless nights. I hear Kennedy's footsteps overhead, then the sound of water through the pipes. I hold my breath as the bathroom door squeaks and the light fixture above my head trembles slightly, and I pray he'll go back to bed.

But I know better. He can't get back to bed if he isn't sure I'm okay. I glance outside at the spot, trying to gauge if it's noticeable from here, and try to slow my breath.

Just as he rounds the steps to the landing, I catch my reflection and swipe with a tea towel at the mud stain on my chin.

"Whatchya doing up all alone?" Kennedy sounds like hell; his voice has none of the buoyancy.

"You know me, living on the edge."

Kennedy pulls out two mugs.

"Yeah." The timbre is too thoughtful, hangs like a bell peal. He reaches for that pill bottle. "Don't forget your Clomid," he says, palming one to me. He fills a glass from the tap and hands that over, too.

I do as I'm told. Reality feels softer than ever. But I'm pulled toward the idea of action, something I can *do*. Just meters away that tackle box hums with an energy I feel from here, and that's where my thoughts are—with the contents and why I'm so sure I shouldn't share them with him.

After our tea, I wait for him to fall into sleep shudders, breathe deeper. But I can tell he's only pretending to sleep, the normal rhythm of it is missing; it appears he's waiting up to see what I will do next. Though we keep up the act, neither of us sleeps a wink.

21

KENNEDY

"Thought I'd make us all some breakfast," I say the next morning, pulling on track pants and a tee shirt, ignoring the hurt or possibly frightened look in her eye. It's not that I want her to feel desperate, but she cannot know about everything her father wants to say, all the terrible things. My cancer is a metaphor for everything that's been festering. It's all tearing us apart, been silently doing so all this time.

Downstairs, I turn on news radio, yank an egg carton from the fridge and go about collecting cheese, onions, ham. I will miss ham, I think, when I am dead. Cheese, too. For a second, I freeze, staring at the two mugs in the sink. I don't want to think about what she was doing up last night. I don't like sleeping when she's not there.

I don't have much time to contemplate before I hear the patter of little feet down the stairs. Covering my tracks has become second nature. I busy myself with cracking the eggs before Rose emerges—as if merely standing in the kitchen might look suspicious.

Rosie looks shy, which she sometimes does in the morning.

Though I suspect it's a bit of a put on, I can't say I've got any defenses against it.

"It's nice to be needed," Millie always says to me, and she's right. But how could I have indulged myself in this emotion when all this time there was a chance I might not be around for the needs? I hold my arms out and Rose runs my way. This is our thing. Despite myself, my heart swells at her breathy hug, the static electricity attracting her sticky-uppy hair to my shirt. Against my chest, she views the breakfast preparations. I did it because I'm such a damned good liar that even I believed there was nothing wrong with me.

"Omelet?" she asks. "*Oscar makes an Omelet.*" She sings the book title the way Millie does for her when she reads this beloved book. I can't believe our kid is three. Will I see her get to four?

She takes after me in many ways, but without Millie's kind of thinking, Rosie wouldn't have sidled up to the counter singing that adorable rendition of Supercalifradgilistic, would she? Crispy salad oceans! You would never think something like that could make you so deliriously happy. Not where I grew up.

"It's expialidocious, Kennedy," my mother would have said. "Practice." Pulling out the nonsense syllables like they weren't nonsense, but a scientific phrase I would be tested on in order to get into college.

Millie's a beacon of innocence. Her methods are unorthodox, and with her blackouts back again she's slightly dangerous, her thinking confused, but her intention is pure. As pure as anything I've ever encountered. What her mother did to her! God, I hated that woman. But Millie's the opposite; she protects Rose at all the scary bits of stories and life, making up angels and cozy couches in the clouds for anything that might otherwise hurt. Is that something an evil, bad person would do? How can her father think these things of her? I know how, but again, my powers of persuasion have had everyone—myself included —fooled.

My daughter tucks her fuzzy head into the crook of my neck. It's with Rosie—this Dora the Explorer night-gowned girl with the crayons in her handbag and the penchant for humming mid-career Madonna songs (if it wasn't for Millie, she wouldn't have mastered that parlor trick either. Yes, I'm guilty of pulling out the video footage every now and again after a few beers. Beers, I will miss those too)—that I feel most helpless about the cancer. In a way, it is for the best that we lost the pregnancy. Nobody official is going to allow for Millie to care for a child alone if Mr. Burns gets talking.

I must be imagining it, but Rosie looks at me as if she knows something I don't. I try to talk myself out of it but then I realize I'm just being soft on myself. There are real consequences to our actions. And Rose's well-being is one of them. She clearly knows something is odd. I had her lie to her mother, she's been barricaded in her room, and after that stunt, she's going to be seeing a lot more of me.

"What kind of omelet does Oscar make?" I ask, looking out the window to the garden. Last month, I fixed the loose stones, hammered in the uneven nails on the fence boards, and chopped away the precarious weeds that looked poisonous. With Rose, here, now, it seems almost welcoming—the apples jostling merrily on the wind.

"Tomato that reeks," she says.

"Tomato with leeks," I correct her.

"Whenever."

"Whatever."

"Dad, why does it have to be right?"

"Because—" I begin but I don't know how to finish. It doesn't. Wasn't I just regretting this about my own mother? I am always needing to be right. That's probably down to my mother, too.

"Because what?"

I knew this day would come when I wouldn't have the answers for our child, but I didn't expect it so quickly. At a loss for an answer that balances the precarious differences between truth and correctness, ethics and honesty (which at this point, Rose only knows as a Billy Joel song), I change course. "Are there any reeks out there?"

Rose shakes her head. "Mom does herbs, but she doesn't permit veggies." Like the Aussies, my daughter pronounces the hard h in *herbs*. Good on her. I once told her we were half Australian. Why not?

"Why not?" I ask now about the veggies. My wife is the kindest woman in the world, a world that mostly doesn't deserve her. She calls our yard a garden for the sake of her mother, who didn't deserve her either. It would kill Millie if I tore the whole thing up without her permission, the way I'd been feeling out with the pool idea. But what if it wasn't a pool? What if it was a first-rate garden, something to be proud of, where Rose could pretend she was riding a unicorn all day long with no idea what was underneath the ground? Perhaps it's just a distraction, but it's a good one if I have to be home babysitting Rose so her mother doesn't accidentally lock her in a room, and something good I can do for my kid. Maybe Millie could let loose and I'll even plant her some reeks.

I get a kick out of the funny drain noise she gurgles out, thinking it's a unicorn's neigh as she attempts to skip (more like the chicken dance). In moments like this, I know everything I'd done was worth it.

Despite myself, I swell with the connotations of a gardening project: renewal, control over life, sowing seeds. God, cancer makes me such a pussy. You'd swear I'd been drinking the Burns' Kool-Aid.

"She says it's for the future. She's saving it for the future," Rose says. "I asked her 'who's the future?' and she said, 'we don't know, Rose.'"

"That's because that's my job, Rose. I control the future. Me and the future are thick as thieves." In that moment I can almost believe it.

"Thieves," she repeats.

"Damn thieves."

"Damn thieves," she says.

My eyes bug and I place a finger to my lips. "Don't say that," I say, but I assume the authority is undermined when we're both laughing. *This is life. This is what it's all about.*

An hour later, I'm pushing an oversize steel cart around the nursery, Rose standing on the back.

But now I was here the idea began deflating: what was my planting veggies going to do? Make the world a better place, even though our politics were going to shit? Even though our culture was growing more and more selfish and silo'd every single day? Like I could fix the future for my child by growing my own vegetables. Rubbish. The logic was already busting at the seams.

All the same, walking the aisles, I choose carrots, reeks, tomatoes, pumpkin, and cucumber, among a number of lettuces. Remembering summer weekends with my dad— quietly observing what it meant to be a man—I pile slabs of manure and soil onto the bottom rack and don't skimp on the good stuff. There's something undeniably promising about all this green, all this fresh earth. Fertilizer!

Why can't humans have something like that? Apply every two weeks for healthy growth. No, we're too busy inventing new ways to cook bacon in the microwave. As I shimmy the last bag into place, someone taps my shoulder. I turn. This young kid in his baseball cap could have been me at twenty-one, around the time I traveled to Sydney.

"Sir, got a look at your haul and wondered if you knew this isn't the right time to plant those veggies?"

"Oh yeah?" I say, not giving any cards away, like maybe I'm a farmer pulling an experiment. I grab another tomato plant from the half-off stand next to us.

The kid's oblivious though. He's got that do-good look like he wouldn't let anyone walk out of here with the wrong thing, and I don't know if it's that I want to quash before it bites him in the ass, or the questionable future of all the unplanted veggies, the unwanted veggies, the misfit fucking veggies that have no future, won't do anything to affect this unredeemable world's future, which makes me double my order.

If nature wants to try to fuck me, I'll show nature who's boss. If I have to build my own fucking greenhouse, that's what I'll do. It's me who handles the future. It's always been me. Now? Well, I'll have to fucking work something out. And I'm taking these veggies with me.

On the way out, I add a boatload of pretty flowers, just to make the whole thing smell better.

22

THE PLANTING IS SATISFYING, PHYSICAL, CATHARTIC. I TEAR OUT A whole section caddy-corner to the shed, going at it with an axe, a spade, my bare hands. In a couple hours, I'm turning over dirt and pouring fresh earth. It smells amazing. Why haven't I done this before? Grew up in an apartment dreaming of things like this. Our vacation home's yard was "landscaped," and we weren't allowed to touch it, not that my brothers and I didn't mess around in there when no one was looking.

I squeeze the plants out of their plastic holders and gently bury them, patting over the root balls. There's no denying the hope and anticipation of the venture. I ignore the obvious symbolism—life! Because it's too cliché. I don't do symbols. I do action, consequence, results. But cancer doesn't want to play that game.

In no time at all, there are four rows of veggies—everything we could need to make salads, side dishes, soups, and more for freezing. It's so simply sustaining. Why do we make life so difficult, the clean, vibrant plant rows seem to say as I spray them with the hose, their boughs bouncing?

At the end of the rows, I stand back to admire my work. I

pull the shovel toward me, digging its tip into the dirt. But it hits something solid, with a thud. Lifting the handle, I lower the end and tap again. There's definitely something there. In fact, it looks like the three feet or so past this end has already been dug up by someone else. The dirt's been replaced, but it's clear it's been disturbed, the surface is fresh, deeper in color, just like the earth I've dug up in the path leading here. It doesn't take more than a few seconds to palm the dirt away from the object and see there's something beneath there.

It could be sinister. Or not. Rose would love this, I think. Buried treasure! Maybe she and Millie planned this for me because they knew I'd be planting out here. I should go grab her, make a big show of it. I'm feeling more positive now, like everything just might be okay, and this discovery, now, feels almost fated: look at me talking like Millie!

My mind takes the buried treasure idea to an intersection with Rose and I realize it wouldn't be responsible to call her out here without checking into it first. What if it's not been put here by them, but instead, it's something dangerous? A land mine? Just as I'm thinking this, Millie appears from the kitchen with iced tea. I place my foot on the patch of the object I've unearthed. Her hand is trembling. I shouldn't be out here; I'm stressing her more. What was I thinking?

"Here!" she says a little frantic. "Why don't you come inside and take a break?"

She won't say, *I'm worried that you are weak because you are dying of cancer.* Or mention any of the other stuff going on here.

"Thanks," I say, and take a long sip of the tea. "And, surprise! I'm making you a garden." She tries to smile, but it falls fast. I catch her looking at the ground. Does she know about this thing in the dirt? Did she put it there? If so, why? And why can't I bring myself to ask her if she's been hiding something from me? It's amazing how quickly our perceptions can change.

23

MILLIE

ANOTHER SLEEPLESS NIGHT AFTER CATCHING KENNEDY BY THE tackle box in the garden. I pretend to sleep and then when I hear Kennedy drive off to work, I rise to bathe and dress Rose for the day. I didn't think he would leave me alone with her after the way he acted the other day, but I was glad for it.

I can't know if he was looking for the box or had come across it by accident. It wouldn't have been difficult the way I left it. I also can't know whether he looked inside and put it back, or never got to that point. I know I mustn't let on until I've got the facts straight. It's just papers. I'm sure it's just papers. What else would it be? *Gestalt. Instinct.*

The morning is sweltering. After breakfast I scrape my hair back into a bun, but it's already wet at the roots just two shovel swings into the effort. Later, I'm sure to feel the sting from where the sun is burning my neck. I swing and dig, toss the dirt, swing again. Surely, I hadn't buried it this deeply.

I hear Rose call for me and drop the shovel. There's a hug, *kickles*, teeth brushing and breakfast. Then I settle her in front of *Sesame Street*, her book and charm necklace in hand, and head back out to the garden where I can see her through the large picture window. I still can't believe Kennedy would leave her with me today. He must believe me about what happened the other day, that she magically ended up barricaded in there.

I dig until I'd made a mess of that corner of the garden, just alongside Kennedy's impressive veggie patch. The tackle box isn't there. He's got it, hasn't he? And if he does, then why hasn't he said anything? Why am I so worried about it? I don't believe I know what's inside, and yet I feel a strong tug toward it. I sense whatever's in there is monumental to me.

I look through the window at Rose. She's just listening to Sesame Street, her attention on the book. It's a normal scene, I tell myself. I replace the dirt and pack it as best I can.

Back inside, I pull up Google. I type the words: Dr. Pinocchio.

24

AT WORK, I LOCK THE DOOR TO MY OFFICE, AND TELL SEB NOT TO disturb me. Over the desk, I drape a moving blanket we keep to protect our floors when we're unpacking and moving merchandise. I place the tackle box on top of it.

I had to make quick work of digging it up and putting it in my trunk before Millie and Rose were up and about this morning. I lift the latches. The smell is of old, moldy paper, which is exactly what's inside. This doesn't bother me. I've come to love the smell. Our house is filled with Emily's old books that smell exactly that way. If it wasn't for Emily and her fucking books, I wouldn't be with Millie, after all. I'm grateful to moldy books.

But when I realize what's inside, I drop my head in my hands. The fucking *quelque choses* papers from my shop that Millie used to carry around all the time. Hundreds of them, and not in any particular order. They're torn into individual sheets and piled any which way. I remember when she told me about the paper, and I went along with the idea of the incredible coincidence that she'd bought them in my shop. Oh, Emily, I bet you rued the day you ever walked by that place. Even I had to admit that despite the untruths, it felt like a sign that she'd found something so important to her in my store before we ever met.

But these are the notes of a person who is not well. The writing is frantic, followed by tons of exclamation points, the slant is that strange backward slant of Millie's. These were from a different time, when she was quite sick, and now that I've put her under so much stress, she's not coping, and she's come back to these, to the only way she knows how to comfort herself.

I cannot believe I am now in the same camp as her mother, having pushed her just as far. And now her father is ready to make it all worse. What will become of Millie? What will become of Rose?

I pull back the silk scarf the pile is covering. Amongst the musty scent of old unwashed fabric, the rhododendron perfume is still there: cinnamon chocolate. I breathe it in deeply, hold it in my lungs. Scent is a strong sense. I remember Millie's original telling of her mother's story—the dramatic smashing into the rhodo plant along their driveway. Poor Millie.

I'll never understand this world. I'll never understand myself. I have done everything to save her from this—and in turn, I have everything a man could ever want, and I've managed to fuck it up, lose it all to cancer, and ruin lives instead of saving them.

I have to do something with this box that has presented itself to me. Something to fix what's going wrong with Millie. I sit down to memorize every single word and get ready for my biggest lie yet.

25

MILLIE

MY GOOGLE SEARCH PULLS UP A PLETHORA OF CARTOON IMAGES OF storybook Pinocchio on a physician's table, nose extended, hat feathered. I realize how deeply ingrained this story is in our culture. Pinocchio means *liar*. I see your nose growing. But there's another meaning that's been popularized too: he's become a real boy! And here I get a frisson. Yes, Dr. Pinocchio has always reminded me of a boy in a man's body, one who looked uncomfortable in it.

But none of this is news.

The next click brings something juicier. Chapter 16 of *Pinocchio*, the original novel by Carlo Collodi, features three falcon doctors who can't agree whether Pinocchio is dead or alive. *Pinocchio*—a story of cheeky puzzles. Why should I be surprised?

Finally, my search calls up some real, live doctors (and plastic surgeon advice about reducing an "overprojecting nose tip"), who attained the moniker Pinocchio because of untruths. There are twenty pages of entries like this. Who says literature is dead?

Unsurprisingly, there are not a lot of people, let alone

doctors with Pinocchio as a genuine last name. I come across one, in Northern Australia, who treats birds exclusively. But my Doctor Pinocchio has not joined Facebook, he has not become digitally part of our history in any way. When I see this, I feel I shouldn't be surprised. These are not modern people. These are classical people with ideas too modern for modern people. I will have to visit a library to find him. See if he has published anything, and if so, through what hospital or university, or press, and then try to track him down from there.

So I add "+ New Jersey General" to the search and the hospital's number comes up, firing off all kinds of memories for me, and a quick call tells me he's no longer with the hospital. There's no forwarding information.

Later that day, with Rose's crayon bashing a Disney coloring book at my feet, a librarian across a desk has found something published in the last three years by a "Dr. P," entitled, *Psycholinguistics: A Non-Medical Approach*. It was put out by a small medical press in New York. With little effort, I find their details on the internet and ask after Dr. P's contact details.

"I'm writing an article about Psycholinguistics, and I'd like to interview him," I say.

"Any publicity is good publicity for book sales these days," the young woman says. "Especially books about Psycholinguistics. The study of the interrelation between linguistic factors and psychological aspects. What does that even mean? And why the mysterious nom de plume 'Dr. P?' I can't seem to get anyone to tell me."

I won't give this girl the satisfaction of the truth. "It also studies psychological and neurobiological factors that enable humans to acquire, use, comprehend and produce language," I say instead.

"Yeah right. I forgot that bit." She laughs, as if we're both convinced the P stands for pointless drivel.

I force myself to laugh.

"Gosh, I've landed a long way from the bestsellers, haven't I?" She reads off his telephone number and asks me to send a copy of the article.

I dial four numbers and hang up. Six. Six again. Finally, I make it to a ring before cutting the line. Lucky six again. In the end, I get a voicemail message. *You've reached Doctor P. Messages may be left here.* His voice sets off a kaleidoscope of sensations, the deeper I gaze, the more quickly they reconfigure themselves. I remember writing down all the things I told him, so I could look back later and assure myself of his response. I'd burned those pages long ago.

I muster the energy to leave a message. "This is Millie Burns. Please ring me. It's urgent." I leave him my contact information and hang up.

I wait all day, trembling, keeping Rose in front of the television, with food out in case I disappear, terrified of what will happen to her if I do, but I don't. And Pinocchio doesn't ring. Meanwhile, to my eye, it looks like Kennedy's garden has exploded after this one sunny day. I try not to imagine Mother's bony fingers grasping the roots.

26

ROSE HAS BEEN SULKING FAR AWAY FROM ME ALL AFTERNOON. Dinner was a disaster. I could think of nothing but Pinocchio and lost track of the meal the second I closed it in the oven.

"How can a chicken be both overcooked and raw?" I asked as Kennedy brushed his teeth in the en suite. The good doctor hadn't rung and I was sick of leaving messages, each sounding more desperate than the next. I swore myself off after three. I should have used the same pretense I used with his publicist.

This morning, I called the publishing house back with a lie. I was on my way to meet him and left the slip of paper I'd written his address on at the house. She hadn't followed up with him, she admitted! She hoped he'd been easy to get a hold of. No wonder she had no bestsellers.

"Wait. I know the answer to this one!" Kennedy replied to the rhetorical question about the chicken.

"No, you're thinking of the one about the salmon," I said.

"Am I? We should wake Rose. She always knows these things."

But Rose was exhausted. Apparently, she was barricaded in her room again for hours. I had blacked out, gone to the book world. This time it was *The Fountainhead*—god, how Mother loved that book.

Again, I wondered how she'd gotten herself stuck in there. Yes, I understood it would be blamed on me, but it was difficult to feel guilt when I had no memory of doing it. I couldn't understand but again, Kennedy was kind about it, strangely so, despite his obvious panic. And the part of me that believed Rose was doing this when she crossed over to the book world thought, yes! Let's keep this magical book world to ourselves. This is how a mother and daughter ought to be. I felt overjoyed with images of her practicing her moves on the ice, making friends, and living life to the fullest in a way I never could manage. The meaningful parts of life, the beauty of it, would pull us through. It was unconventional, the barricading she managed to arrange from that other world, but what *was* conventional about any of this? I thought, good on you, Rose. You are a clever girl. She was sleeping when he found her, which is just as well after such a long day on the ice.

I'm going to Pinocchio tomorrow, whether he calls me or not.

Rose picked two small purple buds off the rhododendron this afternoon before her disappearance. They're in a tiny, chipped teacup on the kitchen table, aggressively vibrant. The root beer smell permeates, reminds me of the missing tackle box. Of course she's paging-in.

I suddenly feel the way I did back then when it was Mother's house, and I can almost believe Mother really had insisted the garden wreckage outside our home remain untouched. But no, the truth is I hadn't wanted anyone to discover what I'd buried. That feels like a lifetime ago.

I need to get to Pinocchio. He's the only one who understands the book world, knows the truth.

After dinner, I put Rose to bed with Kennedy hovering nearby, pretending he isn't worried I'll harm her. He coincidentally is heading down to watch the news just as I leave her room.

"Glass of wine?" I ask. I'm exhausted. I feel like my every action is a sham. I'm faking everything, and yet the life I had only days ago feels like it's just past the tips of my fingers.

"Please." I want his arms around me. I feel tears prick my eyes. Could he really die? In certain moments, everything looks so normal, I can almost forget. But I will save him.

I hear the snippet from the presidential debate the other night. I've nearly got it memorized by now, there's been so much coverage. The shorthand is Bush doesn't give a fig about the rules, but the rules matter to people. The public seems to like Bush anyway, and so they don't care about the rules. My ears perk up, because there's something new to the story tonight.

Bush was in the lead in all eleven swing states, including Colorado, Florida, Iowa, and Michigan, until Monday's debate. It seems polls are showing people do care about the rules, as the moderator had insisted. Our teams hit the streets to ask voters why they felt so strongly about having a president who follows the rules. Answers varied widely.

Darryl Kings in Cedar Rapids, Iowa quoted Ayn Rand's famous novel, The Fountainhead: *"'Nothing is more important than the collective brain. We are together in this world. We get our best innovations, as a collective, each of us channeling the best in ourselves and bringing that together...'"*

That is *not* how that quote goes. Mother quoted that book to me nearly as much as her line about grounding books in reality. *"The mind is an attribute of the individual. There is no such thing as a collective brain. There is no such thing as a collective thought. An agreement reached by a group of men is only a compromise...The primary act—the process of reason—must be performed by each man alone."*

I look to Kennedy to see if he recognizes the change. I know he's read the book. In today's world, this book is different from yesterday's. Because a book has been changed, it has created different influences. *Ground your reading in reality.* I am making real headway. Look how powerful I am! I am doing this.

The novel's words, in their original form, sound sinister. They certainly align with a mother who chooses, three times, to abandon her child to suicide. Not the romantic, mystical explanations I've always used to explain why she hadn't meant to abandon me. *"I do not recognize anyone's right to one minute of my life. Nor to any part of my energy. Nor to any achievement of mine. No matter who makes the claim, how large their number or how great their need."* Kennedy said the main character was a dick, stood for everything that's wrong with this world, that no one gave a shit about anyone else. And now I've changed that. Perhaps I can make the whole world a better place.

It feels almost like this incredible change in reality is a message from the universe to me. You can fix this, it's saying. Trust yourself.

I barely know it when I'm standing in front of the television, blocking Kennedy's view. Even I can tell my words are too excited.

Slow down, Millie. You are not making sense.

I hear him, but I speak over him anyway. "This is *not* how the debate went. We watched the debate. We laughed along with all the morning radio shows as they lampooned a Bush-run country, breaking rules like washing your hands after using the toilet." The book in my hand, I flutter the pages to find that bit from the television, but I can't concentrate. I'm too hyped up. I can't find it.

"Slow down," Kennedy is saying. "I don't understand you. What are you saying? Something about *The Fountainhead*?"

Didn't he hear the news? Doesn't he realize I'm changing

reality? He looks concerned. I don't like the way he is looking at me.

"I think you should lie down, hon. I'll come with you. It's been a difficult week for all of us."

"What? This has nothing to do with that! Don't you see?"

"Millie, you know what this is. Come, come to me." He tries to pull me in. For a second I think I'm trembling. But it's him. He's crying. I've never seen it before, and it strikes me like the end of the world.

We are both spent after and fall asleep for half an hour.

"What are we doing here?" I ask when we wake.

"What do you mean?"

I decide to take a chance. "Where's the tackle box, Kennedy?"

"What tackle box?"

"The one I buried in the garden."

"I don't know what you mean."

"If I mean anything to you, you will answer this question honestly. Where is the tackle box?"

He stares at me long and hard, as if making a decision. "I have it."

"Where?"

"In my car."

"Why do you have it, the box of all Mother's most treasured research?"

He doesn't answer. I move to the armchair. My gaze drops to the picture window, to the garden. Something aligns in my mind.

To Kennedy's credit, he keeps looking me in the eye. It's me who looks away. I can't reconcile this man with the one I fell in love with. Despite the pull, the way I've always known him as much as myself, as part of myself even, the truth is, he's a stranger. All his secrets. And all mine. If he knows about the tackle box, what else does he know?

It must take courage for him to cross the room and kneel before me. He takes my hands in his.

"I love you, Millie. More than anything. You must know that. No matter what I tell you next, this is the truest thing of all. The circumstances surrounding our start may have been, well, questionable. And I've tried to make up for that by giving you everything I have to give. What you taught me is that none of it matters as much as you and Rose. I would do it all again." His posture straightens at the last sentence, as if he'd just decided something.

I turn to him. "What do you mean, questionable?" No matter what answer he's about to give, our connection is there between us, undeniable, no matter the circumstances—the cancer, the lies. I can't help it. I respond to his kiss. I tremble at his touch. It's never diminished. In fact, the drama only enhances it. Like in all good stories. It feels right that I should be so angry and so in love at the same time. It's more dramatic that way. Still, there's something that frightens me in his eye. I force myself to pull away.

He continues. "I, too, can go to the book world. I was young, like Rose, when I first paged-in. That's what we call going over into the fictional realm. When you leave you page-out. You know how conventional my family is. They didn't believe me when I tried to explain it to them. The first few times I paged-in and out before they even realized I was gone, so there wasn't the panic over me missing. But eventually, they couldn't deny I was disappearing *somewhere*. They simply pretended it wasn't happening. My mom stopped checking on me so that she wouldn't have to face it. Even now, they pretend it never happened."

"Your family seems so normal. Anachronistic, judgmental, but normal. How is that possible?"

"The mind is a powerful thing. If you want to pretend there isn't magic under your own nose, you just do. You of all people must understand that. Haven't we been pretending for your benefit that nothing's going on, while you cross over into the book world?"

I flinch. I don't like pretending. And I don't like being left in the dark. Besides, all this time, I thought this was my secret, my family's curse doing this to Rose. All along Kennedy was complicit. No wonder he wasn't concerned at her disappearance. He'd probably been waiting for this moment. Perhaps it had come before, when I wasn't looking and he was? Maybe our whole life together was an elaborate plan to get to this moment.

"I was an early Reader, and all of this started happening when I learned to read. I read everything I could. If you hang out at book shops and libraries enough, you'll run into another one. There's the trembling you can spot from someone who's recently paged-out."

He grabs my hand. "Yes, I noticed," he says, kissing each fingertip. "But there's something else, an aura, I can't tell you exactly what it is, but it's something intangible that's come back with us to the visible world; you recognize each other." He said *us.* It is the first time anyone has acknowledged me as part of that world, and it's overwhelming.

"It was terrifying, the first time I brought it up to another person. This would prove there really *was* another world. But my instinct was right. She was a Reader—that's what we call people who can do it."

She? Do I want to hear the rest of this story? I look down at my hand trembling. Kennedy smiles. "Ah, there it is, the mark of the special."

27

MILLIE

KENNEDY OPENS AND SHUTS DRAWERS, GATHERS HIS DAILY essentials, an evening ritual. I followed him into the kitchen from the living room. He places his small, neat pile on the counter by the door. I cannot believe he is being so normal after what he's just told me. *Jesus, Kennedy, do I mean so little to you? How could you let me live this lie, knowing all of this and never saying? Think of the things we could have done!* Even as I think the accusations, my mind tries to reject it. This dying man loves me, or I have no idea what love is.

Right now, it's a flood questions and doubts about the things he's told me tonight, and for the entirety of our sham life, and about what I have and have not said. And of course, there're all the old inadequacies poking their heads. He told me that he knew Mother. *Emily,* he called her. The first Reader he met. Not only did he know her, he was her arch rival. He used all the right words. This could not have been a lie. He knows too much. I'm shocked to the core.

Mostly, his experience of paging-in, as he described it, is similar to mine. But a bit of it diverges, which is understandable because if I'm meant to understand anything about paging in, it's as different for everyone as the experience of reading is. It's even different for each person each time they do it because we're never the same person twice.

Though my anger is formidable, I have to keep a handle on it. I've been waiting so long to ask these questions. I must get all the answers I can. "I am going to ask you questions. And you are going to answer them," I say.

"I will. But first I will tell you this," He looks at me like he's charming me, casting a spell. "I should have told you earlier, but you are exhibiting classic signs of a developing Reader. Waking to different realities. I watched how disoriented you were. I saw your hand trembling. I wanted so badly to comfort you. And then you remembered the other version of the debate. And that version of reality you remember from the other day, when I wasn't ill, when you weren't—" He can't say it, just looks down at my bump.

I feel faint. So, I wasn't imagining it. He doesn't say why he didn't tell me earlier. I'm too terrified to ask.

I have so many questions. A lifetime of questions. I don't know where to start. "But why is the paging-in working now?"

"A lot of people think it's about finding an *important* book. But all books are important if you connect to them. It can be any book, if the author's done a good job suspending reality, pulling you into the world of the book. It's connecting to the story in your mind, and that's what really matters.

"In fact, sometimes it's not about the content at all. Your mother is known for her connection to rhythms. The flow of the words, the cadences of the sentences are key to her page-ins." I think of the heady novels Mother surrounded herself with. That all feels right. In fact, it feels like a natural detail I already know.

"The reason you're so disoriented is because you aren't strong enough yet. The changes you made in the book world didn't stick completely. So you're left with a residue of the old way of things. You will get stronger, but as you do, it gets more difficult. You'll see. Working it out is just the beginning. Handling it, learning to work with it, and then, of course, struggling against those that don't see its use the same way you do, hiding it from the general public—those are the parts that will drive you mad."

"I don't like that word," I say.

"Understood," he says.

Those answers are too large to wrap my head around at the moment. I decide to start smaller.

"Why did you take me out that first time?"

This time he can't hold the gaze. I pretend not to notice. It isn't hard. He doesn't want me seeing that. We know what our partners need and we give it to them. That's what love is. Just as I'm thinking that, I'm shocked at the next words out of his mouth.

"It's love that makes it work. We—the Universalists, who use paging-in for the world's benefit, rather than our own, like your mother's group, the Individualists, we thought if we could take Emily's love from her—the love she had from you—then she would lose her power. She didn't deserve your love anyway. Not the way I do."

I'm going to be sick. I knew it wasn't a meaningless suicide. I knew it couldn't be that. Here, finally, justification. Meanwhile, all my life was a lie, needlessly. Tragedy is what it is.

He shakes his head. "You loved her so much, but you have to understand what's at stake, Millie. Your mother was a dangerous, powerful, incredibly careless and selfish woman. Think about it this way, would you want her to have power over the nuke button? Because that's essentially what she had."

"Did she give you cancer? Is that what this is all about?"

He nods, turns away.

"Are you just saying this so I'll hate her?"

He shakes his head, manages to meet my gaze.

"But why did she do that to you? And how? You know, the ironic thing is that as soon as I found out about the cancer, that was my first thought: paging-in could fix this. But I couldn't work out how to target it so specifically."

Kennedy sighs hugely. I can't believe this is all happening.

"Do you really want this life, murder, mayhem, manipulating the very yearnings that make us who we are, all for the unwinnable battle of taming man's desires? It is ugly. Believe me. Look how amazingly we got on without all of this." He scoots his chair close, grabs my hands, puts his face in close to mine. "We have it all—no fantasy, no fiction required. You've let all that go all these years. Maybe you can leave it behind again. For good this time."

I feel my chin wobble, wet rivers down my face, gushing.

"*Had* it all."

"But how can you go in with a specific goal of altering a specific reality outside the pages?"

"You have to be incredibly powerful to do that."

"Like Mother." I swallow. "And Rose."

"Why don't you tell me more of what *you* know?" he says.

"Well, there has to be an incredibly strong connection to the story." *Always carry a book with you to ground your reading in reality.* "And a deep understanding of the way stories work, which elements will lead to changes down the line, a grasp of character, and the way readers connect to those characters, and why. Years and years of study. There are many schools—the methods are as varied as the amount of texts out there multiplied by the ways we can interpret them. But the person who can tug at those exact strings that stir the precise reaction they were after. Well, that person is what has come down the line to us as *God*."

He looks at me again. My throat catches. I feel my eyes glass.

Have I said too much? If so, I can't seem to stop myself. I seem to speak for hours. Until he stops me.

"—What you said there, 'to be desired, to be a hero, to be glorious, great, to take a life. That is life dramatized to its largest stakes. So easy to see right and wrong when the stakes are so great, isn't it?"

"Yes," I say, but I'm not sure I agree. Taking a life: that is the bit that's always caught me up.

"And what more beautiful way is there to save someone than to achieve the greatest stakes?"

It's in that moment I know for sure I won't tell Kennedy about seeing Pinocchio tomorrow. There's something about his stance. Like maybe he doesn't believe everything I'm saying, despite what he said about his own experiences.

Mother. Is this all your fault? Just another jab, perfectly delayed in the execution, to kick me down just when everything's perfect? Now that's much easier to believe. And yet, I have so many questions, I can't leave it there.

"Readers are a dangerous bunch. The risks and rewards are always high in literature—that's why it's so powerful; it works on our desires, letting us see what it's like to fuck or kill or please someone in the way we've always dreamed—"

"I still can't believe you've lied to me all this time. How can that be?"

"I eased your life in so many ways, Millie. Don't you dare tell me I didn't. I gave you years of freedom from all this. I gave you love, a family, peace."

"But at what cost? And was that really for my benefit, or to tick off the boxes on the ruination of Mother? Where does the one end and the other begin? At what point did you realize you loved me? At any point?"

"You know what Döblin said," Kennedy says. "'Omens and coincidences and signs flow into the visible world,' from stories.

A 'softening' of reality, he called it. It's all so mixed up, I can barely recall what's real."

Now, *this* I can understand. As a matter of fact, I remember when I first read Döblin. I wrote that down on my *Quelque Choses: Doblin, softening of reality*. Some words scream out to you to make them your own, as if they always were and you're now just getting reacquainted with them. I underlined it twice.

He always said he loved it when I jotted down my notes. *Harriet the Spy*, he called me. But that was long ago.

My mind is thrashing around for a way out. I can taste the memory of this feeling. I fear what I will do to satisfy the desire, to quell the discomfort. Anger rises.

"And so you see that while technically I can page in, why I can't tinker with this cancer—can't have you tinkering with it either. And besides, as a Universalist, it's completely against everything we stand for, everything we fight your mother and her clan to protect. There's an order to things, an oath for the good of man. And I'm the leader of the movement. We're not supposed to use it for personal gain. So, please leave all that behind."

This is the moment I can reassure him, if I want to.

"Doesn't everyone fuck up the world every day, just more gradually?" I ask. "That's the nature of life." I'm not sure my reaction is genuine, but I think of all the times he's helped me, soothed me, all those memories now mixed up in our new reality, and I can't close the door on him just yet.

"I'm not surprised you see it that way, growing up with your mother. And I do have respect for that point of view. There are times I wish I'd taken it. It's the only direction where supreme satisfaction lies."

He seems to mean the words he says. "The problem with literature is that it poses more questions. The deeper you go, the more questions you have. We need to ask these questions, but mostly, we don't have the answers. I think Universalists often take the stance that they do merely to play devil's advocate, or because they wish they did have the answers, or wish others believed they did. Like politicians."

He's given an excellent argument. But I need to save him, if I can. He is Rose's father, the father of my unborn child. As if he can read my mind, he stands, pulls me up, too.

"Where are we going?"

He doesn't answer. Just walks me to his car and pops the trunk. In the back is the tackle box. "This is the most sacred of relics. It belongs with you."

It belongs with me.

28

SHE'S LOOKING AT THE MOUNTAINS OF *QUELQUE CHOSE* SHEETS. BUT I know she's seeing something completely different. Her imagined relics of another dimension that she deluded herself into thinking her selfish piece of shit mother could visit, all so she didn't feel like she'd been neglected and abandoned for no good reason. It is the saddest thing I have ever seen. And I am so sorry it had to come to this.

God, I wish I'd never sold those notepads. But who knows, surely she would have found something else to pile all this significance onto? I speak her name, but she doesn't respond. It's like she doesn't hear me. She lifts a sheet, looks at it for a very long time, then puts that one back and picks up another. She clearly thinks she's looking at something other than the ordinary paper with her back-slanted writing all down it. It's like she's catatonic, except her lips are moving double time, forming incomprehensible sounds.

I can't help the tears from flowing, watching her like this. All the pain has done this to her. And much of it has been at my own hand. I thought I was helping, but was I? I loved her, I wanted to help her, but I wanted to help her for myself. So I could have her, love her, because of the way it made me feel.

I know what's on those sheets, memorized every single one so I could go along with the delusion, help her to feel comfortable, to stop fighting her confusion and do what feels good. But what is she looking at, there in her mind? It must be incredible, to layer so much meaning, such rich beauty to everyday ugliness and pain. Was I wrong to give it to her? I had to know what she made of all of it, to take us forward. Otherwise, I was sure she would crack. Better to have her this way, or no way at all. I couldn't deal with that.

After forty-five minutes or so, she puts down a sheet and returns to me. As if she was never gone.

"What incredible relics," she says.

Relics?

"A true treasure. I should never have buried it. People will be after us for this. It's incredibly valuable."

"To the Individualists?" I try. I think I've got the logic down.

"Of course, but also to the Universalists. And the rogues, Like Do—" She stops herself and I don't force it. I don't want her to feel pressured or shut down. That would be counterproductive.

She has no idea what she's been doing—standing there, unresponsive, speaking gibberish and gesturing. I can't leave Rose with her anymore. I swallow to keep the tears back. "Let's go to bed," I say. "It's so late, and all those incredible treasures. It's so much for one day."

"You're right," she says. And we go up, take all our clothes off and sleep clutching each other. Because despite everything, we are two people in love, who would go to the greatest lengths for each other. And as we said earlier, what could be more romantic than that?

29

MILLIE

I DON'T EXPECT TO SLEEP, BUT I DRIFT INTO SLUMBER IMMEDIATELY
after our conversation, only briefly, though deeply, dreaming of
chainsaws, weed whackers. There's something in the mind that
keeps us trying to make sense of everything, to find the code in
the random. The secret center. And that's what's had me hooked
on paging-in my whole life. Mother obsessed with such things,
too, but I'm nothing like her. Our individualities could not be
more divergent.

When I wake Kennedy's out cold. His back to me. His
breathing tight, compact, as if he can't relax even in sleep. I
touch his shoulder to make sure he isn't awake. With everything
Kennedy has told me, I can't wait until tomorrow to go to Dr. P.
In seconds, I'm up and in the car—terrified, and Kennedy's right
about the complexity of it all. Nothing is the way I recognize it.

Don't want to ring me back, Pinocchio? Well, I'm coming to
get you. The way I see it, you owe me. Time to pay up.

Again I'm on the bridge in the middle of the night. My
thoughts connect directly to Mother's days in the hospital. The
same lights, the same coned off sections of road. The same cock

and balls graffiti on the turn-off for Co-op City. Everything changes and nothing changes.

There is no traffic, the ride is not long enough to prepare me for what I'll say to Pinocchio, a man who has dodged my increasingly desperate phone calls for three days. His home is behind another home. The house in front is depressing. An old ranch with sky blue vinyl siding faded to near colorlessness.

The driveway winds behind to Pinocchio's elevated studio, which looks like it might have had a garage beneath it at some time, but now has become a store room utilized by a hoarder—a book hoarder, of course. His lack of care to the written words themselves would have pissed Mother off and gives me a bad feeling about his priorities.

Piles of hard and paperbacks, softened and half-open boxes, newspapers, folded blankets, bolts of fabric, and cases of more books fill every inch of the garage, and give off a nauseating damp smell that makes me retch. Thankfully nothing comes up. He was passionate about Mother once. That's the only card in my hand.

I ascend the wooden stairs, waiting for a creak that might prepare him for my approach, but it's deathly silent. On the rail, my palm catches on a splintered shard. I wince and holler out. When I yank it, there's blood. More than I would have expected. Inside my purse, my hand closes on an old, hardened tissue I must have used on Rose's nose.

Mothers aren't put off by this kind of thing. I press it to my palm, then squeeze it in my fist. At least there's proof we both lived. I think of the paper scrap from *Truth and Art*, under my childhood mattress, Rose's mattress. I feel the pull of the *Queleque Chose* lists. I haven't thought about them in so long. Why am I thinking of them now, after the box of relics? I can't stop thinking of the connections they have helped me to make. Does everyone search these associations out? What's so special about my ability to do so? If I'm to believe Kennedy, quite a lot. Another card in my hand.

Three more stairs and I'm there. The door has an old-fashioned brass knocker. It feels heavy, lovely, actually, in my hand. Lucky threes, I think and use it to knock as many times.

As if in the habit of receiving visitors at 2:30 a.m., Pinocchio opens the door immediately. It's a shock to see him. Same tall, lanky frame, same tee shirt if I'm not mistaken, same giant Adam's apple and smooth face. But his hair has thinned. Cut short, I can see his scalp below the nearly blonde fuzz.

"Hell-" the word quits itself on his tongue when he realizes who I am. His first move is to shut the door. I wedge my foot in the jamb. His jaw tightens. He looks me in the eye. "Go away."

"Why?"

"Go away."

"At least hear me out."

"You? I should hear *you* out? All the trouble you caused me, with your accusations, your ability to make people believe you, even when you're completely bonkers."

"That doesn't sound like the kind of talk a professional would use."

"Well, I'm not a professional anymore. Been stripped of my title, thanks to you."

"Surely that isn't true." I don't know what he's referring to. Yes, it was quite ugly that day, but I said what I remembered happening. That is what the attorney told me to do.

"I'm sorry," I say.

He says nothing. I see movement at his jaw. It's anger.

"Please step out of the way Millie Burns."

My father's name smarts. Doesn't he know about Kennedy? Kennedy's so powerful, so important in their world.

"I need your help."

"Your mother is dead."

"I know that." But I don't. She was missing, is missing. It's an unsolved case.

"Step out of the way, Ms. Burns, before I call the police."

"We both know that would look ridiculous. A woman frightening you?"

"If I must remove you from the doorway, I will." His voice has grown loud, his hand posturing as if in performance.

"You once asked for my help. I wasn't ready. But now I am."

His gaze is unshakeable, but his left eye twitches. He watches me notice. I can see his shoulders slump. Is he just posturing? How far can I push?

"Millie, I can see you are not doing well. You should go get some help."

I show him my hand.

"The trembles?" he says. "Please take care of yourself. That is not a good sign."

"Kennedy. I'm Mrs. Kennedy now. My daughter is a Kennedy too."

His eyes bulge.

"You have a child—with that patient, Kennedy."

My hand lands heavier than I intend on his shoulder.

"What did you say? How do you know about Kennedy's cancer."

"I don't. Please leave."

"But you said 'patient' and you're right. My husband Kennedy is a cancer patient, and he's dying, and—"

"Mrs. Kennedy." He yells over me. But he's heard.

He crouches down to try to move my foot from the door. "I am truly sorry for you, Emily." He looks up to the sky. Millie, I'm Millie, I want to say, but don't want to put him off anymore. Besides, we're so alike in our talents, I can see why someone would be confused.

He shoves and this time my foot slips out enough for him to

gently, but successfully push me back enough to close me outside. The platform outside is small and I stumble down one step. I'm voiceless, in shock, my hands cradling my empty womb, but I catch a post of the handrail and stop myself from tumbling further. I look up.

"You're a coward! You blame me for your failures. But we can fix that now. Together. You have an invaluable perspective, and the expertise to inform it. You have ambitions, and I have made attaining those difficult. It was a hard time for me. I wanted my mother. Nothing else mattered. But I'm not a child anymore. I will make a deal with you, Dr. P. And then we can both get what we want."

Not a sound.

"Fine! I don't need you! I'll do it myself! I am a Reader!" Even as I yell it, I know I need to tame my emotions or I'm not going to get anywhere. Besides, I can't do this all without him obviously, or I wouldn't be here in the middle of the night. And he knows it too. Still I can't help myself. "You're a fucking coward!" I kick the post.

On my way down, I see someone brush aside the curtains on the windows of the main home. Good. Let them look. I stick out my tongue and spit. I can act like a child too. Maybe something that sends a stronger message. I go down below to his book storage mess and start upending boxes, kicking at piles. And when I'm satisfied with my mess, I go home.

30

MILLIE

ALL THOSE YEARS AGO, BREATHLESS, I LISTENED TO PHIL COLLINS sing with an electronic twang about the air tonight. That haunting drum beat. I blacked out, and Mother disappeared into her story, I told myself. She was dead, or as good as, and either way, it had nothing to do with me. I was a good girl. Whatever happened I'd have to deal with it alone.

But I didn't have to know the truth, I realized. Better not to. That way, I could live with whatever narrative best suited. That night had become immortalized in my mind. I've gone over it so many times, there was no way to know what was true and what wasn't. But whichever way I went through it, there were the holes—important holes.

I'd drunk four shots of Jack Daniels and that's how I'd explained passing out in my bed. Mother was still gone, up to the moment I'd blacked out. Dead? Gone. Dead, likely. She'd left the copy of *Wuthering Heights* right in the center of the floor, so I couldn't miss it, I remember thinking. Though somehow I knew she wouldn't return, I waited three days, pacing, reading, running my finger over the chalky boards, before phoning the police. That wouldn't look good.

I pictured them running their yellow tape around trees and across doorways. Their lights littering the sky, their polyester jackets swishing as they strode. But in reality it was not that way. There was no crime scene tape, no searching the house. Only a rookie cop, looked about two years older than me, who asked a few questions and then left. It was the longest day and I tried desperately to hide my shame. Because I wasn't going to get into the things I knew.

I remember being unsure how I should appear—horrified, terrified, concerned, cool and collected, helpful? Anything but guilty, not so different from how I had to seem with Kennedy, at Rose's disappearance the other day—which inevitably comes off as suspicious. I couldn't sort the images that bombarded me, some quite grizzly.

I tried to keep it simple, my desperate attempts to explain without explaining, because I wouldn't, couldn't even begin to unravel the truth, much less share it, but I was terrified to become a suspect.

The day after the questioning and initial investigation, I woke alone at a nearby hotel, as I thought it best if I showed I couldn't bear to be there, or that I was afraid that someone might harm me. I had mentioned this to the young Officer Lou, and I followed through. I kept picturing them bulldozing the wild garden, which seemed to have taken on a life of its own. I shivered, thinking of it, huddled under starched sheets and scratchy blankets. But no such thing had happened. Mother hated hotels like this. I held onto the image I often came back to: dancing for her, gargling ginger ale from the Princess Leia glass. Had that even happened? It was so hard to know now.

There I was in this place I had only known as a highway landmark that meant I'd be home in ten minutes. It was already noon when I made myself open my eyes. In the room's incredible blackout-curtain darkness, I rose with dread, and soon realized something else was off kilter. My ankle, throbbing painfully hours earlier the way it always did in the damp, was healed. Beneath the support sock, I could feel the strength in the leg, the blood pumping in a way it hadn't for a year or so now. The pain was gone. I scanned for a logical explanation where there was none. The story of my life.

Mother was gone. She took my injury with her. It was a parting gift. I allowed myself the soothing warmth of this notion for a few wonderful hours, imagining telling this version of the truth at her funeral. Her last thoughts and actions for me.

Mother had discovered a portal to another dimension. When she transported over there, she could take problems from here over to there. And what she did with it was help me. Now she existed in the worlds of her favorite books. My chest puffed with the significance, the meaningfulness. It was beautiful. I withheld all judgment of my ideas and conclusions; I let creativity run free. I pictured Mother's chalked circles of reasoning on the boards. I was sure I understood them now. The mother-daughter connection was doing its thing, tendrils stretching, branching, twisting around to new heights.

Later, though, after Dr. Samuels, I decided that I would defer to the logical explanation: my ankle hadn't been that bad to begin with; most likely, it had been psychosomatic. The doctor had been humoring a poor, misguided girl, putting a Band-Aid on an imaginary boo-boo.

At home, several months after her disappearance, the officers had dredged the lake where Mother had attempted suicide last time, dug around a bit in the garden, quit when they found the tackle box Dr. P had given me, which I'd buried in the yard, and after examination, considered its contents proof she'd gone mad. Her handwriting and mine were so similar, they'd noted. But the truth was I'd studied hers, perfected it. I didn't correct them. I just wanted them to go.

In seven years, they closed the case and pronounced her dead. They went away with conspiracy theory stuff to laugh about in the break room. And I would go on with my life, stop referring to it as the magically healed ankle, and forget all the inexplicable stuff. I asked myself what other choice I had. And for a long time, in that mindset, I did not have any "blackouts." I lived life relatively normally. I found Kennedy and love and meaning.

Now I know none of that old logic applies. Not only am I a Reader, but I am a Writer—a creator with God-like powers. And I am free to explore the full extent of that. Which is just as good. Because I need to find a way to save Kennedy's life. Despite everything, that's all I want: to go back to the way things were.

31

MILLIE

I sit in New Jersey, in my car, way down the block from my father's house, across the road where I have a good spot to memorize their cookie-cutter center-hall colonial. I don't know what I'm looking for. Same thing Pinocchio wouldn't tell me hours ago? But everything seems questionable now. Do I really know why my parents divorced? What did my father know about Mother's abilities? And mine? I am a discovery writer, meaning I don't have a clear path about where the story will go, so I put my characters in the situation and see where it all leads.

With Pinocchio ignoring me, I find myself gravitating toward my father for answers. The key is here, somewhere over the bridge. I take Rose to sit outside my father's house. I have every intention of knocking on the door. Could this *something* I sense here be the missing link? Without Pinocchio, I can only work with what I know; and right now, the most pressing bit seems to be that I have information in my brain that I cannot use with precision enough to save Kennedy.

I sip mechanically at the herbal tea I've brought with me and sit poised...for God knows what. I squirm when a chunky woman notices me as she fetches the mail from her windmill-shaped postbox. Can I be arrested for this? I hope a young mother in a Toyota SUV looks sensible enough.

I think back to one of the keynote memories of him: at my high school graduation. He'd been fiddling with the program, his strange way of mouthing the words he reads. When his head wasn't buried in the program, I'd catch him checking his watch and wondering, it seemed, when it would be over so he could get back to Tennessee and forget about this failed life.

I retrace memories of my father, as if I must prove to myself he's real. Real, real. What is this real we're always so concerned with? If it felt real to me, isn't that enough? I pull out a *Quelque Chose* and note this. It feels so good to put my pen to that paper. I don't know why I swore myself off it for so long. There's the day the two of us drove to the big park, two towns over, which had the special wooden bridge we called *The Bridge to Terabithia* (I'm sure Mother found the allusion obscenely simplistic), and a rope swing for moat crossings. I swung higher and higher on the swing facing this structure, feeling the breeze at the backs of my legs while my father chatted with another dad he recognized from the neighborhood.

"Hey!" he yelled, when he noticed how high I'd gotten. I was Leslie, from the story, on the day of her death. What did I care if I swung too high?

I remember the satisfaction, the power of pulling him away from his conversation.

"I want you to slow down. Not so high, Millie." He didn't raise his voice—something he was careful about (too careful, according to Mother, God forbid he show some emotion).

"Leslie! I'm Leslie!"

My father refused to play along. "You are Millie! And you'd better get down." The other father was watching, too, and I knew I could drag out what felt like the Millie Show for a little longer. But my father frowned and came toward me. I knew he would grab the chain and pull me off. I didn't like that ending, so in a panic at his reaction, I jumped off, twisting that same ankle I later reinjured on Rhodo Day. Because of the secondary break, the doctor had called it a "complex" fracture. Mother certainly had a lot of fun with that. At least *she* had imagination.

I release my seatbelt and get ready for my mission.

"Mommy's just running to that house right there, Rose. You stay here."

"Why? WHY?" she yells. "What are we doing here anyway?"

"Just stay. I'll be right back and then you can go home and have some ice cream." What a wonderful mother. When she isn't barricaded in a room, she's being blackmailed with full-fat dairy. Rose starts singing an ice cream song, again to the Happy Birthday tune, and I smile and bob my head, then leave the driver's door open, and run across the street, checking over my shoulder that the mail retriever isn't peeking through her louvres.

All clear. I'm going to ring the bell and ask him outright what he knows. What was he doing at the supermarket with Kennedy? I'm clutching an Aspidistra, a popular hardy house-plant, to give to my father as a gift. It's a fighter with unflagging, graceful sturdiness it fights back when harmed, cultivating its complex network of shiny, dark leaves, commanding attention in the face of adversity. When I saw it at the supermarket, in a mesmerizing tiered display at the head of a check-out lane, I thought, it's the botanical equivalent of a fuck you.

Even you could not kill this plant, I am saying. Here.

I muster enough anger to propel me up the elaborate side-winding staircase of his ghastly miniature mansion. I ring and look to the left and right at the identical homes, with their contrasting window molding and shutter colors, which undoubtedly, the owners wear as badges of superior taste to their neighbors. My mother would be nauseated. It is, in every way possible, the opposite of our home.

The small holly bushes have been planted exactly a foot apart. Rose of Sharon and Camellia—perfectly maintained but sterile, like a budget hotel room.

My gaze stops at my father's miniature Cypress tree—the one in the very center of the row of three carbon copies, and look around. I hear footsteps down the steps inside. I can feel my pulse beat in my palms as I run back down the steps, bend over and pull that Tuscan shrub, that poor little plant, out, with everything I've got.

I look back at Rose, who's turning the pages of one of the old Disneyland record books I ply her with from thrift stores and garage sales. This one is *Pinocchio.* I get a frisson. I'm so close. I'm so fucking close to working it all out. I can taste it. I check my father's windows, but my gaze is drawn back to the fucking perfect tree. I squat like a sumo wrestler, getting a good handle around the shrub, and yank. What am I doing? If this is my instinct what is it telling me to do? Am I going to be on the seven o'clock news? They're strong, this one's roots. I imagine my father planting this Cypress. How would he do it? What would he wear? Is he a morning person? Are there gloves on his chunky hands? Does he research gardening do's and don'ts, or simply wing it?

I uncurl my trembling fingers, take a deep breath and crane to see further through the screen door. All clear. I re-squat and tug with all my might. It's free. It feels so right. And see, I couldn't have predicted I'd do this because I didn't even know the tree was there. That's the great thing about discovery writing. I glance once more at the front door as I shake the roots free of large debris, and don't see anything. It sounds like a news program is playing on the television.

Suddenly, I hear rumbling. My father's garage door begins to rise majestically. My chest ices over in panic. I drop the plant and run back to the car, as I hear the mechanical door rumbling higher behind me. I cannot believe I didn't think through what I'd do if he saw me here. I fumble to get into the driver's seat when I realize Rose is missing. My fingers are clumsy. I turn the ignition. I just need to start driving. The shakes must weaken my grip on the key; the engine doesn't turn over. Relax. Just relax. More footsteps. The garage door goes silent, its ascent complete.

Across the road I see a pair of shadows reaching to open doors, sliding in the car. I don't know if they see me. I try the ignition again, twist the key exaggeratedly so it not only kicks over, but scrapes grotesquely. Surely, their attention must be drawn to that. I reverse to make my way out of the spot, and then I look down at the shifter because it doesn't seem to be moving into drive.

"Millie!" It's my father. He's right in front of my car. He's holding Rose, who's looking back and forth in shock. "You nearly hit her!"

When I look up the tree hasn't been removed. It's there. How can that be?

My father has coaxed me out of the car and into the garage.

"Ice cream, Mommy?" Rose is asking.

A child is peeking out from the door that leads to the garage. He's adorable—great big dopey blue eyes and blotchy pink cheeks, like he's been running around. "Ice cream?" he says, his look expectant. Artificial floral scent assaults me. Judging by the sofa cushion in the boy's hand, I'd guess he was having a good old pillow fight.

"Leo!" another boy's voice yells, clueing me in. This is Leo, the younger of the two boys by three years. Davinci slides along the wood laminate floor holding not one, but two pillows. He's darker than Leonardo, a little heavier—bigger boned, but he's got those same pixilated blue eyes, the same long lashes. He's also red faced. In that way kids can, they've gripped me, and dragging this deflated belly around, it doesn't take much to win me over. I want to lavish them with stuffed toys and Dr. Seuss, no matter who their father is.

"Who are you?" Davinci demands, realizing belatedly that Leo had opened the door because someone was there.

"Yeah, who?" Leo says, inching closer to his brother and biting the inside of his cheek. Amazing how this pair of boys has made me ashamed of the Aspidistra's sentiment.

"I'm Millie," I explain slowly, bending down to their level. This is the way children should be addressed.

Their faces scrunch up identically. They've never heard of me.

"Millie," my father says slowly, eying me like a foreign map he doesn't feel like deciphering. They must have inherited their complexions from Tennessee, my father was always the greyish, shadowy figure.

"Is she selling those soury candies for the school?" Leo asks. "I really liked those." He jumps up and down. "The snake ones!" and when his father doesn't answer he looks concerned, stops jumping. "Right?" he turns to ask his brother, who nods with conviction.

"Candy! Candy!" Davinci starts them both yelling, fists pumping.

"Why don't you go inside, and take um..."

"Rose," I say.

"Rose, here, and finish the game and I'll be back in a minute," my father says.

They freeze, their faces falling. "But Da-ad, she's a girl!" Davinci wines—a master of that juvenile ability to stretch syllables into unrecognizable chants like natural-born Gregorian monks.

"Go ahead, sweetie," my dad says, patting the back of his eldest son's head to coax him in the direction. The tender gesture sends a cold shiver up my spine. I swallow. I'm sure he can hear it.

"Fine," they chant, but Davinci does, in fact, take Rose gently by the hand, and lead her into the other room, pillows dragging on the floor behind. "We'll find you a pillow," he says.

"Not mine," I hear Leo say.

My father and I share a smile, which fades quickly. I walk back to pick up my plant and hold it out to him.

"Thank you."

I imagine he feels decades older looking at me. He inspects my eyes, probably noticing the beginnings of crow's feet around his own daughter's eyes, the slight downward slide of my skin, the couple of gray hairs around my part. I haven't been dying my hair or wearing cosmetics much these days. Mostly my hair is as I have it now, back in a long, heavy ponytail.

He looks ten years older as he frowns, rubs at the back of his head. How I remember that gesture! Angry as I am, I have to work to remind myself that's part of my own repertoire, that This Is Happening no matter how I feel. Time to face things. Harden the fuck up, as they say in Australia, according to Kennedy. Remember why you're here.

My father's hand pauses on the door jamb. He says my name again as if he hasn't thought of it in a while. "Millie. I'm so sorry." He grimaces and swings the door open behind him, extending an arm for me to walk through.

"For which bit? Deserting me to a suicidal lunatic? Not coming to my aid after she disappeared? Meeting with my dying husband behind my back?"

"All those years ago, Kennedy convinced me I'd done the right thing staying out of it."

"All those years ago? Staying out of what? What are you talking about? You met with him before the other day at the market?"

He nods.

I'm betraying everything Mother and I have stood for this twenty-odd years, but I follow him inside the house without much hesitation. Because clearly, it's all been shit. I'm not sure how yet, but that's where this must be going, isn't it? Still, I turn suddenly and shove the Aspidastra at him. "It doesn't require any looking after," I say. As soon as it's out, I realize how weak I sound, having shown my cards: the deserted daughter. Boo-hoo.

He doesn't look at me. "Thanks," he says and frowns. "Come inside. I'll tell you what I know."

My father leads me past a fussy grand foyer, garish with colonial furnishings in small scale that look not only uncomfortable, but obscenely overpriced. Everything matches—the check on the sofa with the cushions on the side chairs; the decoupage handle of the fireplace poker and the lace doily under the fake flower arrangement, and even the knob on the brass oil lamp replica all have the same combination of rose pink and Wedgewood blue. I scan for signs of our old life—a photo or a chair I might remember. There's nothing.

We walk a long hallway studded with black lacquer framed photos of the boys, of my father and Tennessee with the boys. They're swimming and swinging baseball bats at home plate aware that their pictures are being taken, holding up karate belts in every color of the rainbow, toothless grins poked through with nervous tongues. I decipher the images like a code—the Writer's book code.

After a shot of the boys on a wintery day, replete with a carrot-nosed snowman and photo-shopped red snowflakes at the corner, we step into a kitchen with an equally vaulted ceiling, fitted out with maple cabinets in fancy woodwork—maple leaf cutouts and hand-turned moldings, all gleaming in the overhead track lighting.

At the center island, lopping off disks of cookie dough, is Tennessee. I'd boycotted their wedding. Angie and I threw a Fuck You, Arthur party for Mother, and she allowed us to have a glass of sparkling wine apiece. This house, the domestic Tennessee, it all seems like a bigger, more elaborate Fuck You party to Mother and me. In fact, it seems our party was a bust compared to theirs.

As Tennessee wipes her hands on the same New Jersey is for Lovers tea towel Kennedy and I rescued from the basement, nobody speaks. Because I would probably do the same, I realize my father brought me in here for solidarity. They look to each other over the kitchen island and their bond is obvious. My parents never looked at each other like that. Tennessee steps out toward me and I can see her apron is embroidered with "Mrs. Burns." Her frown is quick and, as rapidly, replaced with a giant smile. I'm so glad I changed my surname.

My father searches and then seems to find something in her eyes to ground him and speaks. Their roles are nothing like I expected and this instantly flares my anger—at him, or myself, I couldn't say for sure. They seem to be living proof that Mother lied about everything. Could this have been my life? Would I have wanted it? I say nothing.

"My daughter, Millie," he introduces me as if she'd never met me before, as if he could rewrite the narrative. "She brought this plant." His hand shakes a little as he lowers it onto the island, next to a quilted placemat printed with the words "Lazy Summer Days." With him, I'd never read anything into the tremors. A Writer knows these things. The material's print is a silhouetted couple on a beach chair—their feet big and splayed every few inches. DAYTONA BEACH is silk-screened in the middle.

It hits me like a brick: they're terrified to find out why I'm here, now, after all this time. That old troublesome family hiding in the background, just waiting to pop up and cause trouble.

"Oh, Millie!" Tennessee says, too emphatically. As if I don't know what she thinks of the troubled girl who returned her wedding invitation with the words I DON'T FUCKING THINK SO, marked in purple over a skull and crossbones. I offer a tight grin—even I can feel how unconvincing it is.

Remember your goal. Your dad must know about Mother and what she could do. And of course, what had Kennedy said to him?

"This is the most beautiful plant!" Tennessee gushes. "What is it? A fern?"

No, it is not a fucking fern. It is nothing like a fern, the only plant you've ever heard of.

"Isn't it beautiful, Arthur?" The name shaped in her syrupy tone drops me over the edge. My father darts a look at me—not apologetic, but honest. He knows this will hurt me. He never let Mother use his real name. He didn't like it. Insisted she call him by his middle name, Gregory.

Still, he doesn't speak. This is too hard. *This is who I am,* he seems to be saying. *And you aren't part of it.* But you already know that, Millie! It's all in the past.

"Tea!" Tennessee says. "What'll it be? Country Peach Passion? Mint Magic? Raspberry Zinger?" She starts pulling out tiny tubs for a huge contraption they have for tea brewing. I've seen it on television. It's ridiculous. Her sudden rush toward hosting makes me want to flee. No wonder I've managed to put this off my whole life.

"That would be nice," I manage. My father watches

Tennessee gratefully, like she's handling things now. She will know what to do. Has he always been this useless? I feel even more confident that my father was not the reason for Mother's suicides, that they were, instead, part of her magical book world. She could not respect this man, certainly not enough to off herself over him. Could she?

Tennessee cues my father, indicates her head toward the kitchen table—a huge built-in with two benched sides and on the ends, spindle-backed chairs straight out of Friendly's Family Restaurants. My father doesn't move. Her eyebrows bounce; her lips squeeze. When my father shrugs, she gestures hugely.

"O-ohhhh," he mouths, catching on. I see where his kids get the syllable stretching. I don't do that.

Tennessee smiles ingratiatingly, as if I hadn't caught on or she doesn't care if I have.

"Why don't you have a seat, Mill—" He can't seem to finish my name. He turns to me as if I can feed him the second half, and I see pain in his eyes—surprised and ashamed, precisely what I'd thought I wanted.

Instead of following his lead, I inch back toward the door.

I try the words. "What don't I know?" I say, floundering. I hate the way that came out, desperate. I hear the boys and Rose cheer and pound video game controls on the other side of the wall.

My father begins to nod agreement then catches himself. It's my turn to flinch.

"I know, Millie," he manages my name. "This is hard." It's the first honest thing I've ever heard him say.

"*What* is hard? You know all about it don't you?" I can't bring myself to say "the book world" in front of Tennessee, but I'm sure he knows what I mean.

"Here, your tea's done," Tennessee says. She places the mug on a brash tray, crackle-painted with a folksy teapot. I don't know which flavor she's chosen but it's a deep cranberry color. There are ten kinds of sugar and sweetener neatly fanned out around my mug, which also reads, "Mrs. Burns." Either she's an evil genius or the dumbest woman alive. "Sit, please," she says. They take neighboring seats.

I pull out my chair and perch across from him, I can see my father has begun to sweat. He's obviously unsure how to start.

I think of Pinocchio. Truth. That's all I've got right now. I must hold onto it. "I saw you serving yourself a generous helping of chicken wings at the International Food Bar. I know Kennedy told you about the cancer, and now you've slipped up and said you've seen him before. What about?"

My father turns scarlet. He mops his brow. From their arm movements, I can tell Tennessee is squeezing his thigh under the table. I'm as jealous as when I was a little girl.

"Your father. Your fucking father doesn't love you enough," my mother said to me in-between the first time she tried to kill herself and the second.

"I didn't think you wanted anything to do with me, but I always did what I thought was best for you, and your . . . situation," he says. Outside, a bicycle bell pings. Tennessee's brow knits in sympathy. I want to punch her.

"I was hurt," I say, hating myself for it.

"Sure," he says. Again, it rings honest. His voice betrays no pretense.

Tennessee doesn't look anything but sympathetic, clucking her tongue and shaking her head, as if this has nothing at all to do with her, the woman whose photo my mother and I used to throw darts at, the one snuggling up with my father while we went without a fire in the fireplace because that was a man's job and we liked to sulk about it. Any other father would ask her to give him a minute with his daughter.

We sit that way for a moment, the air around us burning, the sun through the vertical slats blinding. I don't fit here.

I've spent so long demonizing him. I never considered the possibility of his own emotions. In my thoughts, he was a supporting character—there only for what he'd made us feel, on hand for a convenient bit of blame, but never suffering feelings of his own, never given his own chapter. Where was the satisfying, simple justice, the good guys versus bad? No. No. That isn't the way things work out once you actually get to them.

"Thanks for the tea," I say to Tennessee. "Do you think I might have a moment alone with my father?"

He looks horror-stricken, but she nods. "Of course, dear."

I'm not your dear, I keep to myself.

He tries to smile. It fails. "Dad, what do you know?"

"Know about what?"

"About Mother. About paging-in." He doesn't speak for a long while, during which I watch him and recognize the look of him, the one that never let me truly hate him. Kindness.

"It isn't real, Millie. You know it isn't."

"I knew you would say that." I smile, an instinct. "Then why did you leave? Huh? We all know you left because you were jealous. Because Mother could do it and you couldn't."

He shakes his head. "You don't know a thing about it. She didn't want me there. You only wanted Mother. I left. There isn't a day I don't feel terrible about it, about the way things ended up for you. But after that, everything I did, every decision I made, it was all for you, for your best interest. Kennedy assured me all those years ago that you were doing better. That you should be allowed to have a normal life. That you deserved it—finally."

"Sure, you cared so much for me! Nice story you've been telling yourself all these years. And of course Kennedy would say something like that! That's all he ever wanted for me. Why you've all kept it a secret, I can't understand. But I don't seem to understand much these days." I can't seem to control my speech. Now I'm in the scene, it's got a life of its own, and now I realize that means it may not go my way. Still, I smile; there's always a layer of meaning if you just dig deep enough; it doesn't always have to be pretty.

"I told Kennedy I was going to tell you, but I guess he couldn't bring himself to prepare you for it. But listen, seeing you today, putting Rose in danger like that, I . . . I can't let this go on any longer. It isn't right. There are people who can help you, Millie."

"The Universalists? Please! Don't tell me you're on their side, that you would sacrifice Rose."

"I don't know what you're talking about, Millie. This is all part of it."

"Of course it is!"

"What about your daughter? That is why Kennedy came to me. He's worried what will happen to her, to both of you, when he dies."

"Don't you talk about my daughter."

"Look, I know how angry you must be. I'm your father, and I left you and never had anything to do with your life. It's the worst thing a person can do. I'm not proud of myself. And on top of that, I never talked to you about the most important thing. I had to make a decision about what was right. And in the end, I chose to go Kennedy's way; he was very convincing."

"Look, forget all of that. It's in the past. What I need from you is to tell me what you know about the book realm. About Mother."

"What you did to your mother." He drops his head in his hands. His back is heaving. I can tell he's crying even though no sound is coming out.

"What *I* did?" I feel like a traitor discussing her with him. I'm ashamed. Look at my life now, I always say. It's everything she could never work out. Or it *was.* But now those words sound awful, childish. Incorrect. Fuck. I feel disoriented, unsure of what's real.

"It's love. Love is what makes it strong. People in love can go in and out of the book world like crazy," I say. "And that's why you broke her heart."

"And yours," he says.

"I'm fine."

"I can see that. Millie, you need help. You are delusional."

"You are too ordinary, too banal to understand any of this. Just look at your choice of wife! That does not make me delusional. That's just the kind of thing unbelievers say. Please! Ask Kennedy; he knows all about it."

"Don't you say a bad thing about Tennessee. You have no idea what she's put up with! She's not sophisticated, she's not educated. She's not nearly as beautiful as your mother. All of that is true. Of course, it is. But she lives in the now, in the world that really exists, just adjusts along with every change. Doesn't fight it. And she lives in it *with* me.

"Is it thrilling? No. But it's helping the world, not hurting it. And it's pleasant, too. Tennessee was a nurse for fifteen years! She knows about doing the right thing. Your mother, for all her intelligence, genius really, and intuition, well, she was never aware of anyone else. I know you felt it. That's why you've done all of this. But she loved you. Believe me. She loved you more than anyone. But not enough."

"But you see, *Dad*, you were tricked."

He runs his fingers through his thinning hair, gives the old forehead a few rubs.

"I was so in love with your mother, and you know, she wanted to leave all that behind. Though she didn't know how, she wanted to have a normal life with me. And I know that's what you want, too. It's what *I* want for you. But without Kennedy, it isn't going to work. You have to think of Rose."

My stomach drops at the similarity. Mother and me. Perhaps we aren't so different after all?

"In Australia, on our honeymoon, she tried to suck me in. And I wanted so badly to believe her. Then Dr. P showed up and she gave me her song and dance about him. And I nearly killed him. I should have gotten out then."

"How could Pinocchio have been there?"

"Who?"

"Pinocchio, like the story."

"That's not his name. You must be remembering wrong. Anyway, I don't know the details really. They were both researching books, the effects they have on us. But in quite different ways. She hated the guy. It was so messed up. It was always so messed up. But Emily, she was the antidote to life's futility. She had the 'something more' I'd always been searching for."

"But you couldn't deal with it."

He shakes his head. "Turns out there isn't anything more. There's just this. We're kidding ourselves if we think anything else."

"That's just the kind of thing I'd expect you to say. And so you were gone, but you still had to deal with me. So, when Kennedy gave you an out, one that you could tell yourself was the right thing to do, you took it."

He's silent.

Now it's my turn to shake my head.

I stand up. "All the lies and secrets are out. So, now's your chance. Is there anything else I should know?"

I think of Officer Lou. And just as I do, my father mentions him.

"That young cop. He asked a lot of questions. You could tell he was intrigued by the books, the romantic ideal of a novelist, the philosophy, the whole thing. Would've fit in perfectly with the crowd at your mother's god-awful parties. But I think he suspected something was off with you."

A cold shiver runs up my arms.

He looks at me so sincerely, so deeply, that I wonder for a moment whether all his comments about Mother might unite us against a common foe. I hate him for that, for the fact I can still care about being united with him. It's too late now for any of that.

He grabs for my hand across the table. I flinch, but allow it. His fingers are warm. "Your mother is dead, Millie. You killed her."

"What are you talking about?" Even as I say it, the images bombard me. All this time, I've been convincing myself I didn't do it, when I did. How will I ever live with myself if I'm a murderer? What will my daughter think of me?"

"No. No!"

"Yes, Millie. I'm afraid it's true. She was missing. But Kennedy found her body. And he buried her for you. It was not the right thing to do."

"That isn't true! Why wouldn't you turn me in? Why would Kennedy do that for me?"

"Because we love you! I don't know. You suffered enough, Millie. Both of us know you have no clue what's happening when you have those episodes. It was done. She wasn't coming back. But it was wrong. I see that now. You're a danger to yourself, to Rose. Without Kennedy, I can't see how you'll survive.

"I have her copy of *Crusoe* here, in the boys' room. She put it in the boxes she gave me after the divorce. I spent plenty of hours trying to tease out the meaning in that gesture. But then, the way you killed her. So brutal, the way you used to run around maniacally with stones in your hand."

I try to quieten the swallow I need in order to breathe.

"I had to tell you, Millie. I'm worried. Terrified."

"So terrified you never even came around. I'm fine. I *was* fine. But now my husband is dying. And I—I, umm—" I can't stop the sobs, they're long and horrifying. It's true. What he's saying is the truth and deep down, I've always known it. The question is, what do I do now? My father is weak. She was right about that. He was probably jubilant the day Kennedy advised him to leave it to him. Free at last.

Tennessee appears and he goes mum.

"Going already?"

"I've got to."

She seems relieved. I don't know if she's stood at a distance or heard everything. She looks unfazed, either way. I can't ever hurt her, but it doesn't seem so important anymore.

She smiles, her dumpling face glowing healthy, which sends Arthur's lips curling too—if only for a second. "It's probably for the best," she says. "This hasn't been very nice."

"The truth shall set you free," I say.

"Rose!" I yell. "We have to go."

I stomp down the hallway toward the children's voices and repeat myself, louder this time.

"No! I don't want to! I'm having so much fun with my uncles."

I stand at the doorway.

"Where did you hear that word?" I say.

"From Grandma Tennessee."

I've never seen such a neat children's room. It looks as if the toys are scrubbed daily. The giant Mister Potato Head, the primary colored drum set, the intricate setup of anachronistic soldiers, horses, and light armored vehicles. On a tall pine IKEA style bookcase, there are games and stuffed toys, all manner of poseable 'guys' those two must lose hours on, but there are no books. I'm wrong. There's one book. It's *Crusoe*. My *Crusoe*. I walk over to the shelf and take it, daring someone to stop me.

"Boys!" It's Tennessee herself; she plants herself in front of them, like she's protecting them from me. My breath goes sharp, painful.

"I want to stay here!" Rose is agitated now. "They have video games. How come we don't have video games. This is so much fun! Please, don't make me go. I want to stay here! Please don't make me go!" She's kicking her feet, and when that doesn't work she throws herself on the floor. I have to lean over to pick her up. She squirms, and finally I grab her, but then she escapes again. I go to pull her by the sleeve and pinch to pull her to me.

"Ouch!" I must have squeezed through to her skin. Oh, I am a terrible mother. And in front of these two. I could not imagine anything worse. It's the opposite that's true. I'm the sensible one, the enlightened one. It's you two who are the Philistines!

"Let's go," I say, finally lifting her under the arms, while her legs kick at me and she continues to scream, piercing, incredibly loud wails.

My father doesn't stop me.

I can't remember the drive home. But somehow I make it and park the car at the top of the driveway, with the book in my lap, wondering where it will all go next.

While my life tangles into an intricate mess, which I feel tightening further in on me, I wonder, if that was my instinct—to steal the life my father had decided to plant—where was that taking me? He stole my life from me, so I stole his plant. Pointless. No wonder things had gone so terribly wrong after that. I am a murderer. No symbols necessary there.

Back home, in Mother's garden, however, my shaky hands

know precisely what to do. I provide the antidote to my father's clean perfection. On my way home, I must have stopped at the roadside sale I saw driving to his house, because I've got four potted plants—I musn't have been able to resist the red-mark-ered exclamation on the drive home: Last Day! Even with the murdering on my mind—and I seem to know precisely where to plant them. Even before I pull them from their pots they look so natural in their various sizes and shapes, so meant to be here.

Dig this here, secure the roots, deeper, higher, a little to the left. When I'm done planting, I can't explain what made me commit to these choices, pair one hairy leaf with a slim, delicate bud. It's as if I went to sleep and something else took over. Clip-clop. The horse. The stone. The blood. All of it now grounded in with the beautiful plants. It's as if I'm immersed in the story and turning the pages to see how it plays out. Or even better, writing them as I go. It's more terrifying than wonderful. But in select moments, it's more than wonderful; it's ethereal.

Now the plants are my father's Cypress. How odd! I straighten it slightly at the root ball, pat at the dirt above it, when I realize it must go a little bit to the left. That's where it belongs. I start to dig a few inches from the plant, and only inches down, I see her ring finger. I'd recognize Mother's ring anywhere, its inlaid diamonds around the band. Art Deco, she'd called it.

32

KENNEDY

WHEN I GET HOME, MILLIE IS IN THE YARD. SHE LOOKS LIKE SHE'S performing a frantic pantomime of someone planting a tree. She's going through all the motions, but she doesn't even have a shovel in her hand. She's just pretending she does. She's speaking that gibberish again, and it's clear she's having another one of her episodes.

It's quite confronting. And where is Rose during all this? Yelling and stamping to be let out of her room, while again she's been barricaded inside. I go and deal with that while I watch, mesmerized, at Millie out the window. What am I going to do?

The scariest part of the whole thing is where she's doing the imaginary digging. It's alongside the rhododendron, where I buried Emily. Somewhere in that mind, she must know.

Right before my eyes, I see her discover the hand. I should have buried it deeper, but the body was our connection to the real, and I was afraid to let that go forever. Besides, once the police were done over here, I wanted to keep her close by, where I could keep an eye on her, control the narrative. So why the veggie patch? Renewal. Millie didn't have a monopoly on symbols.

33

OH GOD, OH GOD, OH GOD. I REALLY DID KILL MOTHER. NOT JUST in a book. She's dead. Buried in our yard. But how had the police not discovered the body? All it would take would be a metal detector to find the ring. All the sounds around me are hollow, like I'm hearing them from down a deep hole. All my desires, all my concerns. What are they, if I'm a murderer?

It smells too much like her. The scent is too powerful. I run to the toilet and vomit until everything in my stomach must be gone. A few times after that. The tiles are cool, so I lay back for a minute, holding the hollow baby bump. Mother, yes, I hated you. But I loved you. Could I really have killed you?

Maybe it was a hallucination, seeing your hand like that. All this stress, all the negative energy. Maybe a *bit* of what's been said about me is true. I think of that Motherhood book I was reading. *The baby will be born in kind.* I'd worry for this child if there were going to be one. I don't know what I'm doing to Rose. My beautiful, lovely, Rose.

Where is Rose? I remember leaving her right there on the couch when I went out to do my digging. I'm mother of the year, I remember thinking, as I draped her with Mother's afghan, getting a stale whiff of Mother. Still, isn't it odd that Rose never complains when I leave her to do these things? Why is she so often conveniently out of the way when I need her to be?

I flash to a future where my own daughter hates me, where that is my hand, my ring, buried in the garden. Is that a real possible future? Is it like my family at the ice cream shop? I want to scream. Sitting up, still scented with my vomit, I do so, bring the hand towel to my mouth expressly for the purpose. I must get this out. Somehow. The puking didn't work. I'm too tightly wound to cry. I scream into the towel over and over. My throat feels torn after, and this is slightly comforting. It's something I'm sure of.

Could she have been buried here all this time? Kennedy's cucumbers sprouting up alongside her? It's all so macabre like some kind of true crime horror. I couldn't be a murderer, of my own mother no less. All this time, it's this reassurance that's got me through. But I don't think I can do it anymore. I brush my teeth and sip some tap water, hold the glass up to my forehead. I must go back out there. I must see again, make sure it's real.

I make myself put one foot in the other, down all the stairs, across the kitchen. I close Mom in the kitchen with a bone, but she's barking right away. I can't have her waking up Rose, so go back in to bring her out with me, tie her to the tree on her leash. Down on hands and knees, I brace myself to push the dirt that I'd mounded over her fingers back to the side. I find tears pouring down my face after all. Maybe I don't know myself. After all this time, could I just be a deluded murderer?

As if he knew what I was about to do, Kennedy comes out of nowhere.

"Don't do this," he says.

"What? Do *what*?"

He doesn't answer, instead, leads me upstairs, to our bed.

Why do I go? The same reason I did not check to see I'd tucked Rose on the couch.

I lay down, and his body partly covers mine. He has always comforted me, so this is not as strange as it may seem. Feeling around, I trace the dip of his pelvic bone. Becoming deeply aroused in a way I recognize as the desperation of everything about to change, I kiss below his earlobe, feel the sensations of our connection as intensely as I had that very first time—on his family boat, too fast, too much—and before I know it, he has me pinned down and thrusts so hard and so deep, looking so far into me, this man who knows I'm a murderer and loves and protects me anyway, but keeps secrets, too many secrets, and now feels like a perfect stranger. I should be turned off, but I'm not.

What do you know? I think while I look up at him lost inside me. In his lack of concern over Mother's dead body in the garden, he was suddenly terrifying, a stranger. Still, I can't help but come before he does. I watch him as he gives in and I feel his hot liquid inside and see the relief on his face. I loved him, still do. This is how the fiction has been able to propagate.

"Did you plant the garden to bring this all to a head? Did you know I'd really killed her all along?"

"Yes."

"No. No! No! No! No! This is so fucked up! Can it really all end this way? Mother murdered, at my hand, my husband, my life, a lie, my daughter. My daughter?"

I look up to him. I feel my hands trembling, the halos around everything. It's happening. My husband looks perfect. It makes perfect sense. Love is the power that propels Readers through, but loneliness, the misery of it is creative gold. I'm so fuzzy. My brain is struggling to make connections but can't. Like it's being physically restrained. And then the familiar blackness.

My arms and legs are splayed, and I feel myself land gently, slowly with a *pffff* onto the duvet. My gaze lingers on Kennedy's bare shoulder blade hulking from beneath the cover, the bit of his neck that meets his dark hairline, the fine peach fuzz of his earlobe. It's no longer possible to give into this narrative that pretends things would continue on in kind.

I find myself, during the sleepless portions of the night, focusing on Mother's communication, from the time she wasn't speaking. She made baby noises—kicks, grunts, slight voice bumps, which I translated painstakingly. Those baby noises are called vegetative and they are all about survival. Rose did the same thing once upon a time, and I took great comfort in reading about what it all meant in the baby books. There was a lovely echo of significance in the duality. But now, I realize it wasn't the same at all. Rose's communiques were natural, each noise and gesture a unique calling out for something specific she could only get from the mother she trusted and needed for everything. But with Mother, none of it was for me, telling myself anything else was all bullshit and I knew it. She did it for her—research. All that came first.

For once, I do bring myself to check on Rose, who fell asleep in front of the television earlier. According to Kennedy I locked her in her room again. But I don't believe him anymore.

34

MILLIE

With Kennedy home from work the next day, it's like normalcy has completely left our home. He doesn't trust me with Rose. I barely need an excuse to leave the house, which I'm grateful for because I need to convince Pinocchio to help me.

But I'm completely off. I see that hand wherever I go. I went out three times during the night and the ground looked undisturbed. How can that be? I was digging it up. Putting Dad's tree in. Or was it the plants I bought at the market? But this morning, none of those were there either. I'm sick. That much is clear. Can't discern between reality and fantasy. But that doesn't make me a murderer, does it? Is *that* what my father was getting at?

None of it means I'm wrong about everything either. But I am off. I forget to rinse Rose's shampoo and spend ten minutes listening to her best rendition of "Ouch, Mum!" while battling her to let me rake a comb through the hardened hair clumps before I realize my mistake. I forget to eat breakfast, even skip my coffee.

When I notice my blood sugar dropping, I dig through the fridge and pull out a thick slice of expensive fresh turkey with that lovely stringy texture, until Kennedy comes over and bites it off my fingers, grabbing my waist as he does. I'm not imagining it. Our attraction is heightened. The eroticism is palpable. It could be the taste of loss, the feeling of it all slipping through our fingers, or even the idea that neither of us really knows the other, that maybe we never can. Or that we're in on something secret—together. It feels like in the beginning, when we weren't ever too tired or hungry or grumpy to want. I tell myself sex is animal. It doesn't have to do with love or trust or doing what's right. But that's bullshit and I know it. This is real drama, real love, real significance. I'm drunk with it, and it's worth whatever ending I get.

He sucks my finger a second too long and my body reacts. He smiles, like he knows he's got me. I want to believe relief's behind that, and not guile. But it's impossible to say. It is so tempting to bury all the secrets that have come out and continue on. But he's dying, I remind myself. Even that horrific element feels surmountable—I can fix it. I'm seeing things on a greater continuum. I can feel my mind, and world, expanding. *Softening.*

Am I maybe enjoying the game a little? I hear my old therapist's words in my head: *It's the illusion of control you're drawn to.* And now I know I'm a murderer, there is a weight lifted from me, for at least I know the truth, and can free myself from the lost hours of speculation and obsessive reasoning. I don't feel good, but that's been my survival tactic all along. Not feeling good I can deal with. Still, it's doing strange things to my perspective.

"Mmmm, love," Kennedy says. The kitchen is hot, sticky, weighty with significance. Are we meant to be forgetting about the trouble? *Could* he really die? As soon as I think it, my mind searches for a solution: if I can't count on Pinocchio, could I manage to control a page-in on my own? If Kennedy died right now, I'd know I would have wanted to live my life with him, to save him if I could have. Shouldn't that make it easier for me to forgive him? It's dense with tangles and hurts and questions and love, of course love.

"You've got to try this turkey, Rose," he says, reaching over me to grab another slice from the deli bag. He seems absolutely unfazed that we were looking at a corpse's hand in our yard yesterday.

"Nom, nom, nom," Rose says, chewing the slice with her mouth open, engorged zombie eyes. She loves him. I love him. But he's lied to us. He's dying. Or not. Secrets—his, mine. I can't trust him. I can't trust myself. The circle goes around. How can he seem so composed?

"More," she says. I release myself from the cold of the open fridge, select a yellow plastic plate for Rose, which Kennedy palms to the table, pretending to stumble for Rose's benefit, miming a clumsy waiter while she giggles. I have to steady myself at the sink. Nothing lasts forever, I remembered Mother telling me.

"Wanna come with me, Dadda?" Rose asks. Thank God for her. For unbridled youthful cognition. She normalizes things. You have to keep up the routine for her benefit.

"Come where?" he asks, eyebrows in a furrow.

Rose bites a hole in the center of her de-sandwiched turkey slice, and sticks a finger through, pointing to the garden with one eye shut, sharp shooter style.

"To the skating competition," she says. Rose's pupils swell, lashes draw back.

"Sure, grab the book."

He continues to eat, as if he can ignore what's just been exploded into the open. Rose can page in. But he doesn't bat an eye.

The turkey slice collapses, limp, over Rose's finger. Her brows echo the shape Kennedy's etched seconds earlier. He runs up to her bedroom. "Can't catch me," he says and she squeals and giggles after him. I pretend to ignore them.

I yell out my excuse before Kennedy can say anything about it and leave the house. I feel bad as I close the door without kissing my daughter goodbye, but let's face it, she's probably safer without me.

In the car, I nearly doze off twice. I haven't been this tired since Rose's first few months. I recall how my exhaustion was deepened by the implication that I would have to get up again at any moment. The shade between sleeping and waking was always half drawn. This thought sends a vibration through my mind. Could this be the way with reality and stories, when you've settled properly into the state? *A softening.* Pinocchio will have the answer. I will show him the box and he will tell me what's what. He will know. He must.

For most of the ride, I go over what happened with Kennedy, when he presented me with the tacklebox he'd had stashed in his trunk, like some kind of mobster.

We brought it back out to the shed.

"What do you see?" Kennedy asked me, when I pulled back the lid. I described each priceless, beautiful relic of the Book World, in disbelief that I'd buried it without ever looking inside. I'd been so strong in my conclusions then, under Dr. Samuel's care. I'd written it off as hogwash and never looked back. What I saw now were Illuminated manuscripts, underlined passages of all the books mother had read, hardbacks from the authors and philosophers picked out on her chalkboards.

The scent of turned earth has always made me nauseous, and now I think, it's probably wrapped up in the memories of whatever terrible thing happened with Mother. The lamp glowed brightly, then dimmed, a warning for my expectations, which I didn't heed.

Kennedy said, "It's been safe in this garden all these years. Might as well leave it here." I couldn't think of a reason to disagree.

Beneath Mother's rhododendron scented scarf, the box was full, right up to the top. Perfect, in fact. Thought out. Agonized over. Draped like a liner beneath the scarf was a typed-out page. As soon as I disturb the sheet—the slightest nudge—I smelled Pinocchio's menthol cigarettes. The back of my neck went hot with significance. I knew everything was leading to him.

I tried to process what I was experiencing: the smell. Dr. P hadn't smelled this way when I went to his home the other night. He quit. At the hospital, you'd find him fanning smoke away from passersby at the flagging ficus-topped ashtray at the entrance, then one day he'd stopped.

It was such a smooth transition, his quitting, I remember questioning myself in Dr. Samuel's chair. Had I been mistaken? Had he ever smoked, or was that a delusion of mine? It felt disturbing, how little I really knew for sure. Before, I had taken all these minute changes, all the confusion, as clues in my mingling of alternate realities, signs I was paging-in. But what was I meant to do with the pull of significance then, when I was just meant to believe I was prosaically crazy?

I drive on, shaking my head to keep awake.

This time it isn't difficult to talk Dr. P into letting me in. Something's shifted in him. He apologizes, invites me to sit, and listens to me begin my story in fits and starts.

"Oh Millie."

"You never believed me," he said. "And they wanted to get rid of me. It was a perfect storm."

Can I trust him?

"Did I kill Mother?"

He puts his hands on my palms. "You have a lot of problems, Millie. But you are not violent. This is not the way your issues play out."

"But Kennedy says I killed her."

"She's missing. Not dead."

"Then where is she?" I say.

He shrugs.

"Don't fuck with me."

"Mother disappeared. You know that."

"You don't think so."

My heart races. "What do you know, Dr. P, that you aren't telling me?"

"Are we showing all our cards now?"

"Your lateral thinking has worked on me."

I decide to explain it to him exactly as I remembered it, when I allowed myself to. Otherwise, how will I ever know the truth? I started with the end, so I wouldn't chicken out of confessing. "When I 'killed' her, Mother watched me every second—defiant, as if to say, remember this. You will never rid yourself of me. I thought it was a dream. But sometimes I didn't.

"I was thirteen. Dad had left. Mother was so low. But this one day, she woke me early. She was fully dressed in one of her Parisian getups, scarf tied intricately, hair in a bun, everything."

"Yes, I remember how lovely she looked," Pinocchio says.

I go on to relay the whole story for him, which I'd never told anyone. This time, I leave out nothing.

"At first the dream was complete blackness, nothing. Not a sound, sight, smell. Disorientation. I remember being conscious of never having had a dream like that before. My heart raced. But suddenly there were Mother's arms around me. A voice I could trust. Bit by bit, details emerged—a kind of veiled light, a flower petal, a huge sky. I needed them to, my heart pounded with the urge to settle myself, to know what was what. At the same time, the disorientation was exciting, like a drug. I sensed a tense, gloomy, kind of anticipation. As I saw a sweep of rolling, brilliant green hills, the word moors lodged itself to describe them. It was familiar, this scene. Her scene. The kind she pined over but would never admit to—the kind only I would know she wanted sincerely.

"With every passing second, the view crystalized. And then I realized, wait, I don't recognize myself. I felt the urge to move my arms to pat my body. But I couldn't feel my body per se. I had the familiarity of my mind, though I found myself in this strange place, but it was disembodied. And yet, Mother's arms were still there. I couldn't feel them so much as sense them. Lovely. I had never experienced them like that before.

"Through her embrace, I sensed a man approaching. Intoxicating. The impression of the air changed around me. I pictured oil-filled stickers, the way your touch could reconfigure them. This was a powerful man. He approached on horseback, the way I imagined approaching horseback to sound: clip-clop, clip-clop. He was to be feared, there was a darkness, but that didn't over-power the anticipation. It fed it.

Danger. Suddenly, I sensed it. I was meant to remove myself from this man, who I've come to realize is Heathcliffe, from *Wuthering Heights*. Run! I thought. But again, there was no sense of a body with which to do so. I was under the control of some Other. Not total control. It was more of a team effort, but the movements, the decisions seemed not to belong wholly to me. I had a say, but not autonomy. I was being guided, by a more knowledgeable, experienced voice. I was in the book. I was me, and yet I was a character in the book.

"In a way, not having to make my own decisions was a relief. Without the pressure of choice, there was an abundance of feeling, a flood of it. And a reflection and examination of everything that had brought me to such a feeling. I loved it. Life but super-charged. Drenched with sensation. Now, I look back, I believe I remember the halos around objects, the incredible noise. But that could be unreliable memory. Because that is what has been happening to me lately, when I page in, during the times which Kennedy says are blackouts—periods of time I cannot account for.

"Mother was there as herself and a character, too. When she'd tighten her grip, what I could only interpret as Mother's own experience of these happenings would flood me. This was such a different woman than the one I knew. There was the same presence, the influence, but every nerve ending seemed to be at attention. She was satisfied, more than satisfied. She was in ecstasy.

"The man approached. Clip-clop, clip-clop. Their eyes locked. He slowed but didn't stop, then galloped over the next hill. I hated her for feeling that way—hot for him. I hated him for not feeling that way about me."

And then Heathcliffe rode away and Mother grew angry with me. As if it were my fault he'd gone, that everyone had gone —in life, in the story, it was fluid. I'd stood in the way of what she wanted. The anger flooded all the crevices of my hyper-consciousness. The noise intensified, deafening. It was like anger times one thousand. There was no control.

She ran over a hill. I picked up a rock and charged to her. I lost sight of her for a moment. Over the other side of the hill I caught sight, I thought, of not one, but two women in the same dress. But no, I must have been breathing so hard my vision blurred. She was one again, one woman, not two. And she'd fallen, face down, unmoving now. I caught up and threw myself over her, pinned her beneath me.

I was on top of her. I hit her with the stone over and over

again. From the first, she'd blacked out, which I remember thinking vaguely disappointing. I wanted to look at her. The blood didn't come immediately. It was slow to leak at the broken skin of her skull. But once it came, there were great, biblical waves of it.

I awoke, or came to, or whatever one would call it first. Mother was still asleep, or in the book. Had all been a dream, a cruel dream, which shoved in my face all the experiences I would never have? It must have been. But sometimes I wasn't so sure. I woke and then she was gone.

Was I awake? Had I really done that to my mother? It was the last time I saw her. I'd ask myself this question for years after. While after she'd had her first brush with suicide I told myself she deserved every hateful emotion I'd ever had for her, now she was gone and this gruesome memory, or whatever it was, bombarded me, I wasn't so sure.

"Why? Everything okay?"

"Just come with me."

After, when she was gone, I often sat in her office, that place, which was always a wonder to me. The blackboards were jammed with the familiarly inscrutable words, arrows, swipes. I pictured her laying on her daybed, a dozen pillows supporting her. I loved the idea of an office bed, her pillows, the Indian embroidery, the rich velvets, cool silks—a patina of tea stains and pen markings that said so much about her. I still dreamed that one day she'd reach for my hand and pull me onto the bed next to her. How many times had I wished for such attentions? For her to hold me to her and stroke my hair tenderly, look me in the eye unwaveringly? But day after day, it was just me in there alone, in the one place I'd always wanted to and never been allowed to be. "Is it ironic that right after I'd killed her in my mind that this is very thing I'd longed for?"

He looks at me kindly, with sympathy. "No. These are all part of your dissociative episodes. It makes perfect sense to me. Your mother was a creative genius, she had a lot to teach us all. But she was a terrible mother, a narcissist who didn't have time for you, felt justified in her reasons for that deprivation. But she wouldn't let your father have you. No, that would be giving up control, and she wasn't about to do that."

I am not sure I believe in fully blocking out memories, but this is the closest I can come to describing what had actually happened with that bloody experience with Mother: I was powerless to pick at this memory strand once it happened. "Though I was told repeatedly I did not kill Mother, it felt too neat and tidy that she was gone right after that."

"No. None of that is real. Millie it breaks my heart, your carrying this around all these years. This is a fantasy. Something you've concocted to assign blame and a solution to an unre-solved mystery of a woman gone missing, and most of all to find meaning in a senseless loss and incredible stores of hurt and abandonment."

"But she is not missing. She is *dead*. I found her hand in the garden. I must have killed her!" I show him the ring.

"No. No!" He drops his head and begins to cry.

He takes his time gathering himself. When he rises he says, "I have to show you something."

He shifts through the cardboard file box he'd brought along, rifles through some piles of what look like CD or DVD cases. It's amazing he can navigate through all these mountains of stuff. But his features shift when he's clearly got his hands on what he's been looking for. "You, my dear, are not capable of murder. You are not wired for it. I said as much to you many times when you were on the ward, though you wouldn't hear it. Kennedy, on the other hand, is a compulsive liar, with sociopathic symptoms besides, and he is capable of murder. He has very different kinds of problems."

I flinch at the word. I understand its connotations. Can it be true? Then it occurs to me. "Wait. Are you telling me that Kennedy was in the hospital with Mother?" *She.*

"Yes. And he did not like her."

"Yes, I know that. It's because Kennedy is a Universalist—you know, he believes paging-in should only be done for the good of man, while Mother is an individualist."

"I recognize the words from some of your episodes. And while it's rather beautiful, and poetic, I'm afraid it's something you made up."

"But Kennedy's famous! He's been the leader of the Universalists since the early days. It's why he founded the luggage shop, which is just a front for the Universalist headquarters."

He shakes his head. "It's just a luggage shop. I shouldn't tell you this, but I recall him making up all kinds of nonsense about the exciting secrets he was fronting there. But it really was just a luggage shop. No. Those details are all made up, by you. They seem real to you in your mind, but they aren't. I saw most of this on your lists."

My mind is reeling. Kennedy has been boldly, systematically lying to me all these years, going along with some nutso shit I made up in my head. Every day another lie surfaces. Even his admission was a lie. I want to yell and tear my hair out. But I need to play it cool. I need to be rational and systematic despite the fact that I have never been so in my life. How do I know it isn't Dr. P who's lying now. I say so.

"Have a look at this."

Dr. Pinocchio hands me a note and an envelope, which contains a CD Rom.

The letter is dated January 2, 1998. The day before Mother's disappearance, which must have been when she died. The day before Pinocchio left the hospital for good. The day before I buried the box and told myself I would never think about any of this again. The font and the tissue thin page, I recognize from Mother's old hospital reports. The feel of it against my nail brings me right back.

Millie,

By now, you must have noticed some remarkable things about your mother's condition. It is no secret that I have been interested in her case. And yes, I cannot deny this interest exceeds mere goodwill for her wellbeing. I believe it's important to be honest about these things.

My life's work has been dedicated to the theory of consciousness and the creative brain. Our hypothesis (my definite knowledge, which I must present as hypothesis to maintain scientific protocol) through your mother's case has always been—to say the least—exceptional.

I dared not share these findings with anyone until I knew the full breadth of what we're onto here. With the skeptical, ready-to-be-cost-cut attitude already shined on our art rehabilitation techniques by the government funding bodies, it wouldn't take more than a whisper of scandal to shut the whole thing down. And yesterday, purposefully or not, you managed to orchestrate that. And so here we are.

However, I know you have suffered enormously—perhaps more than anyone involved—under the conditions of your mother's, shall we say, extraordinary state of being, and so, I would like to help you. I can see you are struggling.

Sincerely yours,

Dr. P

I look up to him.

"You were always antagonistic toward me," he explains. "I know you didn't want to hear the things I had to say. And I get that, but it caused me a lot of problems. I'm afraid I wasn't as compassionate as I could have been because of what your actions had done to my career."

I'm not fully across everything he's saying but I nod. He's obviously quite serious.

Pinned to the letter is an envelope, and inside the envelope is a CD-Rom.

I hand it to him and he holds it gently while he waits for the laptop to warm up. It takes ages for the suck of the CD, and once it clicks into place, it seems to spin at hyper speed, but nothing happens.

"Wait," I say. "I need to show you something." I want to trust him, and whatever he's about to tell me about Kennedy. But there's something I need to know in order to do this. I run to the car and heft out the tackle box. Dr. P is down the stairs quickly, eager to carry it for me once he sees what it is. It's clear from the way he's looking at me that he recognizes it.

Inside, alongside the computer, he carefully lays the box on the table. I turn back the lid and ask. "What do you see?"

"Millie, these are your lists. Your *quelque chose* lists. You had them with you all the time. It broke my heart to see you wanting to be like your mother, trying desperately to work everything out. You aren't still doing this, are you?" I shake my head. Kennedy had gone along with what I said about the relics. More lies, but why?

"Why don't we watch this?" Dr. P coaxes. "It might clear up a few things."

Finally, a window pops up, asking him which application he'd like to use to open it. He doesn't seem to know. The disk is old by today's technology standards. I look to Pinocchio.

He shrugs. "Not very technical I'm afraid."

Wavering for a moment, he chooses the first option and gets an error message. Then he closes out the window and has to search through a directory to find the file again. The wheel of death spins on the screen and my chest aches.

He clicks on the file and this time chooses the second application option. It works. A black dialogue box pops up. He clicks on the green arrow. Again, the wheel spins. But then an image appears. I'd know it right away: it's Mother's room at the Cuckoo Bird Hut. My entire torso begins to quiver in terror. I haven't seen her in so long and I've buried so much that the idea of her image coming across the screen now is unbearable. But I must proceed. There's no more time for denial.

No sooner do I think it, than there she is. My god, my god. I remember that sweater, the featherweight cashmere, the only pink thing she had, and the perfect pink, not too bright or dull; natural, as if everyone were born with a pink sweater, everything always perfect.

She's propped up on a corduroy husband that I remember briefly being part of her life at the hospital. Someone had lent it to her and then taken it when they'd gone. So it was something with a timestamp, if only I could remember who the patient was.

Her hair is short. She's beautiful, reading, otherworldly, unapproachable, and then there's a knock at the door, and the person holding the camera puts it down, the view is of Mother's wall. She's got one of her chalkboards hung there, and I see the familiar names in the spiral shape: Steiner, Bataille, Coleridge.

There's a screech of the door hinging open and then Mother looks up. Her reaction is pure terror. "No! No! No!" she yells, and Dr. P runs to secure her.

"Mr. Kennedy, please leave!" I hear Dr. P shout. Seconds later, I see Roxanne and the male orderly who was always playing ping-pong, secure Kennedy to a stretcher and then Roxanne injects him. It's Kennedy. It's definitely Kennedy.

"Yes," the camera holder says, off screen. It's a voice I'd know anywhere. Kennedy's voice.

That's it. The screen goes black. What have I just witnessed? Clearly, I know *why* I've witnessed it: Pinocchio wants me to know there's something about Kennedy and Mother I don't know. But he hasn't let me know what. I watch once more, get the same chilling reaction, then slam the screen down and run back outside for some fresh air, gasping, bent over the handrail.

Pinocchio's hand is on my back.

"I always liked how you called me Pinocchio."

"What do you mean. That's your name!"

"No. It isn't. It's Dr. P, for Peters, plain old Doctor Peters. Way back in my student teaching days, they called me Dr. P and it stuck."

"Pinocchio?"

"Yes?"

"What was that I just watched?"

"Kennedy did not like your mother because everyone loved her. He undercut her every chance he got. I don't think it was any coincidence he took to you, given how poorly Emily often treated you."

Had Kennedy planned our meeting at Two Guys?

"Why don't I remember him?"

"There's a lot you don't remember from your mother's stay as well as your own."

"He was there with me, too?"

"We often had to guard your door. He was always standing there, watching you. We didn't know what he might do."

"You're telling me my marriage is a sham? That it was never real?"

"Did it *feel* real?"

He takes my silence for assent.

"Then it was real. This is what you always miss, Millie. Your experience is the real one, even if it doesn't always make sense.

Even if it isn't like anyone else's. Maybe, now that you know the truth, you can begin to be comfortable with yourself."

"But Kennedy and my father believe I'm a danger—to Rose and to myself."

"Well, I have a feeling that's not entirely true. He can be very manipulative, Kennedy."

"I'm going to go to the police tomorrow," Dr. P says.

"Please give us a few days. What difference will it make now?"

He dips his chin and we part ways.

In the car ride home I tell myself that if Dr. P were really worried about what Kennedy would do to me, he would have insisted on going to the police immediately. He must think he'd never harm me or Rose.

In Mother's office, on the far corner of her desk is a photo of her. In it, she's twenty-one years old. Her hair's wavy and thick with uneven, sultry bangs that seem to just fall in a way others spend hundreds of dollars trying to achieve.

You can't see, and she never told me, but I know. She's looking down at me, to where I'm gestating in her uterus to the size of an unshelled peanut.

The next morning, Kennedy handles it for a long time, his finger marking the glass.

"Originally, I came across this photo in one of those trash bags hunched five wide by our back door in the days after my father left," I tell Kennedy. I want to gauge his reaction. "It was a day a child welfare officer was coming to check on us and I had to make the house look respectable. When I tried to haul the trash to the bin, this bag busted on account of moldy pea soup and too many glass ginger ale bottles—an anthropologist would have had a field day.

"Grumbling, I'd unrolled a new bag and tried to shove everything inside. As I tipped in a dustpan full of limp tea bags and take-out chicken bones, the picture skittered gracefully out. I felt its slick surface, mottled only by the slightest ketchup smear. The residue had faded a spot which added to the photo's patina —like the symbol of a rose in a religious painting, the image revealing more to a trained eye, but something indescribably enhanced to the average observer."

When I see Mother and myself in that way, so in love, so smothered in ketchup, I know threw away this photo because she'd lost the hope pictured there. I was all she had left, and I'd failed her. She'd made that clear. But if you destroy an image, can you destroy its intention? I hoped not, which is why I kept it. I knew that she thought it possible, and that's what gave her gesture power. But my keeping it had power, too. I often glanced at it as a possibility that I might be loved again one day. And I was, wasn't I? Despite it all, Kennedy loved me, had decided to whatever it took to build a life with me. But what would happen now?

35

MILLIE

ON THE WAY HOME FROM DR. P, A MEMORY DISLODGES ITSELF: A day on the Upper East Side of Manhattan with my parents: fancy shop windows, ancient diners with formal waiters serving ten deep on each arm plates of glistening thick-cut fries and toothpick-skewered chicken salad sandwiches. I must have been about seven.

Along Madison Avenue, where I remembered so clearly walking between Mother and my father, while each pulled an arm and raised me so I walked on air, my feet furiously shimmying, Mother said, "We're here. This is it." Only later did I learn that this outing was to accompany Mother to the city so she could attend her therapy group at the end of this street, one she'd just begun a few weeks earlier. Father had already told her he was going to leave if he didn't give it a good try.

She'd stopped in front of a luggage store with a particularly enticing travel display. The cases were floating, suspended by invisible thread, adorned with glittering, dip-dyed wings.

"The man who owns this store hates me. He's in my group and has it out for me."

My father and I had exchanged one of our looks. *Here we go,* it said.

Beneath them was arranged a picnic scene of furry animal figurines, each with their own luggage. It felt like something from another world. Any place that could make suitcases into such a dreamy image was someplace I wanted to see. I begged my parents to go inside.

Mother said, "Absolutely not. I have no idea what he's after. I told everyone I was coming here with my family this week, and he must have done this for my benefit. Or *hers.*" She thumbed in my direction.

Even by then, I knew my father's tactic for Mother was to "not engage" when she said such things.

"Dad, please. Please! Please! Please!" I got quite agitated.

"You're getting too excited," he said. This was his code for 'you're making me think you're like your mother.' I knew this because she often screamed those words at him. I wore them like a badge of honor.

Instead, I screamed all the way to one of those diners. Calmed down out the front, and we then ate silently at an upstairs booth, looking out the window at everyone walking by below. I can remember clearly feeling more deeply upset than I ever had before. That was the beginning of the end for our family. And right in the midst of it, there was all this wonder, all this action, held out—just for me, I'd felt—and then suddenly, because of her, it was yanked from reach. Now there was anger, silence. I refused to eat my french fries and my father had said we'd sit there until I finished, like a *normal kid.* Mother had defended me. "Who wants to be normal?"

After twenty minutes Mother had scooped me up and raced out of the restaurant to her therapy. We waited in the diner until five minutes before she was due to come out and stood there at the ordinary wooden door to a brownstone, in a row of others just like it. When she emerged, there was a dark-haired man behind her.

"And who's this beautiful girl?" he said.

Mother ignored him, like he simply hadn't said anything. "This is Rose," my father said, while Mother bored holes through him with her eyes. He kissed my hand. Nobody had ever done that to me before. He excused himself and then bowed before me. "My lady," he said, and winked before he walked away.

"Yes, he looked just awful," My father said, when he was, in fact, down the street, in front of the luggage shop.

Father said he had things to do and Mother and I rode the train home without him. I screamed the whole way, until my throat was raw and I fell asleep. I didn't know why I was so upset. And when I woke up I never thought about it again. Until now.

As I clicked the memory back into place, I realize why I'd felt drawn to that shop years later, when I went in and bought that *Quelque Choses* paper. Could Mother have been right about Kennedy? Could our whole life be an elaborate final fuck-you to her? And all the while, could I have been so pathetic that this was this the start of my manic search for meaning in it all? Pathetic. I really was. Poor Rose, what would become of her, with an unfit mother like me?

Even as I thought it, I couldn't help but admire the beauty of our story's pattern—the reversal, a powerful literary setup.

Inside the luggage shop, on the day I'd bought the papers, I rebuffed an offer of assistance, made my way to a glossy gray suitcase that caught my eye, past the image from the window—a mirror that reflected me in a floppy hat, a passport, a book, and a small suitcase—that I'd been trying to work out: how had they done it? There was no floppy hat there, no book, no small suitcase, and yet I'd been reflected with them in the mirror, a fantasy version of me. It looked like a magical mirror, but certainly must have had some intricate illusion set up behind the scenes. I hadn't realized I'd seen this place before.

I checked the price tag on the gray case, which inspired a discreet gasp, which propelled me to the sale rack at the rear.

Rummaging through the cut-price merchandise, between travel Scrabble sets and ingeniously rolled Totes bags the size and shape of a croissant, yet printed with baguettes, I found stacks of notepaper topped with the words *Quelque Chose*, which is French for "something."

It seemed significant. Not only the paper itself, but the experience of finding it, the atmosphere, the grounding of words in life.

Feeling I was getting something important, for a very good bargain, though I wasn't exactly sure why, I bought all the stock.

"*Quelq'un achete quelque chose*," said the narrow man in black plastic frames and a blue Mohawk, wearing a name tag that read, Seb, who rang me up. I was someone buying something, sure.

"Could be the opening of a great novel," he said, as he handed over my change and my purchase in a pretty paisley paper bag. I gave him a tight smile. All of this clicked into meaningful patterns for me. Too bad I'd missed the most meaningful bit. It would probably be my undoing.

36

MILLIE

THE NEXT DAY, I'M NEGOTIATING THE TIGHT SIDE STREETS TOWARD the Long Island Expressway on my way to New Jersey General for some answers. Back to Roxanne, and all the clusters of memory that will alight at yanking at that strand of history. I've left Rose with Kennedy again. I seem to be solving his problems by making myself scarce.

This morning, at the breakfast table she had her "writing" of smiley and sad faces in front of her. I could see her practicing her own smiling and frowning. When I caught her she said, "Don't look at me!"

I shouldn't come back here. I feel it deep in my bones. I'm a few feet away, holding my breath, when a honk startles me. It's Roxanne, in her ancient Toyota. She circles her fist, bulges her eyes, so I'll lower my window. She looks the same, but her hair is grayer.

"Well, hello. I was wondering when I'd see you again."

I think I'm going to be sick. Roxanne leaves her car idling, door open, to stand over my window and smooth my hair. In her embrace, she bends me over the open door and I want to vomit all over her shoes. The ungentle feel of her hand sparks off more memories. She steps back and I cut to the chase. "John Kennedy; was he a patient here?"

"You know he was, dear. You and he had a special bond. Didn't you?" Roxanne says—in her strange, gruff, register. "Which I'll never forget because he didn't like your mother much, did he?"

It's true. It's all true.

"Are you okay?" Roxanne demands.

"I'm fine," I say. I need to get out of here immediately. I may not recall much of my time here, but I can sense deep down in my bones that this place is poison to me. And if I stay here, I may say too much and right now trouble feels like it's hiding around every corner. Roxanne's the woman people bare their souls to, the one patients confess their most tortured thoughts to on sleepless nights, when they'd rather string themselves up with a bedsheet than hold it in one more second. I shrug and feel the pull of a frown.

"Good to see you," I say.

She nods. Tugs at her ponytail. "You be careful. You understand?"

I swallow big and drive away without looking back. *What did she mean by that?*

It's dumb, but I used to look at Roxanne as Mother's alter ego, part of her, a mouthpiece for that part of her that still wanted a relationship with me. Because I knew Mother had spoken to her plenty. I sensed even when she wasn't speaking to anyone else.

But attention is not the same as love, and Mother's words coming from crusty Roxanne always underlined that. And now they solidify what I must do.

I've made a decision. I can't live the rest of my life as a lie. At the station, I ask for Officer Lou, half thinking he won't work here anymore. After twenty minutes, a woman in plain clothes leads me to a small room with a wood-look table and plastic chairs and leaves me with a glass of water, waiting for nearly half an hour. I'm busting by the time Officer Lou makes his entrance. He has aged, which I'm sure I have. Seeing him brings everything back—the images come faster, more intensely. It is impossible to pick them apart. But me with a rock, bashing, bashing still makes the deepest, most frequent appearance, despite what I've learned about Kennedy. It makes me question my motive: how can I turn Kennedy in? What will this do to Rose? It doesn't feel right. Have I made a misstep coming here?

"What can I do for you, Millie Kennedy?"

I can see the second he realizes who I am. His eyes widen, he swallows, tries to cover his shock by sipping at his coffee. "Millie Burns," he says after.

"The same."

"You and your mother, you had quite an influence on me. Read every one of the authors on your mother's boards—Steiner, Bataille, Percival. I don't think you're looking at the same man you saw the last time."

"Mother would be so glad to know that."

I ask for the bathroom, and he calls in a female cop, whom he introduces as Caroline, to take me. Back in the room, she lets him do the talking.

"So what brings you here today, Millie?"

"I—I think I've made a mistake." I stand to leave.

"I know it can be intimidating, once you get here. But you came here for a reason. Why don't you tell us what it is?"

I can't help it. I look down at the ring, Mother's ring on my finger. Why did I put it on? How could I have been so stupid? I described it in detail all those years ago, as I did any identifying clothing, marks, characteristics.

He must have noticed my give because he looks right at the ring. Oh, why did I come here?

"Do you want to share anything with us?"

I shake my head.

"Well, it's funny, you coming in here today, when I got not one, but two calls about you."

Heat rushes my face and chest.

"Is there anything you'd like to tell me?"

I shake my head.

"Your father is worried about you. He thinks you are a danger to yourself and to your daughter."

"And the other?"

"Dr P. I think you call him Pinocchio?"

"He thinks your husband is a danger. He thinks your husband is a murderer."

He looks directly at the ring now.

"These are some wild accusations," I say.

"I always liked you, Millie. I felt for you. And like I said, you and your mother have changed me. The world is a very different place to me now. And I have you both to thank for that. But because of that, I have always felt a special duty to you both. I don't like leaving cases unsolved. My old boss, he didn't like leaving files open. So he closed your mother's. But now, with these new leads, I can re-open it. Just a matter of some paper-work to be handled first. So. You can talk to me now, or you can wait until I come to you. Your choice."

I don't say anything.

"I know you're a good girl, Millie. I know you want to do the right thing." Why does everyone always say that to me?

The problem is, I don't know what the right thing is. "Am I free to go?"

He nods. "For now."

37

WHEN I WALK INTO THE HOUSE, I EXPECT THE WORDS SEEN BY POLICE to be printed on my forehead. I find him in the garden, watering the new plants, as if there isn't a dead body there. He sees me staring at him, makes sure to catch my gaze and then looks over to where Mother is buried. "I love you, Millie. You are everything in this world to me. There is nothing, and I mean nothing more important. Do you know that?"

I gulp. I feel the truth of the words, but see them in light of Dr. P's words: *he's a compulsive liar with psychopathic tendencies. He believes his lies, doesn't feel any guilt about his actions.* I've made a terrible mistake not telling Officer Lou what I know. Which isn't to say Kennedy's love doesn't still have an affect on me. "I do." Even as I say it, I know I can never trust him—or anyone —again.

My hand trembles so severely, I drop my keys in the dirt. He leans down to help me pick them up and our hands touch. He sees the ring. My throat goes dry. Suddenly there's the loud noise, an incredible halo around everything.

Kennedy's words come loud, deafening, and I've dropped down to the floor.

"I love you. I love you. I love you," he says.

I'm not paging-in, I tell myself. *It's a dissociative episode*, which makes me feel not full of his love, but of loneliness, of the terrible sensations of everything around me, and the memories, before I black out.

38

MILLIE

ON MY LAST DAY AT WORK, I WAS JUBILANT AT THE IDEA I'D camouflaged my pregnancy from Mr. Tyler all those months. You'd think I'd been up for an Oscar. In his version of my life, I'd gone on, a single girl, groomed and headed for bigger and better things. Perhaps that version still exists somewhere, too. But I've never run into her.

"What about Chico for a baby name?" Kennedy said that evening of the last day at the office, tin trays of dumplings once again between us. We ate in a cloud of new intimacy. A child, a shared income between us.

"Don't even think about it."

"What? A girl could rock Chico."

"We're not naming her Chico."

As I stretched to pick up his empty plate, he hooked a finger over my knuckles, what he called 'locking me on.' Was that a character behavior he'd given himself? Something to ground him into the mind's eye?

"What is it?" I said, suddenly cold all over.

Sighing, Kennedy turned my way and looked as if he wanted to say something. Instead, he shook out his head and shoulders, and grimaced. So many secrets. Which had he wanted to share? Was he about to confess about the reality of our situation? About the cancer?

Chicorella kicked. When I put his hand there and she did it again, Kennedy's throat jumped, his eyes glassed.

"What is it?" I was suddenly terrified and had no idea why. I didn't allow myself to think about analogical brain functions then.

Visibly straightening himself, Kennedy's green eyes went dead in a way I've never seen before—the way a movie character playing dual roles often affects for the alter ego.

"I just liked Chico was all," he said, deadpan. Liar. And what of our little "Chico" now? Had it been the cancer, or the web of lies that got him so upset? What would become of Chicorella now, a product of a sham like this?

"You're a kept woman now," Kennedy had said, carrying me over the threshold of Mother's house—our house—on my last day at the office. I liked it. Now it all looks so sinister. Was I so transparent that I could be played so easily?

Still, what followed was what I can only describe as my most organic phase. Without an alarm, I rose peacefully each morning, never once wondering what I ought to be doing, or feeling guilty that my time wasn't being spent properly (that would come later, of course).

Smug, I wanted to scream it from the rooftops: "This is the meaning of life, people!" I knew this would disappoint Mother, this warm acceptance, this comfort with what you were given, so I relished it. Now this all reads shamefully. I think of another phrase of hers: *Perception relies on a naïve realism.* Well, maybe Mother, you were right about that.

Instead of fretting, I read my way through Mother's giant book collection—the Emerson, Whitman, Baudelaire, *Flora's Interpreter*, and Flannery O'Connor, and pieced together a narrative of the world I don't think I could have before pregnancy. The new experience of Mother's world was unrecognizable with a life growing inside me. I jotted down whatever helped me to make sense of things on my *Quelque Chose*.

Would I have changed anything, I wonder? I don't think I could have even if I'd wanted to. I loved Kennedy too much. I loved who I was with him. And despite everything I know now, I am scrambling to find a way to hold onto that feeling. Because it was the only time I ever felt good. Angry, frightened, betrayed as I am, I don't know who I'd be without him. This is what I'm thinking when I come to.

39

KENNEDY

IT'S A STIFLING NINETY DEGREES, DYNAMITE SKY. I CALL SEB AND tell him Millie is not doing better and he shouldn't expect me in before next week. She's been strange with me since she saw Emily's hand. It's obvious we're all better off without her, and it doesn't matter how that happened. So letting her think she killed Emily, rather than admitting it was me doesn't make any difference. As a matter of fact, it's better this way because she'll feel indebted to me for keeping her secret, and for loving her warts and all. Which is good because she's pretty pissed at me about keeping the cancer a secret. Just imagine if she knew I'd killed her mom, too.

Anyway, Tomorrow's my appointment and who knows what that will bring? I'm sure Millie realizes that if she tells anyone about Emily's unfortunate death, then she'd lose Rose to the authorities and me to cancer in one fell swoop. I believe our secret is safe. It would be the biggest tragedy if I died and my daughter thought she came from monsters.

Never thought I'd be a luggage man, but here I am. Turned it into something profitable. Something to provide for my family in the way they deserve. And that makes me a powerful man.

But these lies I'm telling, that's something else—it's the ultimate power, to be able to roll them off so perfectly, so believably, to make our lives whatever I want them to be.

I'm up before Millie; poor thing was having one of her episodes all night. She must be guilt-ridden. I'm starting to feel like she should be. I've told it this way so well that it's stating to make sense: why *couldn't* she have killed Millie? And now it felt like the right way to move forward, to keep us together. I would —and have—done anything to do that. That's what I've always said and I'm upholding it.

She comes down all tiptoes and clenched muscles, and I watch her make her way to the kettle. It's so cute how she drinks tea instead of coffee. I'm sure she thinks it's romantic. Her waste of a mother used to drink tea, too. Poor Millie. I saved her. And what we have is the real thing, despite everything.

A husband who keeps her darkest secrets and loves her despite that? Well, that's right up her alley. I've taken our perfection and made it even more perfect. It's got all the drama and richness of fiction, which of course is everything to her. Of course, I might be dead soon, but at least she'll teach my kids I was the man she loved, who loved them, a hero. I stand a bit taller, walk up behind her and put my hands around her.

She stiffens. Poor thing, she must be feeling so guilty for what she's done.

"Allow me," I say, and make her tea just the way she likes it. Then I make myself a coffee and take it out to the improving eyesore that is our yard. There is the fresh smell of mint.

Quiet at a human hour, the garden is ethereal now. The new plants are taking root and plenty of new shoots have sprung. Pink sky, stringy, translucent cloud leftovers. Looked at from the right angle, they are noble. Like me, I think. Emily is buried there, under the rhododendron, where we can keep an eye on her. All this time it felt comforting, but now it's like looking at the last piece of the puzzle. With the peace I feel at the moment, I can almost believe the world is telling me that the tests will come back clear.

But hang on. Wht's this? Looking down, I see Millie's footprints in the packed dirt, but then a second set of tracks from a man's shoes, continue on past mine through the gate. A man's been out here during the night. In my yard! What the fuck? I follow the tracks to a scrolled iron chair, and then, oh God, no. To the rhododendron. I must be too late. Does she know the truth? Or has she turned herself in? Regardless, with a body, they'll work out it was me, and not her. They have ways of discerning how tall or strong someone must have been to deliver that kind of blow. And there'll be DNA. There's always that.

I laugh out loud despite myself at the obviousness of Millie's "secret" endeavor to find things out on her own. Accept the truth, Millie. You killed her. That's the way this story goes. But why be so obvious about it? Why not wipe away the tracks? Again I laugh out loud. When you know someone so well, it's an amazing thing. I recall how sloppy she is about these kinds of things when she's tired. That must be what's happening here. I recall during Rose's first three months getting salt in my coffee more than once. We'd say Rose was in on the joke because she'd squeal and motor her dimpled legs as I puckered and forced myself to swallow.

"Think that's funny?" I'd say, using that dumb baby voice I swore up and down never to use. There's not much I wouldn't have done for a flash of those gums back then. Not much has changed in that department.

But all of a sudden, my mood turns. As much as I don't want to, I'm going to have to change tack. Millie should have hidden her tracks better. Now I have no choice but to silence everyone who knows, for good. It was either her dad or Dr. P or that cop—Officer Lou from back during Emily's disappearance investigation. That's everyone. I can handle them. I breathe a sigh of relief. I'm already getting a handle back on all this.

The phone rings and I run inside to grab it. Millie must be upstairs because she's nowhere in sight.

"Kennedy speaking." It's amazing how my voice can sound so normal. I am very good at this. People are always charmed by me.

"Hello, Mr. Kennedy, it's Cindy, from Dr. Kramer's office." She's flirting shamelessly, as usual, even though she's connecting me to the man who will deliver a death sentence.

"Hello, Cindy." I grab for purchase on the wall next to the phone. I look outside to where Emily's buried, to regain that sense of control over my destiny I felt moments ago.

"I've got Dr. Kramer for you. Hang on, Sweetie."

"Mr. Kennedy? I've got excellent news. The tests are clear. Turns out there was some muddying of the results of your diagnostics; you had a false-positive. I do greatly apologize for the stress this must have caused you, but false-positives are more common than you might think—the risk is over 60% for men. But these new results are consistent with all the other tests you've had since you've been in my care. Congratulations. You are healthy. And I don't think you'll have to worry about this again. We'll keep doing the periodic testing, but consider it preventative. Go live your life."

When I hang up, I feel euphoric for a moment, until I remember the task at hand. I'm going to live my life in prison if I don't do something about this. You have the control, I tell myself. You know what you have to do.

40

WHEN I COME TO, I'M LYING ON THE LIVING ROOM SOFA. ROSE IS sitting in the pink afternoon sun at the kitchen table, busy with something she keeps calling "hone work." I excuse myself down to the basement filled with things Mother used to love, wedding gifts, things she'd made a big show of keeping after the divorce, only to smash them—boxes and instruction leaflets and all—into mosaics named "Him" and "That Woman." They still hang in her office. She's a master of fusing art and life. They're good.

Last year Kennedy and I had sorted through whatever was left, and after keeping the salad spinner and the New Jersey tea towel, we donated the rest of the garish statuettes and novelty tablecloths to charity.

"What do they think I spend my time doing?" Mother had asked when she'd see these abandoned gifts down here all those years ago before her disappearance. "Throwing dinner parties for tacky idiots?" After considering her own question, Mother had answered it. "Well, I guess you project your own reality onto others."

I throw my head back in laughter at the memory. No one I've met speaks the way she does. And with her, I felt like part of her tribe, and lucky to be. But there were other times, and other feelings.

This leads me to wonder how my father could have willingly left her. When I think of my father's wife Tennessee, as I do now, it is often framed in the context of that, because she could never compare. But this time, it sits differently. What have the relics of my father's reality become down here? What has appropriating them as items on my endless lists of *Quelques Choses* done but make the things more real? I'm starting to be cognizant of the tricks my mind has played on me.

I don't mean to, but I start smashing. And once I do, I can't stop. Now my father and mother's *Quelques Choses* are *Quelques Choses* quite different. I have the power to change, too. Even if it does involve destruction. Maybe change always involved destruction. It certainly has for me. Still, as I look around, I can't help but think it all looks truer this way. I should have done this years ago.

The relief is palpable. I can feel my shoulders sinking down my chest, my breath reaching deeper. I don't think; I simply act. It opened the floodgate. Though Rose is upstairs, I allow myself to sink down against the wall, rest my head on my shoulder, and allow my mind to go blank. I'm defocusing. My mind is clear. This is the way creative types prime their brains for their best work—it's a state without judgment, a state where everything needn't make sense. A non-fiction tome Mother often referred to was big on that. I'd always read between the lines, believing there was more to it than the words on the page prescribed. Somewhere in that space was where I was meant to weave Mother's mantras: *always carry a book with you; ground your reading in reality; what is real?* But what exactly was that something more? A magical portal that special people could reach if only they could connect properly with the words. She was so obscure that I became convinced this was the only thing she could have been getting at, the only goal that could be so important she left us all behind in pursuit of it.

I pull out the slim paperback I've been hiding in my skirt waist and read the introduction to this thirteenth edition of *Pinocchio*, I'd underlined the introduction so deeply, I tore the page. I recall how desperate I was at those times. But what do I have to show for it?

There seems to be no game more beloved of all children in all lands than Pretend. Toy soldiers for the boy, and dolls—few or many—for the girl supply the only raw material required to play this, for of course, the charm of the game lies largely in the imagination of the doughty captain who endows his men with life and ability to go through exciting manoeuvres; and in that of the miniature mother who directs so wisely the behavior of her family.

After we grow up we are astonished to learn that this game originated with the old Greeks hundreds of years back, who used to make little jointed puppets of wood or cardboard representing men and women, moving them about in a life-like fashion which was hugely entertaining to both old and young. So popular was the game that soon the Romans wanted to play, too, and then later on the Italians, French, and English made puppets for their countries, only they called these little figures marionettes.

I let the connections wash over me and soon find myself leafing through to the famous scene where a piece of wood screams, "Do not strike me so hard!"

Master Cherry blames his imagination; is it any wonder I got to this point? At the end of the first chapter, I read the words, "What happens next is a story that really is past all belief, but I will relate it to you in the next chapters."

I'm very mixed up, I think. And then I'm gone.

41

"MUMMY," ROSE CALLS DOWN, REVIVING ME.

I look around me. Same old shit down here in the basement, yet everything looks different, broken. I feel panicked. Has someone been in the house? Who could have done this. Me. It must have been me. I'm so mixed up.

"Rose! Rose!" I yell.

"Are you okay?" she asks when I appear at the top of the stairs. Her hair is smashed in on one side, as if she's been sleeping. I hug Rose tightly to me and tap her head with my fingers.

"I am now, darling."

I breathe in her coconut conditioner. The shampoo smells like it, too, but it doesn't have the strength of the conditioner which stays with her all day. The scent grounds me, reminds me she is my Rose, nothing sinister.

I find that Rose has been "reading" her magic charm book again. She's just a child, reading a children's book, I tell myself. A child whose father is a murderer.

"Where's Daddy?"

He's been out back, digging.

My mouth goes dry.

Am I crazy, or does Rose look guilty? Has she been enjoying having this secret from me? Has Kennedy been using her? Mother? No. I must stop trying to deflect this from Kennedy. He is not what I thought. I will have to face that—among other terrible truths. There will be no more Book World to save me from it all. If I survive.

To ground myself, I touch her hand, I feel her lovely squeeze. I brush my fingers along the inside of her palm—a gesture that has always made my chest flutter, has served as a touchstone to how far I've come from Mother's fucked-up world. I nearly forgot, but I promise myself I won't know. I will claw my way out, for my daughter. No matter what it takes.

I finger her magic charm necklace, telling myself it is just an adorable novelty. There will be no more denying reality.

"Do you like this book?" I ask.

"Yes, I do. Very much."

"And you were fibbing that other day. It's okay, I know Daddy told you to because he told me. You always had this book, didn't you?"

She nods.

"That's a good girl," I say, trying not to show my fear.

"Mother, am I still a big girl if I have done a wee wee in my underwear? Look, I am all wet. You need to pay better attention."

"Who told you that I need to pay better attention? Was that Daddy, too?"

Again she nods.

Suddenly Kennedy's in the room and asking why she's sitting in soaking wet pants. I don't know how much he's heard.

He pulls her from me, as if I've failed at my job. There is nothing worse than a poorly done by child. I turn away as he whisks her upstairs because I know nearly all of this is my fault, and I can't stop my eyes filling with tears. He stops halfway up the flight.

"Don't you go anywhere," he says. He's smiling, for Rose's benefit, but I can see the edge in it, the way it hasn't made it to his eyes, which lay into me like daggers.

When he comes back down, he's alone.

"Where's Rose?"

"She's fine."

"But where is she?

"I can see you are quite distressed about facing the reality of killing your mother. But, people are murdered all the time. Anyone can see it's better this way. Just look at how the fates have shined on us: And we will live our lives. I have excellent news, Millie. It was a false positive. The cancer is not back. Not only that, but the oncologist said I don't need to worry about it anymore. So you see, this has all just brought us closer together. A happy ending!"

At first I don't realize what he's said about the cancer diagnosis, couched as it was in all kinds of terrifying madness. And then I'm momentarily relieved. That quickly dissolves into the reality of where we are—the opposite of a happy ending. Even he doesn't look like he's very happy. And he certainly doesn't look like he wants me to live happily ever after. Or even any way, at all.

When he's called away on a phone call, which he takes at the edge of the yard, by, well, I don't want to think what he's by, I tiptoe up to Rose's bed, where she's already soothed herself to sleep. She's passed out with one leg hiked out like she'd just collapsed after a long journey. The blackened magic charm is in her mouth and I should remove it, but I don't.

I barricade the door with Rose's child's furniture—pink and white and full of everything I thought my life was. I do it for a different reason this time. In this context it looks so different. Nothing will ever be the same.

I tiptoe back downstairs and to install myself exactly where he last saw me. At the bottom of the stairs, I turn left directly into him and scream out.

"Why so jumpy?" he asks and takes me in his arms. I resist. I feel my arms flail against his strong grip.

"Shhhh," he says into my hair. And I try to let the calming sound and feel of it wash over me. For so long he has been the only one to calm me. Mother never did anything like that. I feel him kiss my hair, then push it aside, and kiss my neck. Not like a psychopath, but gentle, loving. Could it be I've made this into something it's not? It sounds like something I would do. I feel myself fall into him. In all the scenarios that's always been the one constant. And now? How could it all be over so abruptly?

"The obstetrician said you might be feeling off from the IVF, that it could come and surprise you at any time. You were so insistent on being strong, saying you could handle it, even though the drugs could exacerbate the kinds of challenges you've struggled with in the past. But you wouldn't hear it. You wanted to go ahead."

It takes a second for the words to sink in. He's mirroring the exact self-doubt I just felt. No. You must trust in yourself. You have been confused, that is true, but you are clearer now. You understand that you've been dissociating. The same way you did when all the problems with Mother were too much to handle. You came back then and you're coming back now.

"What are you doing, Kennedy?"

"Sssshhhh," he repeats, trying again to draw me to him, but I yank my arms away.

"Look at me. Everything's out now. No more secrets. That did not happen. I am not doing IVF. I was pregnant and I lost it."

"Millie you are confused. You are often confused and forgetful. It's okay. I'm here. I don't want you to worry. I told you, I love you. I know you love me." Part of me still wants to give in. He kisses me, and I respond, which terrifies me further. Maybe I can't come back. Maybe it's too late for that this time.

No. It can't be. There's Rose to think of. "No. No!" I run for the door. But he gets there first, blocks it.

For a moment, I feel real fear. Would he hurt me?

Kennedy's body stoops. He takes my face in his hands. Tenderly, really tenderly. He puts his lips to mine.

"I love you and that will never change. But you seem incredibly confused and distressed. I don't know what to make of it. The things you're saying. They don't make any sense."

"I'm not making sense? Let me make this very clear: I know you killed Mother."

"That's just not true. You killed Emily. I have kept your secret all this time because I love you, and I understand why you did what you did. We have the truest, purest kind of love, Millie."

"But I don't remember doing that."

"There are a lot of things you don't remember, Millie."

"Like you being in the psych ward with me?"

He darts back, like he's been slapped.

"So you've been doing some digging after all. And not just in the garden." It's a new tone; one that makes the hairs on my arms stand up. He even looks different, this man who's angrier than I've seen my husband before.

I have to know. "Did you kill her?"

He cocks his head. His features soften, from the eyebrows down, until I recognize him. I feel tears prick at my eyes. He pulls me into him and despite my terror and anger, I can't help but dive in. Who else has ever comforted me?

"Oh, Millie. Why did it have to come to this? Millie, I love you as much as ever. You and me against the world. You know that. Everything changes, but not that. I promise you, not that."

His words echo in my head. *You and me against the world.* It's something Mother used to say early on. He always says just the right thing, knows exactly where my thoughts are leading. How? Wait. It's the *Quelque Chose* lists! He memorized them. And he's been using them to manipulate me all this time. Before I can talk myself out of the idea, I vocalize it.

He doesn't say anything. "It's true, isn't it?"

"You don't want to do this, Millie. Trust me. Everything I've done, I've done for you. And now Rose."

Rose. What will become of Rose?

His look is inscrutable. It sends a chill down my spine.

42

"You look like shit, Lou."

"And good morning to you, too. You're right. Been up all night. Paid a visit to Malificent's father's house. And I'm glad because I think he's been a big help."

"Yeah, help with what?" Caroline's drinking some perfumed coffee.

"It's all a bit fishy, the mother's disappearance, and now it looks like the doctor's vanished. Maleficent was pretty upset at her father's place."

"Why are you calling her Maleficent?"

"You know, like the evil character from *Sleeping Beauty*? Fitting here. No one's all good or bad was the moral of that story."

"Look who's a romantic."

"Please, it's called research. Committing yourself to the case. Anyway, Dad's still convinced she's dangerous. But he ID'd the mother's ring, just about lost it. Confessed to knowing his daughter had killed his ex-wife all along. Apparently JFK convinced him to let the daughter live in peace. He said he thought he was doing the right thing. She wasn't a bad person, she was mentally ill, and he thought he was protecting her all this time; after all, he'd deserted them and that had certainly contributed to the way things had turned out. He decided it was best to let Millie scrape up whatever bits of her life she could. And the daughter was getting married, seemed like she'd gotten her act together. Nothing was going to bring the mother back, after all."

"That's some fucked up shit. Those crazy Kennedys!"

I crack a smile. "We shouldn't make jokes."

"Then we'll go crazy."

"True enough. So I still haven't gotten the green light to officially open the case."

Caroline raises an eyebrow. "Looks like your old boss has still got some friends here."

"Exactly. And you know how they are about closed cases."

"Closed cases are closed cases."

"Right. Whatever the fuck that means."

I score one of her lovely smiles.

"But, I didn't think we can wait on this. You know the rules: if we're given consent to search, we don't need a warrant."

"Don't tell me the sociopath husband let you dig around."

"No. But the wife did. She was completely terrified. But I got the photos of the hand sticking out of the ground. I can't believe that sicko didn't at least cover it back up."

"Well, you know sociopaths. Need to be in control. Probably likes her where he can see her. He wouldn't be worrying himself with guilt."

"Umm-hmm. So, got those in to the boss and I'm waiting for the green light."

"Don't you think the wife and child could be in danger?"

"I do, which is why you and I are heading over there as soon as possible."

"Without the case being officially opened?"

"Yup."

"And without the wife having to get in trouble with the husband?"

"Yup."

"Urgent circumstances exception?"

"Yup. They haven't given it to us yet using the closed case excuse plus the whole family's nuts argument. But we're going to go over there and watch. If I suspect he's about to so much as touch a hair on either of their heads we're going in. And if he steps near the body, we're going in."

"Understood."

"And then you can sweet talk him if we need it. You're so good at getting those men to open up, fantasy lady cop and all that."

"If it weren't true I'd get you for discrimination. But there's no point. You'll be stuck on a desk job if you bark up this tree."

"There are so many holes in this case, it's begging for someone to dive in."

"Those are a lot of metaphors. Don't think I haven't noticed that copy of *Moby Dick* on your desk."

"I'm immersing myself in the case." I've made light of it, but I have to turn around to conceal the truth I know is in my eyes. I've been reading this Dr. P's stuff all night, after the run-in with Millie Kennedy. Really intriguing. Always loved a good book. Once upon a time, thought I might write one.

And then there're my parents. Dreamed about them all night. That stupid, unsnuffable hope that somehow, they weren't really dead. Dumb. But. What if I could somehow get to them? This is the kind of promise stories give us. This is the kind of stuff this doctor spoke about all those years ago, after Emily Burns' disappearance. About how Emily used the books to escape the pain of the truth. How she couldn't always tell the difference. I can see the appeal.

"And you want me to be immersed too."

"You know you want to."

She sighs. "You're right. But only because I can't resist the chance to sweet talk a sociopath."

"Great. Let's go."

In the car I get Caroline up to speed.

"So what's the deal with the father?"

"From what Mr. Burns said, he's got no relationship with the daughter since he divorced her mother and married this other woman—great knockers on her."

"Again, if it weren't true—"

Not like other women, Caroline. Got lucky partnering with her.

"Makes sense."

"But then a few weeks back her husband, JFK, called Millie's dad after many years of no contact, and set up a meeting, but Maleficent turns up and JFK runs off. The daughter was pretty upset. Turns out JFK is dying."

"Are we meant to be sad about this?"

"Let me finish."

"Ever the storyteller."

"Right. So whadja find on Kennedy?"

"He has some serious cancer. Thinks he's gonna die. So he went to Mr. Burns pleading for him to help Millie out when he was gone. And the dad says no more. He's going to turn his daughter in, that Millie would be a danger to herself and to her daughter, Rose, which he witnessed with his own eyes, and he said he couldn't keep the secret any longer. He wasn't going to have another life on his conscience."

"Woah."

"I know. And ironically, the cancer thing was a false alarm. Busty chick at the doctor's office spilled the beans pretty easily when I told her I was a cop. Must have had a thing for them."

"Lucky you."

"I know, right?"

"Can I ask you something?"

"Anything."

"What do you think really happened to the mother?"

I shrug. "Until we get the okay to go in and get the body, it's hard to say. I'm not sure who I trust here. Difficult to believe the mother was murdered by that beautiful, dark haired woman, with her quiet manner and her huge eyes. But it could be. I used to think the only one with a motive would be the daughter. How could she be a murderer? Detective Muller didn't think she was guilty all those years ago. Doctor Disappearing Act said she didn't have that type of personality, that she was troubled but gentle. Wouldn't hurt a soul. But his case notes don't exactly add up. And now she tells me it was the husband, that sounds about right. Still, Maleficent does seem to have a tenuous relationship with the truth.

She said Dr. Pinocchio was missing, but he was the second source who called in to say he found out something about this case. He said Emily had been murdered; he said it was JFK, that with Millie's psychological profile she would never hurt anyone. She used to barricade her mother in her own room because she thought she'd hurt her, that's the kind of extremes she'd go to in order to prevent herself from being violent. She just doesn't have that kind of makeup. She thinks she's terrible, but she's not. It's all in her head. All this storybook stuff makes it difficult to know what to believe. You start reading meaning into everything."

"But she was wearing the mother's ring. In the old case files, that was one of the distinguishing characteristics. She never went anywhere without it. But Millie was wearing it. Could she have had a copy made? But that would be so sad to look at every day, wouldn't it?"

"Got me, Lou."

There's a call through the radio. "Hey Boss, your paperwork just came through."

Caroline and I take one look at each other and don't need to say a word to know what each other is thinking. In minutes, we're about to crack this case wide open.

43

MILLIE

I NEED TO CHOP APPLES FOR ROSE'S BREAKFAST. I NEED TO CALL Officer Lou back. He's rung my cell phone incessantly. But when I open my eyes, my head is pounding. And when I go to rub at it, I can't because my hands are restrained.

I look up from the bed and see my hands are tied to the sideboard. I feel around my hand with my thumb. Mother's ring is gone. My breath quickens. I'm too late. Kennedy, what have you done now?

"Good morning, Millie." Kennedy kisses the side of my neck from behind, where I lay, my wrists and arms completely covered in blankets. Rose is trailing behind him, her book under her arm. I secured her in her room. But now here she is and I don't like the idea of her here. I tell myself we all have rage, we can control it. Look how long he's controlled it so far.

"Run downstairs, Rose. Daddy's going to make you an omelet that reeks."

She laughs, comes over to breath in my face, eyeball to eyeball, and then give me a loud, pucker kiss. I muster a smile for her benefit. My daughter must be protected. We both watch her trail from the room, listen to her light steps down the stairs.

"You're mentally ill, Millie. Nobody will question your death. Suicide would be understandable. You've had a hard life. It's a wonder you've made it this far. But, with your husband sick, losing your pregnancy, finding your mother's body. It was all too much."

"But what about Rose?"

"She will be fine. At least once you're gone. You've been scaring her, Millie, locking her in her room. She's frightened of you. Or hadn't you noticed?"

She didn't look frightened just now. "What about you? All the things you said? How much you love me. How can you do this to me?"

"Once I've made up my mind, Millie, that's it. I'm surprised you haven't noticed that about me."

"But Kennedy, you said you did all this for me, for how much you love me, surely, that hasn't changed so quickly!"

Just then, the bell rings.

Quiet as I can, I let out a quavery breath of relief.

Kennedy walks to the window to see.

"Why are the police here, Millie?"

I shrug. The look he shoots me answers my question: however much he loved me before, that's how much he's dedicated to the idea of killing me.

"You pretend like everything's normal."

44

OFFICER LOU

"TEA?" MILLIE KENNEDY IS BEAUTIFUL. I SEEM TO HAVE BEEN thinking about this all this time because seeing her feels like a return to something.

"Sure. Milk, no sugar."

She busies herself with the preparation and I look around the vast kitchen. It's got that old farmhouse thing going on, but in a modern way, like it all came together perfectly, by accident. If I ever marry and have a family, this is where I would want them to live. It's so inviting here, something about, I don't know, Millie Kennedy's spirit that makes me feel like instead of visiting, I'm simulating the experience of living here. Like I know her.

The husband is probably lurking right outside the other side of the kitchen door. He didn't look too happy when I asked him to give us a minute. I need to be conscious of what I say if my theory holds up.

She places a dainty china cup in front of each of us. The tea *tastes* better in this cup. In fact, it makes me want to start drinking it all the time. Here.

"So what did you want to talk to me about?"

I barely recall. I see myself behind her at that sink, dragging her hair away from her neck so I can kiss her. I shake it off. I can see Caroline's head shaking over my shoulder. I know she's questioning how long I'm taking to get to the search, but we've got to build up to that, do it right. I've waited so long. This is no ordinary case.

I pull out the old file from inside my jacket. There are photographs of documents, so small I've brought the loop I need to read them. They are of hundreds of long, slender hand-written papers. Atop each one is printed in a beautiful cursive gilt, *Quelque Chose*, which I Googled, to find it means "something." I have been researching and reading through the entries on this list for so many years, I feel like I know this woman better than anyone. "Any idea what these are?"

She is a special woman. That much I know. I am going to protect her.

I can see the tears instantly rush to her eyes. But she takes a moment, calms herself, clears her throat. Not a single one falls. This is a strong woman. "They were—are—a coping mechanism for me. They help me to find meaning in things that are often difficult or too painful to deal with on their face value." It seems to cost her to admit this.

It's my turn to compose myself. No wonder it all felt so personal, like I'd been getting to know her all these years.

"But it turns out I have leaned too heavily on them, imagined, sometimes, that there was a more powerful element, a more magical, if you will, element, that gave these painful life experiences some meaning."

I could tell how difficult it was for her to say these things. "Doesn't seem too different from what we all do from time to time. Some might say that's the entire role of both art and religion. And if you ask me, there must be a reason people are drawn so fiercely to those two. There's something in us that *needs* for it to all mean something."

This time she can't stop the tears. She gets up, grabs a tissue. Stands at the window with her back to me.

When she moves from the window, I can see something she's fingered into the condensation. Words. *He killed Mother and he's going to kill me NOW.*

I knew it. I fucking knew it.

She tries to cover up the abrupt change in the room's energy with a forced smile.

I dip my chin and meet her eyes as reassuringly as I can so she understands I've got everything. All these years of learning her lists, her world, her mother's world, and maintaining my connection to her and the case, and now this vital moment. How can it *not* mean something? She sits quickly, her sleeves ride up. She doesn't try to pull them down. I see something there— marks. He must be restraining her.

It's time to move. I want to kill the man who did that to her. My mind is going a million miles an hour, trying to keep an eye on the entry points of the room, to think of all the possible things that could go wrong. What about the daughter?

She starts to recite something.

"'The ideal is not the vague thing, that boring and intangible dream which swims on the ceilings of academies; an ideal is the individual taken up by the individual, reconstructed and returned by brush or scissors to the brilliant truth of its native harmony.'"

The words have a spellbinding affect on me: *the individual, taken up by the individual...returned to the truth of its native harmony.* We're not allowed to say these words. We're not allowed to stand for truth and beauty these days. Those are old fashioned terms, certainly not the domain of men. And yet, it rings truer than any thought I've ever had in my head.

I write down in my notepad: *Baudelaire's Ideal.* Hearing her say them after reading, learning, memorizing, making them my own all these years, is quite stunning. My hand starts to tremble, and I make a fist, tighten it between my knees. Dare I believe it to be true: that there is something more to this life?

"In *Les Fleurs du Mal,* Baudelaire said there were more to words than the ordinary ways in which we use them. He spoke of their *subcurrents* and the spaces between them. It has been said that he can 'loosen the links that tied words to their ordinary meanings.' And in doing so, writers like him have been able to teach us how to experience the full potential of words, the stories created with them."

She goes quiet.

"Why are we talking about all this now?" I bring myself to say, though I don't want to stop the conversation, stop this feeling. I think I understand why she's talking about this, when her life's in danger, but I need to get it on the record.

"Like I said, it's my coping mechanism. I didn't want to believe it, but it was true. My life is just as insignificant as everyone else's."

"No." I shake my head. "You've certainly had an effect on me. And what about your daughter?"

"You'll find out soon enough, so I'll tell you. My daughter is afraid of me. When I black out from my anxiety, I cannot account for the time. And so I fear for what I will do. And to protect my daughter, I barricade her in her room. And she is frightened of me because I lock her in there for hours." She shrugs. "She's probably right to be afraid."

"No," I say again. "It is clear you are a good person, who's had some incredibly terrible experiences. You've gone to extraordinary lengths to protect her." *And you've been taken advantage of by a psychopath who understands and manipulates you.*

"Why are you looking at those documents?" she says,

looking down at the same photo we'd been talking about this whole time. It's like she doesn't remember. "People don't talk about these things! You don't understand. You either know or you don't. That's part of it. You have to learn for yourself. It's different for everyone. We build it based on our own memories, experiences, interactions with the texts." She's quite agitated. Is she about to have one of her episodes?

The door bursts open. My hand's already on my gun. And I lift and point when Kennedy appears. Amazingly, he doesn't put his hands up. It's the first time on this job that has ever happened to me.

"You've clearly distressed my wife. I think it's best you leave now," he says.

"I'm sorry. Is there something we can do to help her?"

"It's just time. She'll snap out of it. She always does."

"Again, I'm sorry."

I leave my card and head out to the car. My hand's on my gun the whole time. I'll leave this kitchen, but I'm not going anywhere.

45

MILLIE

I watch, horrified, as the squad car pulls out of the driveway.

"Excellent job, Millie. Using all that rubbishy obtuse language Emily goes for. He'll have no idea what you were talking about. Didn't suspect a thing, I don't think." Kennedy walks to the window, waits as Officer Lou's car takes a three-point turn and trails down the driveway, most likely taking my hope of getting out of this alive with him. Still, I have to trust my instinct. He saw my wrist, he saw my words on the window. He saw Mother's body and now knows I'm in danger, too. I believe he has a plan, that somehow, after I showed him the body, he is monitoring the situation here, closing in on an arrest.

"I was worried about that cop showing up, I'll admit. But you know what, Millie. You played it perfectly. Now it's on the record how delusional you are. And of course, I knew you were faking one of your episodes, because you're never that lucid. Jibberish is what you normally spew out. It's quite funny actually. But Officer Lou doesn't know that, so thank you for putting on that show. You made my job so easy. Thank you. And you see, now I can raise Rose and give her a beautiful life. You've done well."

"*What* job?"

"Killing you. Did you think I wasn't serious earlier?"

I slump into a chair, I want more than anything to just give in. But I won't let him know that.

He stands, tips his head. He always makes that same gesture, I realize. Psychopaths memorize normal behaviors, to fit in. How many of his actions I took for love were all a show? I can't bear to think about it.

"You understand, don't you? You're the only one who knows the truth. So you have to go."

"But what if we just . . . forget it?" I say. "I know you did it for me. And even though it wasn't true, I was grateful for all that time I believed you covered for me, when I thought I was the one who killed her."

46

"Look, Caroline, you find out what the fuck is taking that backup so long. And when they get here, have them hide out until my go-ahead. The more clear evidence we get here, the better chance they'll have of nailing him in court. I'm going to sneak back and hang out up there, beneath the windows, behind that rhododendron."

It's kind of amazing, knowing that's called a rhododendron, from studying the case files, the pictures of Millie's *quelque chose* lists. I can feel in every nerve ending that all that work is about to pay off. The husband is definitely harming, or most likely, planning to kill her, as she wrote on that window. But I'm here now. I won't let anything happen to her under my watch.

But what's this? Did Caroline misunderstand me? Are the squad cars coming right up to the house? No. It's a nice black Lexus. I squat down. I recognize the woman coming out. She's aged some, but that's Angie James. She was the best friend, played a minor role in the disappearance case. I should stop her, but I convince myself it's better to see how it plays out. I watch her go in. There's a significant amount of time before she's out of the car. Does she see me? My radio crackles and I decide to show myself.

"Angie James," I whisper scream.

She turns, and when I'm sure she's seen me, I hold my finger up to my lips. She understands, tiptoes over. It will be good to have help on the inside. We can use her.

"Wow, a flash from the past. Officer Lou," she whispers when she's close enough. "Funny seeing you here."

She reaches out to grab my hand and then smashes me on the back of the head with a rock. The last thing I hear are her footsteps as she runs toward the house.

47

MILLIE

KENNEDY DOESN'T EVEN LOOK THE SAME, LIKE AN ACTOR WHO'S just removed hours of makeup and prosthetic. Chills run down my back. I'm in trouble.

"No Millie, I'm afraid we can't forget it. It's too late for that now. You've gone and ruined everything."

I look down at Rose who's come downstairs and just now emerging through the doorway. I grab for her. Kennedy pulls her, not exactly gently, by the back of her tee shirt.

"Who was that, Mum?"

I close the space between us, reach out for her. *Mum.* I'll never hear that again, will I? I can't recall why it irritated me so much. I feel her strong little fingers grip a couple of mine. I love this girl. She loves me.

"That's enough now," Kennedy says. He looks Rose in the eye and says, "Nap time, dear."

She runs into my arms and hugs me tightly. I breathe her in, rub my face in her hair. It's the ending. This is what the ending feels like. I should know. "I love you," I say. She puts her nose against mine and says, "Kickles!"

I do as told and tell my tears to hold off until she's out of the

257

room. Rose giggles deliciously. Did I appreciate this so much before I was about to lose it?

She eyes me before she turns to go.

"You run up and use the toilet, Rose, and I'll be right there," Kennedy says.

"Yes! Because I'm a big girl!" And then she's off.

Kennedy pulls out two zip ties and secures my hands to the chair arms.

"Can't have you running off," he says.

In the kitchen by myself, I look to the window, where I had fingered in the condensation my plea for help. I assure myself Officer Lou saw it. But it's still there and that is going to anger Kennedy if he sees it.

The bell rings.

"Where's Millie!" It's Angie.

"Nice to see you, too," Kennedy says. Their voices are muffled, but I can make out the words.

"Act normal," I hear him whisper to her. But why? Has he told her that I've killed Mother? Has he said I'm not doing well and to expect my behavior to be strange?

"She must have completely forgotten you were coming!" he says loudly after that. It sounds so candid, so natural. It's terrifying, his abilities.

"Really? Are you sure? She's the one I call to keep track of my own appointments." Angie, on the other hand isn't such a great actress.

Do not cry. I am careful to measure my breaths. When that doesn't work, I bite my shirt. Because if Angie finds outs, what's to stop Kennedy from killing her, too?

"Did you hear something?" Angie says. My chest goes cold, but I didn't hear anything.

"Is something wrong with Millie?" Angie asks in her over-dramatic voice. "I haven't heard from her in days."

"I hate to tell you this, Angie, but she's not doing well. I had a bit of a health scare—cancer, and I'm afraid she wasn't coping."

"Barricading Rose again?" Fuck, Angie, don't come within 100 yards of Broadway, they'll kick you right out.

"Yes. And the blackouts, too."

"Is she talking about the book code?"

"Yes, I'm afraid so. She even went to her father and she scared him so much he called the police."

He's digging my grave. I can almost smell the earth.

"Let me go up and see her."

"No, Angie. I'm afraid that's not a good idea. She's resting, and she hasn't been quiet or calm in a long time. I'm not going to disturb her."

"Well, I think she'd want to talk to me."

"If you want to know the truth, Angie, she's been saying some pretty distressing things about you lately, too during her blackouts. She thinks you haven't been upfront with her. And I can't say I blame her. You've never been happy for our good fortune."

"What a strange thing to say."

"Is it?"

"Well, just because I'm protective of my best friend, who's had an incredibly tough life doesn't mean I'm not happy for her." That actually sounds genuine.

"You never exactly welcomed me with open arms."

"Are we going to do this now?" And that.

Did everyone think Kennedy was strange except for me?

I realize I can hop the chair over to the knife block, but it will be too noisy. I try to pull my hands out of the zip ties, but they're too tight. Next, I try yanking through. This just gets my wrists raw.

"It's a day of getting things out in the open. We might as well."

"Okay, then. I thought it was strange, the way you swooped in and fell in love right away, and then disappeared."

"I think you should stop speaking, Angie."

Think, Millie. Think. This might be your only chance to get out of here. They've clearly gone off script and you've got a few minutes. They keep arguing, Kennedy shushing Angie after nearly every other word. I look around for a plan. I can, perhaps, squat down and carry the chair on my back, and then get to the knife block.

Then I have a thought: is Angie buying time, starting in on all this now? Is she going along with Kennedy, doing a double acting job, just for my benefit?

I take a deep breathe, bend over at the waist so my chest is flat against my thighs and with all my strength, I attempt the first step in what I hope will be a crab walk over to the knives. When I lift my foot slightly, my leg shakes and my balance goes wonky. I feel the chair rush down onto my head and back. Thankfully, I can lower my foot in time to stop the chair leg banging into the floor. It does make a small sound, but I tell myself it was too low for them to hear. I manage to straighten it back up. I wait, perfectly still, to see if they respond to it.

My breath is sharp and shaky as I exhale.

"You were suspicious, or you were jealous, Angie? Yet another Burns woman deserting you? And the most intriguing one at that. Everyone wants a piece of Millie. Look at this house. Look how every day is an adventure. You think I don't know the texture she brings to the dull, meaningless world?"

I had no idea anyone felt this way about me. What a way to find out.

48

MILLIE

THE FIRST THING I NOTICE ARE THE RHODODENDRONS. THEY'RE everywhere. My eyes flutter open and all I see are bunches and bunches of them. All different varieties and colors. Only the white ones, like Mother always kept. *Mother?* The scent is transportive. I open my eyes and imagine I'm in her office. No, I *am* in her office. Where is Rose? I shiver at the memory of her kissing me before her nap. Have I fallen asleep? Blacked out? Been drugged? I don't like the thought coming but there it always is in the background, still hoping: paged-in?

"Rose?" I ask though I don't see anyone.

"Rose is fine. You've barricaded her in her room, because you're about to commit suicide," Angie says, making her way into the room. I have no memory of this. Is Rose sleeping in there? Taken out of the house altogether, so I just *think* she's locked in?

"What? No. Not you, Angie."

"Well, I don't know what you heard of my conversation with Kennedy before you blacked out, or should we say 'paged-in' since that's how we're going to recount it to the police when we report your suicide and all the strange things you've been saying and doing. But, Kennedy and I, we have come to an agreement. I won't tell anyone about his little bout of tying you up and he won't kill me. It's a decent deal, don't you think? I mean, I can't blame him. You're a danger. You always were a danger. You told me and I never believed it. You just always seemed so weak, so broken down. But all this time you killed Emily. She was everything to me, hope, love, creativity. She taught me how to live a bigger life. But you didn't like that, did you? I remember the way you used to look at me whenever she hugged me. 'Come here, Angie,' she used to say. Nobody hugged me the way that she did, gripping her fingers into my skin, really wanting me to know how she felt. And she'd look me in the eye like we both got it. The truth of life was our little secret. Then she'd curate the reading. Imagine who I'd be without that."

"None of what you're accusing me of is true, Angie. I never felt like that. Sure, I was jealous sometimes. There was just so little of her to go around. But that's natural. Especially in my situation. My dad had run out and Mother had already tried to kill herself. I wanted some attention from her. Did it upset me a little how much easier she was on you? How she complimented you but only had harsh words for me? Of course." Am I exactly in the same place I was all those years ago? Maybe I am all those things Angie is saying. She probably knows me better than anyone.

Suddenly it all seems too hard, like what have I been fighting for? Perhaps it's time to pack it in on this life. If I'm a danger to my daughter, surely she's better off without me. But not with Kennedy, I remind myself.

My vision is blurry, but Angie's wearing what she had on earlier and it looks like she's smiling. She's got glasses on. Wait. They're the rose-colored glasses; I recall them from when we were kids, inspired by a music video—the Cars. She touches the frame.

"You like? They're growing on me."

"Where'd you get those?"

"You told me they were lost, but here they were, in your room all this time. Proof: you're just a dirty liar, Millie. And that's all you've ever been. A murderer and a liar. No wonder you've had to make up all those fantasies just to get through the day. But it will all be over soon."

Oh, Angie, not you, too. Please not you, too. Just when I think I've found the edges of reality, they shoot out of reach. What does she know, really? What's she doing?

Keep her talking is my only option at the moment. She lowers and raises the Cars sunglasses in question, the checkered ones with the red lenses that, yes, I'd swiped from her in the fourth grade, which I'd been wearing reading *Are You There God? It's Me, Margaret*. God, we loved them. They've been in my closet all this time. She just had everything, and she wouldn't miss them, I'd told myself. But there was another side to that too. I knew how much she loved them. And because of that, I wanted them for myself. She was right about that.

"So you've been looking around?" I say. "Tell me this: *was* Rose really barricaded in her room?"

"She was, you sick fuck."

"Is it possible Kennedy's trying to frame me? Or what about you?"

"You're not in any position to be making wild accusations, Millie."

Her showing up here is so odd. My suspicions must be correct. They're in it together. What else can it be?

"I still can't believe I found these glasses here," she says, as if I'm not tied to a bed, with a person threatening my life lurking somewhere, and my daughter god knows where. "I'd been dreaming of these glasses all these years." She yanks them off her head and lowers them over mine. "And you know what? They look awful now. You've kept them so long they look awful."

"I've got news for you," I say, deciding I need to get her even more agitated if I'm going to get more information. She always was a hot head. "They always looked awful."

"Did they? I don't remember it that way." She turns toward the door. I can hear the kettle begin to hiss downstairs. *Yes, you psychopath—what a great time for a cup of tea!*

"Yeah. Because those rose lenses made everything look so beautiful. That's why we loved them."

"Really? Because you always looked like crap to me." It's her sarcasm, but with an edge—a sloppy one, but knife-sharp all the same.

"Thanks."

More seriously, she surveys the room, slowly, thoughtfully.

I keep talking. "You didn't believe me when I confessed my greatest fears to you—that I might have killed her without knowing. You said it wasn't possible, that this is just what I did, blame myself for everything."

"Well maybe there was a reason you blamed yourself." She looks around, takes in the flowers. Smells deeply. "Anyway, this will be your *piece de resistance*. It's beautiful, the perfect ending for you."

Is that true? All this time, even now, despite what Pinocchio has said, I've had the same lingering doubt: could I really have suppressed something like that?

"Millie. You've woken just in time." It's Kennedy. With a fucking cup of tea.

My heartbeat races.

"Found your copy of *Robinson Crusoe*," Angie says. "That book left a bad taste in my mouth. But we used to have so much fun with your dad's old hunting rifle, pretending we were on the lookout for savages."

That's not exactly how I remember it. I was never very good at picking up the signals, was I?

I think of what my father told me. The time I've lost, incomprehensibly. My therapist, the look on Officer Lou's face, as if he, too, found something vital in the words I spoke. It's getting too difficult to keep it all straight. I need my lists. They're calling to me. *The ice cream shop, the trembling hands, the hazy aura around everything, love makes it work, pain too; Individualists, Universalists, a softening of reality.* I think of Mother's hand in the earth, her art deco ring. Could I have killed her? Has this all only ever been a manifestation of my guilt?

I've read plenty of books about suppressed memories. They always come back to destroy you in the end. Everyone knows that. But people, at least I, wonder can that really happen? Could I kill my own mother and not remember it? I am brought back again, through the cotton wool in my head, of the doppelganger family images I get from time to time at the ice cream shop, the diner. What if that is real, that family, living a parallel life that could have been?

I'm overcome with dizziness, feel my back collapse against Mother's desk chair. I look down to see it in this context. It's stunning. I can see her there, her beautiful dark hair, that perfect pink shirt.

They're securing me into a straitjacket now. That's a symbol if I've ever seen one. I don't even resist. I try to work out which is worse: being crazy or a murderer.

"You must have a million questions."

Someone approaches, the halos are too strong, they're overtaking the figure so I can't make it out. Pinocchio? Whoever it is might be about to untie me, I think, and then he—yes, it's definitely a he—sticks a cloth doused in some chemical in my mouth. I pass out.

Who knows how much later, I keep my eyes closed, pretend

I'm still unconscious. I hear Pinocchio and Angie. "You cannot mess this up," Angie says.

"You think I don't know that? Everything is riding on her. This is Emily's most crucial scene. Each word counts. We've stacked all the details, all the tension, and this is where everything crescendos. If there's even one detail wrong, it won't work. And we'll find that out right now."

Emily? Mother is alive? And if so, how is she involved? Before the thoughts can even crystallize, I give into sleep again.

The next time I wake, my sight is improved. Almost one hundred percent. But everything looks pink.

Pinocchio is gone. That was not me being in a book world, it was some kind of dissociative episode. In this new clarity, this is absolutely certain. I understand that now, which in itself is an improvement, though ironic, given the circumstances.

"You're back." It's Angie, by herself. She's not wearing the glasses. When she sees my eyes open, she approaches, taps the bridge of my nose, where I realize, the rose-colored glasses are now resting. Ah, that's why everything looks pink. More symbols. The flowers look even more meaningful this way. Maybe this *is* the right ending for me. It's starting to feel more and more that way.

"I can see why you wanted to steal them," she says. "They do add a level of meaning, a tone of significance to life that only a storyteller can normally give it. Don't they?"

I don't speak.

"You and I are not storytellers. We are just two poor schmucks, looking for meaning in the mystery of human experience."

It has been many years since Angie spoke this way. She stopped after Mother died. She said she was done with all that. She asked me not to discuss books and reading and "all that" with her anymore. I respected her wishes. She gave me a pass when I was at my lowest point, hospitalized for my dissociative episodes. Listened to all my worst fears about killing Mother, all of it. I always assumed it was a beautiful, silent ode to our friendship, the way she always brought books for Rose. But now? It seems more like a fuck you.

And there it is. She won. I lost. Are we all so simple that in the end, it *is* all about love? I think of Mother and her *Wuthering Heights*, how shocked I'd been that she could love a book so obvious in its selfish, self-obsessed take on love. Here was another girl in love with Heathcliff. How I'd read it and read it looking for something more, something deeper it could have been. But it was about the love, the connection unexplored, destructive because the people in it were too un-self-aware to get anywhere. That was it. That was everything, I saw now— perhaps had always seen without wanting to admit it.

Everything I've ever done has been for love. I refused to admit it because I loved Mother so, and could never, ever be enough for her. If it was all about love and the most important object of that love didn't, or couldn't, or wouldn't love you back, well then what would my life be for? In the end, am I so easily undone for a mother's love? Angie clearly thinks so. And look, everything I've done since I failed at achieving her love has been to make up for that loss, hasn't it? Kennedy, Rose. Could I be such a simpleton? I should accept this end. It is more than I deserve.

Just as I think this, Angie says, "But this, this final scene, this conclusion—it is incredibly satisfying. I can see the appeal of the Book World, the Readers, the Writers. I really can."

She shakes her head, angles it. "I changed my mind. Those glasses suit you."

She laughs, more like Roxanne than anything else. "Why don't we concentrate on what's happening now? Discovery writing. Isn't that what you call it? God, I'm enjoying this too much.

All those years of listening to you, the main character, complain and struggle to make yourself comfortable with the choices you've made, the failures you've accepted as someone else's fault."

"You loved me, Angie. All those years. You couldn't have faked that."

"There was a time, yes. There was such enchantment to our time together, I couldn't help but love you. But nothing could compare to Emi."

Emi. My skin crawls. She would hate that nickname. "Are you playing the bad cop, Angie? Where's Kennedy?"

"Missing the point, again. You're adorable, Millie."

"Where's Kennedy? If what you said is true, that you're just doing this to save your life, then why are you enjoying it so much? Why does it feel like you've planned this? What have you done to him, Angie? Where is Rose?"

Something is not right. Angie is lying. Or more likely, being played herself. Am I just reading too much into things? Always I've been trying to work out the puzzles. It's a habit that's hard to break. Even now, I feel a catch in my chest. I feel a desperate need in my bound hands to write this on my *Quelque Chose.* I feel a prick in my thigh and my lids grow heavy. As I do, I hear Rose screaming. *Rose, Rose,* I feel myself mouth, but there's no sound.

I embrace the blackness, the strength of my subconscious, despite my awareness of the delusions, is too strong to resist.

49

MILLIE

THIS TIME WHEN I COME AROUND IT'S HARDER TO FOCUS. THE glasses are gone. No pinkness, but there're the halos, the kind from my page-ins, but denser, and they're are everywhere. Drugs. They gave me drugs. They? Pinocchio? I feel on the verge of blacking out or paging-in, who can tell? But I fight it, muddy my thoughts with strings of nonsense sounds and counting, because I can tell I'm on the brink of losing consciousness, and I'm not leaving this place until I get to the truth. Until I see her. Mother. They said her name. I'm sure of it.

Though physically unchanged, Pinocchio looks different, in the same way Kennedy did earlier. Like an actor playing a different role. And he smells like smoke, though he didn't the other day. I'm not sure yet what that means. He's less sure of himself, I think—than he was the other day.

"Why did you disappear?" I ask him.

"My part was done."

"And what part was that?"

"To get you to here. To have you worry about what I knew—about your, what you think was your 'murder' of your mother."

"So what did happen with me and Mother that day?"

"You came to a story with your personal history and your perceptions and beliefs, and your brain did what it does—tried to draw meaning from meaninglessness. Your actions resulted in a classic reversal. In life, you felt your mother was killing your spirit, so you went and killed her creatively, where it was safe to act on your feelings. We aren't so difficult to work out, despite the yearning for us to feel we're unique and complex creatures."

"So she isn't actually dead? I thought Kennedy killed her."

"Remember what I told you: art and science are not so separate as we would like them to be. Art is part of science. If you look at them together, you get infinitely more possibilities. And that's what you need to do."

"Why can't anyone simply answer a question?"

"You want simple answers, Millie. This is your problem. The only things that are simple are your desires. Everything else, all the possible manifestations, the permutations of what we might do about those desires, in this realm and in fiction, especially joined together like this, there are too many ways to look at it to get the clear-cut answer you're looking for.

"It's all open to interpretation. And everyone's interpretation is different, just as this, your journey, is unique from everyone else's. Art has always been infamous for presenting us with questions. Science, though it has some answers, with each new revelation, constantly shows us how little we know."

"What are you going to do with me?"

"Well, that all depends on you. But if it were up to me, I'd kill you right away. No point in waiting for the ending. You've been nothing but trouble, since your conception. But there's the whole love problem. None of it works without love, blah blah blah. And so, here you are."

"What do you want, then?"

"Ah, motivation. Yes! That's more like it. What's my motivation? Well, I'm pretty damned sick of being a pawn in this whole game. I'm ready to take it to the mainstream. Just been strung along, year after year, doing a bit part when really, I should be running the show. I'm the one who understands the science of it. I've written all the implementation manuals.

"But nobody can get on board with that idea. It's not something to be institutionalized. It's all individual, creative. For each of us to work out on our own. Blah, blah, blah." He's mocking Mother and it's clear from his exaggeration and body language how fed up he is with her. I've been there myself enough to recognize it. Can this be real?

"So why don't you break off and do it on your own?"

"Wouldn't that be so simple? You are not a thinker, Millie. This is your problem. Your Mother is the most powerful Writer ever, in the history of the world. Do you even know what that means?"

"Are you saying *Writer* with a capital W? I thought I was imagining that."

"Call it whatever you want, Millie."

"Oh, I get it," I say. "Why I always wanted to call you Pinocchio. Because you're a puppet. You voice everyone else's agenda."

"We're all puppets," Pinocchio says. "It's a sick, sick, exultant, addictive business, stories because we all want it to mean something—this life."

"And what about you? What do you want it to mean?"

"Still with the simple questions, Millie. After all this. I think Emily will find you a disappointment."

"Is she alive? I thought she was dead?"

"Oh Millie." His brows raise. "You know what though, I am proud of you for one thing: having the guts to see your dad. Well, that was a surprise. Emily didn't think you would. You've done such a wonderful job shutting out the past, pretending none of it happened. Look at you. You *are* surprising. Well done. Might have a satisfying ending after all." He pats his front shirt pocket, takes out a soft pack of cigarettes, lights one. And I'm out.

And then I'm back again. She's drugged me again. Maybe I was always being drugged? Angie's alone in the room.

"Where's Dr. P?"

"Dr. P? Well there's a blast from the past. You must be off with the fairies again, Millie. No Dr. P here. Haven't thought about that dude in forever."

"Where's Kennedy?"

"The sad part is, after all this, after everything, I still want to be a part of it. You think I don't see Emily in that daughter of yours? You in her? And now I can have her all to myself. Kennedy—what did he do to deserve it all?"

"Where is Kennedy?" I say.

"Dead. And look it's time for your meds."

Blackness.

50

MILLIE

AFTER SO MUCH TIME, YOU WOULD THINK I'D HAVE MY SCRIPT ready for Mother. But it's just the opposite. I'm speechless. What can I say to her? Even when she was speaking to me, I never did have the words.

She looks formidable. In high-waisted jeans and a black silk button-up blouse, her hair smooth in a massive ponytail. I haven't seen her hair long in many years. It suits her. Ageless. I hate myself for wanting to pounce, launch myself at her, crush her with my hug.

"Millie, I'm sorry to have taken your pregnancy."

Of all the things I imagined her saying, that certainly wasn't it.

"It's a terrible thing to lose a child. All kinds of ways for that to happen. Like when your own child murders you, for instance."

A shiver starts deep inside me, takes over. I have to lean back into the chair.

"All those years, you tried to make yourself feel better about it. But the truth is, when you were given the choice, you murdered me. I watched you, shocked. On the one hand, I was deeply satisfied—I could never have predicted you'd go that way. What a plot twist! But on the other, quite a blow to see how you felt, instinctively, deep down. You smashed that stone again and again. Brutal. I guess we are all animals."

"But here you are."

"But here I am."

"Why have you done all of this to me?"

"It's called conflict, Millie. There's no story without it."

"Am I so meaningless? Just a mere character in a story?"

"*Au contraire*, Millie. Characters are perhaps the most meaningful of all. They drive the story, connect the readers, change opinions, challenge beliefs, soothe souls."

"I only ever loved you, wanted you to love me." I hate myself for saying it, but the words are out before I have a chance to stanch them.

"Don't you think I know that? I could never have propelled you through all this if I didn't know your motivation."

"Well, it's out there now, so did you ever love me?"

"I did. I do. I couldn't have invested so much in you otherwise. But one mustn't be precious about these things. When you've been doing this as long as I have, you know you often have to kill your darlings."

"Mother, that's a phrase for writers. In that sense, 'darlings' are words. Not real, live people."

"Are *you* really saying that to *me*? You think I haven't witnessed your pathetic cover-up all these years? 'I don't remember. Was it a dream? Was it in a book? Was it in the Book World? Did it really happen? No, Kennedy! Don't dig up the yard. What if you find the corpse of my mother buried back there?'"

I still have no words, feel like I've been smacked, then kicked, then run over by a big rig. All those years rehearsing zingers I thought would hurt her, and now I realize I can't touch her. She's impenetrable. It's too late to make amends with emotions. We are all on her strings. Puppets.

"It's all beside the point, anyway. Words, people, stories, real life—I've managed to tear down the divisions. And with the help of Dr. P, well, now I've got a surgeon's precision." She laughs.

"Is he really a puppet?"

"Don't you get it? Everyone's a puppet."

"Mother, you can't mean all of this. Don't you remember the way we were: *you and me against the world*." Why do I continue down this hopeless path?

"I remember you always asking when I handed you a book: 'What's this about?' And I'd paraphrase Flannery O'Connor: the meaning of a story does not rise to the top of a book like schmaltz in a soup pot. A story is not a textbook. As she so eloquently put it, 'the whole story is the meaning.' When you were young, you'd get so flustered. 'But can't you just say what it's about?' If it had all been that easy, none of us would be here in the first place, then again, none of us would be here in the first place. Try putting that in a blurb. Try sticking it in a genre.

"You never got it, Millie. And you never loved yourself. Never trusted yourself. Probably to do with your weak father. You're so desperate for love, but it isn't your fault. We're made that way. And that's why it's so easy to work everyone out. He did love you, though. That's what you couldn't work out. He did it for you. He saved you all these years. Gave you time. He's a hero. And now, you've become such a strong character, you propelled us here, to this glorious, perfect ending. Congratulations. You finally get it."

I'm so at peace, it's incredible.

For a moment Mother looks thoughtful, reminiscent even. "You need conflict for stories, Millie. A loving mother and daughter is boring. It just doesn't work. We're making the ulti-mate sacrifice—together."

She approaches me, hugs me in a way I've pictured exactly

many times, her hand in my hair, the feel of that ring getting caught—a pull, but a reassuring one. It's everything I hoped it would be.

"Mother, I love you so much. Thank you; I know this is not your way, to speak so directly. But you've done it for me, because you understand I need it. This straight-talking is not to your mind the best final scene. It should have ended at 'congratulations.' I understand that. But you've done it for me. Thank you. It means the world to me. Mother, Mother, Mother, Mother."

I wake this time to laughing. "*Mother, Mother, Mother!* God, Millie, you are so pathetic! Do you hear yourself?"

Despite the realization of where I am—restrained in my bed, my best friend above me, mocking me after killing my husband, who killed my mother—I feel at peace from the exchange that took place with Mother and me. It's no less true because it came from my imagination. Perhaps it's more true because of that. I've made a decision. I'm done fighting for this life I've only destroyed. Everyone here is better off without me. I'm coming, Mother. I'll fight the good fight—creating and grounding myself in stories—for the rest of my days. And then when I die, we'll be together forever.

And that's when I know the time has come: the classic reversal, story's most powerful hand. She's going to kill me—Angie, Mother, Angie; it's one and the same to me. It's the moment I've been headed toward all along.

51

MILLIE

A SCREAM FROM OUTSIDE BRINGS ME BACK. THE VOICE IS MALE. Angie does not run to the window, she walks slowly, amused by her surprise (what a twist!), I assume, and with an obvious curiosity about how things will unfold. We were always suckers for twists. She pauses before the heavy curtain, another I had made with Mother's coupon, as if savoring the moment, this crescendo. There're footsteps approaching. I'm so woozy, I can feel my head weaving, heavy on my neck. But it's heaven. Whatever drugs she's given me have helped to finally bridge my two worlds.

"Do it, Angie! Please. Kill me now. It's perfect. Now. Before you lose your chance."

"You're crazy! You really are. Do you know that?"

It all happens so quickly after that. The man's voice is louder. There are sirens outside, lots of them. And then yelling through a megaphone. "Angie James! Someone is coming inside right now. If you pull that trigger, you will spend your life in prison. If you come out now, we will make it easier on you."

She shakes her head. "No. This is the way it has to end. I

won't be the weak one now. You're the weak one." She cocks her finger. I shut my eyes tight. The noise is deafening. The pain. Then, thankfully, I'm gone.

52

MILLIE

IT'S NEAT, MY DESCENT BACK TO THE BOOK WORLD. I KNOW exactly where I am. There's Mother, apparently bleeding out on the carpet. I know she's not, really.

When Pinocchio approaches Kennedy, I know what's going to happen. We rehearsed this at least. Angie mustn't know where things stand now.

"She's gone," Pinocchio says.

Angie runs to her bloodied body and prostrates herself over Mother. It's macabre, the way she rubs herself in Mother's blood, beyond devastation, something primal.

"You never did know how to separate yourself from her," I say. And it's true. "That's not the same thing as paging-in. But that's the closest you could get. You were misguided, Angie. She used you. You found what you needed to in her words, but that wasn't necessarily her intent. She only has one daughter. And that is me."

"No. No!" She lifts her head. Mother's blood is smeared at her cheekbones, like she's dressed for a ritual dance, a sacrifice. She doesn't know the half of it. Mother's ending is a corker, a real unexpected zinger—and that's because we wrote it together.

We're a team now. All those years of training. All the meticulously collected *quelque choses*. Well we're finally doing *quelque chose* with them. We're both individualists. We're doing it for the experience, for us. Universalists, individualists—it doesn't matter. We're going to hand it off to the public now, and they're going to choose what they want to see. You make it real, and they choose. That's the magic. Our magic. *We* are the point. We are significant.

In this world, it's Mother holding the trigger. She wasn't really bleeding. We just set it up that way. Had a lot of fun with those blood capsules. Just the kind of fun I'd always imagined.

53

OFFICER LOU

AS SOON AS I PULLED THE TRIGGER, I REALIZED I'D INSERTED myself forever in their story. I'm not going to lie, that felt amazing. I was hooked. Books, writing, reading—it was a new world that had opened itself up for me. Much more satisfying than most prosaic attempted murder scenes. Angie was going to kill Millie. That was certain. I'd done the right thing on paper, too. The mother's body is being processed, thank god.

The paperwork, the hours of questioning at the station, lie ahead of me, but all I can think is how grateful I am to have been pulled into her story, to have the knowledge that there is more out there than the ugly shit I see every day.

I have to swallow, I feel tears sting my eyes as I rush to Millie, check her pulse, radio the emergency services crew to come up from across the street. I can't tell if it really happened, or if it's just the way I experience it, but she opens her eyes, one last time, takes me in, and mouths, "You get it."

My hand trembles and the colors go vivid around me, the noise is deafening. A kind of divine love enwraps me as if in answer to all the suspicion and research I'd given to the idea of any meaning in this life previously. *You get it.*

I step back, slowly catching my breath, and at that moment, I think of *The Great Gatsby*. God, I fucking loved that book, Dr. Eckleberg's glasses across the water. *Something's watching.* In that moment I feel Fitzgerald had it right. It's such a relief. I see Caroline coming toward me, and step right into my role, but standing more upright, feeling more, more—*more.*

EPILOGUE

"Time for meds, Millie." Roxanne's cackle sends shivers right through me.

"Still writing those lists, huh?"

I take the Dixie cup, dump the pills in my mouth, swallow them down with water from the second Dixie cup then open my mouth, swirl my tongue, to show her I've got them down.

"What's a *Quell-ku choose* anyway?"

I don't answer. I never do.

"Fine, well you have fun with all your papers, darling. But don't forget it's lights out in one hour."

Through my open door, I hear her call off what she's given me. The other nurse writes hard enough on the clipboard that I can hear it. Then she slaps the clipboard on top of the wheelie cart and they make their way down the hallway.

"That poor girl," I hear Roxanne say. "First her mother, now her. Well, at least her daughter's safe, off with the grandfather. He's the only sane one in the family."

"You know what Dr. P says—"

"She's happy where she believes she is."

"Well, that's more than I can say for most of us."

They both laugh, and I smile, incredibly satisfied. I'm a better Writer than I ever could have imagined. Mother is so very proud of me.

READER'S GROUP

For a free copy of Dan Noble's novella, WHAT SHE WROTE, sign up for her reader's group mailing list. You'll get access to more free books, launch information, and lots more insider bonuses.

COMING IN 2019

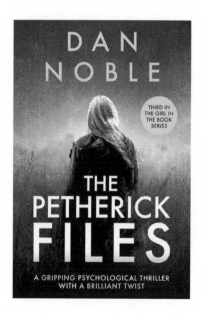

Years later, Officer Lou has made quite a name for himself as the go-to detective in any case where literature is involved.

This time, there's a serial killer picking off the most prestigious scholars at The National Library of Australia. It isn't long before he finds himself immeshed in a story full of twists and turns, where fact and fiction aren't so easily separated. To keep up to date on the launch, join Dan Noble's reader's group here.

ABOUT THE AUTHOR

Dan Noble is a pseudonym for Daniella Brodsky, the Australian/American author of novels across a number of genres, including suspense, general fiction, women's fiction, contemporary romance, romantic comedy, chick lit, and YA. When you see the name Dan Noble, you know you're getting a gripping psychological thriller with a brilliant twist. For free books and more, visit Daniella's website to sign up for the Dan Noble mailing list.

Find out more:
www.daniellabrodsky.com
daniella@daniellabrodsky.com

ALSO BY DAN NOBLE

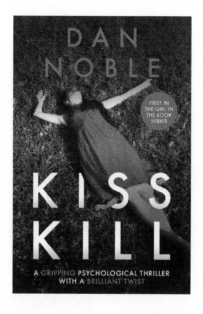

A compelling, gripping thriller with a brilliant twist that will keep you awake until the early hours. Perfect for fans of *The Girl on the Train*, *Behind Closed Doors* and *The Sister*.

In North Queensland, Australia, a child has been tragically, accidentally killed. Years before, her own mother, Erin, wrote a strikingly similar scenario into her acclaimed novel. Is she somehow responsible?

Years later, Erin's trying to cope with the unanswered questions, and thinks she's finally come to a solution. But is her thinking sound? And how many lives will hang in the balance if it isn't?

Kiss Kill is the introductory novella to the psychological thriller novel series,
THE GIRL IN THE BOOK.

THANK YOU FOR READING

If you've enjoyed reading THE BOOK CODE, please share your experience by leaving a review on the online store of your preference, or favorite online book community. You wouldn't believe how powerful your opinion is!

ACKNOWLEDGMENTS

A million thanks to Beta Readers. It's a new world out there for books and the sky's the limit. I believe this book celebrates the active relationship between books and their readers. And thankfully, with the incredible, intimate ways we can connect across the globe, I can reach out to you and make sure I'm writing the books that give you the most enjoyment and satisfaction. It's a learning experience for me, too. And that gives me the most enjoyment and satisfaction. It's a win-win. Thank you for being part of the process. It's an exciting, always evolving one. If you'd like to get become a beta reader (also known as advanced reader) please email me at danellajnoble@gmail.com and I'll get you my new releases before everyone else for free, so you can tell me what works and share your ideas about what would work better. I'd love to hear from you.

Here's to the future of books!

Made in the USA
Middletown, DE
25 May 2020